meet me on Blueberry Hill

praise for
Meet Me on Blueberry Hill

"I truly loved this book. Lisa did a phenomenal job bringing Asher and Sadie's story to life. I have enjoyed the entire series so far but (and maybe this is too early) Lisa may have written my favorite installment. I loved the depth of the characters and the realistic reactions to being hurt and being jaded. But her reminder that God will never fail us brought it all together in an inspirational story."

—KATE, GOODREADS

"We always do what we don't want to do especially when family needs us. Sadie and Asher's story is beautiful. Meet Me on Blueberry Hill will be a story you return to read more than once."

—JESUS BEACH GIRL READS, GOODREADS

"What a sweet contemporary romance read. Sadie and Asher both were hurting, had scars from their respective pasts, and needed healing. This is a story of forgiveness and healing with wounded characters who must decide to come out of hiding and embrace the life God gave them."

—ALLYSON, GOODREADS

"New-to-me author Lisa Jordan is now an auto-read author for me!"

—THE LITERATE LEPRECHAUN, GOODREADS

JONATHON ISLAND ◆ SEASON 1

meet me on Blueberry Hill

LISA JORDAN

sunrise
PUBLISHING

Meet Me on Blueberry Hill
Jonathon Island, Book 4

Published by Sunrise Media Group LLC
Copyright © 2025 Sunrise Media Group LLC
Print ISBN: 978-1-963372-85-4

Scriptures taken from the Holy Bible, New International Version®, NIV®. Copyright © 1973, 1978, 1984, 2011 by Biblica, Inc.™ Used by permission of Zondervan. All rights reserved worldwide. www.zondervan.com The "NIV" and "New International Version" are trademarks registered in the United States Patent and Trademark Office by Biblica, Inc.™

For more information about Lisa Jordan please access the author's website at the following address: lisajordanbooks.com.

Published in the United States of America.
Cover Design: Sunrise Media Group LLC

To Susan May Warren and Lindsay Harrel—
thank you for shining your light at the end of a very
dark year. I'm so blessed by the opportunities you
have given me.

"When you pass through the waters,
I will be with you;
and when you pass through the rivers,
they will not sweep over you.
When you walk through the fire,
you will not be burned;
the flames will not set you ablaze."

ISAIAH 43:2 NIV

Jonathon Island

Meet Me on Jonathon Island (prequel novella)
Meet Me at the Grand
Meet Me on Lilac Lane
Meet Me at the Fudge Shop
Meet Me on Blueberry Hill
Meet Me at Sunset Cove
Meet Me at the Christmas Cottage

JONATHON ISLAND
N
W E
S
Jonathon Family Home
Sullivan Pumpkin Farm
Lake Shore Drive
MacBride Resort
Sullivan Way
State Park
Airport
Jonathon Blvd
Quinn Ranch
Sugar Maple Ln
Blueberry Hills Neighborhood
LAKE HURON
Sunset Cove
Barrett House
Partridge Ln
Dahlia Dr
Lilac Ln
Zinnia Blvd
Poppy Place
Rose Rd
Blueberry Blvd
Pinnacle Dr
Blueberry Hills Park
GRAND HOTEL
Main Sreet
Downtown
Marina
Marina

One

A SHER QUINN JUST WANTED THE nightmares to stop.

Until he found redemption for the tragedies of his past, they would continue to haunt his sleep.

The sound of splintering wood, the creaking of timber, and a crash jerked him from the same dream that plagued him repeatedly for the past five years.

Sweat slicked his chest as he dragged a shaky hand over his weary face. He forced his ragged breathing to slow and stared into the darkness, trying to erase the images flickering through his head.

Impossible.

Nothing would remove the echoing screams or the sear of flames as he fought to escape his metal prison.

Thunder rumbled outside his bedroom window.

Lightning slashed, throwing brilliant light across the wooden floor.

The storm.

Triggers he didn't expect to turn his gut to mush.

But he didn't have time to wallow in the past. He needed to make sure Henrietta Hudson, his elderly neighbor recovering from hip replacement surgery, was safe.

He couldn't have more deaths on his conscience.

Not your fault.

How many times had his counselor said that?

Lies.

Someday, he'd believe him.

Maybe.

Until then, knowing he couldn't save them ate at his conscience.

He snatched an olive-colored T-shirt off the floor and jammed it over his head, his fingers scraping against the puckered skin along the left side of his neck.

Scars that served as a reminder.

He pulled on the tan cargo shorts he'd kicked off earlier, then shoved his feet in a pair of worn leather flip-flops.

Grabbing the flashlight kept by the door, he hurried down the stairs, through the house, and into the storm.

He raced to the stable to check on the few horses still on island. Scents of hay and warm animal flesh mingled with the steamy air fraught with storms that shook the island.

Jagged fingers of lightning sparked across the blackened sky, casting shadows over too many empty stalls.

Pegasus nickered.

He ran a hand over the Percheron's muzzle. "Hey, Gus. It's okay. The storm'll be over shortly."

Next to him, Ginger bumped his shoulder with her

nose. "Hey, sweet girl. This isn't your first storm. You'll be okay."

After giving each of them another pat, he plunged into the night air, dark as smoke, the light in his hand doing very little to shine a path through the storm. Rain pelted his skin as he sprinted across the yard. His feet slipped and he nearly face-planted in the soppy grass. He kicked off his flip-flops and raced barefoot to his older neighbor's front porch.

A long limb had smashed through the side railing of the white storybook cottage. He'd need to come back first thing in the morning to clear it and make sure there was no other damage.

Swiping water and hair off his face, he rang the doorbell. Barking sounded from inside the house. Georgie, Hetty's Lhasa Apso, scratched the other side of the front door as the porch light flashed on.

Squinting against the glare, Asher gripped the door-frame and let out a breath.

She was fine.

The door yanked open.

But Hetty wasn't standing in the doorway.

Asher took in the dark-haired woman a little younger than his thirty-three years and dressed in a gray tank top and navy running shorts that showed off long, shapely legs. Her long hair tangled around her face. She tried to push it out of her eyes as she scooped up the barking dog. "Georgie, that's enough." Then she squinted at him. "Yes? Can I help you?"

"Is Hetty okay?"

"Who?"

"Henrietta Hudson. She lives here. Is she okay?"

The woman cradled the dog against her chest. "Why do you want to know?"

He jerked a thumb over his shoulder. "I heard a tree come down, but it's too dark to see anything. I just wanted to be sure Hetty's okay."

"My grandmother's fine. She sleeps through anything. Doorbells too, apparently. I didn't realize it was storming until now."

"You've inherited that trait from your grandmother." He tried to crack a smile, but her steely look showed she didn't share his humor. He stepped back, hands up. "Sorry to disturb your sleep. Just wanted to make sure everyone was okay."

"Yes, we are. Thanks for checking." She shot him a sleepy smile, then started to close the door.

"Wait."

"What?"

"What's your name?"

"Sadie. Sadie Hudson."

"The copywriter. Your grandma's mentioned you."

"And you are?"

"Asher Quinn." He jerked a thumb over his shoulder. "I manage my aunt and uncle's ranch next door."

"Right, the reclusive neighbor. Gran mentioned you as well. Thanks for ensuring she was safe. That was kind of you, Asher." This time she closed the door and secured the deadbolt in place.

A moment later, the overhead yellow glow from the porch light went out, shuttering him in darkness again.

Taking a deep breath, he exhaled loudly then launched into the rain.

Back at his aunt and uncle's house, he padded up the stairs and to the large guest room that had become his over the past year. He flicked on the lights, then shivered against the fan in the window. He changed into dry clothes, then grabbed a towel out of the small bathroom and rubbed it over his head.

What he wouldn't give for a cold beer.

But he'd given up drinking eighteen months ago. The same night his aunt and uncle rescued him from the depths of his self-sabotage.

Only the nightmares resurrected the desire to hold the cold beverage in his hand, to feel the icy liquid slide down his throat. As he pounded back bottle after bottle, his troubles disappeared.

But only for a while.

Instead, he reached for his water bottle on the side table, then chugged until his parched throat was quenched.

He pressed his back against the windowsill and eyed the queen-size bed with its twisted sheets that spoke of his restlessness. Instead of crawling back under the covers where sleep would elude him, he dropped in the dark brown leather chair in the corner that gave a perfect view of the TV sitting on the electric fireplace. He set his water on the floor and reached for the remote.

Stretching his legs out on the matching ottoman, he stopped on a random channel and threw an arm over his eyes. Maybe he could fall back to sleep to the droning of some mindless show.

"In this episode of *Where Are They Now?*, what happened to the rock band Phoenix? After the fiery tour bus crash that claimed the lives of nearly everyone on board, including the band's famed lyricist, fans are wondering where Eli Noble, the lead singer who was the only one to escape, has disappear—"

Asher scrambled for the remote and shut off the TV. He tossed it on the ottoman, then strode across the room and grabbed his phone that was charging on the side table. As he sat on the edge of the bed, he thumbed through his contacts and tapped on a number.

"'Ello?" Corbin Gray's gravelly voice sounded in his ear.

"Hey, man. Sorry to call so late, and it's been a while, but you said . . ."

"Yeah, yeah, no worries. I'm here for you. What's going on?" His counselor's deep voice mellowed with sleep eased the band around Asher's chest. "Another nightmare?"

"Yeah." Asher dragged a hand over his face. "It's storming tonight. Maybe the thunder triggered it. I dunno. Woke up to a tree falling. Literally. It's too dark to find it right now."

"What was the nightmare?"

"Same one—the crash. I can't get anyone out. The screaming. The fire." Chills skittered across Asher's puckered skin. "I'm so tired of this."

"I'm sorry you're still experiencing them. What you're feeling is valid. Anxiety manifests itself through our dreams. Anything else stressing you right now? Where are you, by the way?"

Asher waved a hand around the room. "I'm still living in paradise, man. What do I have to stress about? My aunt and uncle's place on Jonathon Island is as far out of the spotlight as I can get. I'm managing their ranch while they're on their year-long RV tour. I'm caring for horses who are kinder than most people. So, nothing out of the ordinary."

"Right. Glad you're still there. I went to Jonathon Island as a kid. Before the hotel burned. We had the best pastries at this family-owned bakery."

"The Hudson Bakery. Hank and Henrietta Hudson ran it. Hank passed a few years ago. Hetty—Henrietta, I mean, retired after she lost her husband. Too hard to do on her own. She's my neighbor."

Asher thought back to Hetty's granddaughter, who didn't like her sleep disturbed by things like storms. Or fallen trees. Or concerned neighbors, apparently.

"The five-year anniversary is coming up."

Asher didn't need a calendar to remember the day burned into his memory. He grunted.

"Perhaps the approaching date is coming out through your dreams. How are you feeling about it?"

Asher dropped the phone on the table and stabbed the speaker button. He jumped to his feet and paced in front of the rain-splattered window. Lacing his fingers behind his neck, he wrestled with the words stuck in his throat. "How do you think I'm feeling about it? They're dead because of me. The choices I made."

"Asher, they're dead because of the accident. This isn't your fault."

"I should've said no when Chet and Dom pressured me to let them drive. They were over hours but insisted we drive through the night—and the storm—to get to the next venue on time. My bus, my fault. I couldn't save them."

"Have you read the police report your uncle gave you yet?"

"No." His eyes slid to the wooden dresser where the sealed envelope lay untouched in the top drawer.

"Maybe it's time. Then you can forgive yourself and begin healing."

Asher ran a hand over his jaw, his fingers scraping over the rough skin on the left side of his neck. "My burns are healed. I have the scars to prove it."

"I'm talking about spiritual healing."

"Yeah, well, I'm the last person God wants to hear from." An ache formed behind his burning eyes. "Listen, man. Thanks for picking up. I appreciate it. I'm going to try to see if I can crash for a little while before I need to feed the horses and muck out their stalls."

"You know where to find me, day or night."

"Thanks, man. Appreciate you." Asher ended the call and dropped back on the chair, face in his hands. He picked up the remote and found a decades-old comedy playing. He stretched out. The laugh track echoed in his head as he closed his eyes.

Now that the storm had lessened to a soft rain, maybe it would lull him to sleep.

If the nightmare didn't come back.

He needed to find a way to reconcile the past, to be redeemed from his mistakes.

Then he'd find healing.

Maybe.

Someday.

Sadie Hudson had one month to put her life back together.

If only the mistakes of the last year could've been washed away by last night's storm. Returning to Jonathon Island was supposed to give her the peace she'd been craving, but the consistent turmoil in her chest made her restless.

After her mother had come down with the flu and wasn't able to care for Gran as planned, Sadie sought refuge at her grandmother's cottage nearly a week ago to help care for her while she recovered from her recent hip surgery.

And caring for her meant giving her breakfast at a timely hour.

Smothering a yawn, Sadie dipped the remaining slice of homemade bread into the egg and milk mixture and then placed it on the heated cast-iron griddle on the middle burner of the stove.

Bubbles snapped and sizzled as the French toast cooked. She lifted a skillet off the adjacent burner and rolled the sausage links. While those finished cooking, she poured a small glass of orange juice and set it on the towel-lined tray next to Gran's steaming cup of English Breakfast tea.

Journey's "Don't Stop Believin'" came on the oldies station through Gran's Alexa that sat on the kitchen counter.

Sadie sang along with the eighties song as she moved through the cottage kitchen with white cabinets, gray countertops, and original hardwood floor.

She turned off the heat and plated the French toast and sausage. She added the food to the tray, then carried it out of the kitchen and down the small hall to Gran's first floor bedroom, humming the lyrics to the song now playing in her head.

Palming the tray, she tapped quietly, then opened the door. "Gran, you up?"

"Come in, honey. I was just spending some time with the Lord."

Sadie pushed the door open with her foot and headed into the room. Georgie, Gran's seven-year-old brown and white Lhasa apso, raced between her legs and bounded onto the bed.

"Georgie, get down. You're hurting Gran."

"Oh, he's fine." Gran wrapped her thin arms around the fluffy nuisance and gave him a hug. Then she moved her red leather Bible and matching journal off her lap and set them on her nightstand. She smiled at Sadie, her blue eyes reflecting the serenity Sadie always found comforting. She finger-combed her silver bangs away from her forehead. "What's all this?"

Sadie placed the tray on the bed in front of her. "I made French toast and sausage. I wasn't sure what kind of tea you wanted, but I found some English Breakfast in the cabinet next to the stove."

Gran pressed a hand against Sadie's cheek. "Thank you, love. It's perfect, but you didn't have to go to all this trouble for me."

Sadie laughed. "You're the one of the few people in the world that I'll do anything for."

"Same here, honey." Gran lifted her cup. "Did it rain last night, or was I imagining it? Thought I heard pounding, then Georgie barking."

"Yes, a pretty intense one. In fact, your neighbor came over and checked on you."

"Asher?" Gran smiled. "He's such a nice guy. Sorry the storm woke you."

Sadie waved away her words. "I couldn't sleep once the storm settled down, so I did some work until my alarm went off at six."

Gran exchanged her teacup for her fork and cut one of the sausage links in half. "Why are you setting an alarm? We're on island time, love."

"Island time or not, I need to stay on routine. I can't afford to become lazy. I have four weeks to figure out my future. I picked up remote copywriting work to pad my bank account until I can decide what I want to be when I grow up."

"Trust the Lord, love. He has a plan for you." Gran held out a hand and wiggled her fingers.

Easy for her to say. Gran's faith was rock solid.

Sadie reached for Gran's hand and gave it a gentle squeeze, then sat on the edge of the bed, careful not to upset Gran's tray. "To be honest, Gran, the thought of dealing with SEO, keywords, meta data, and content creation for the rest of my life digs a pit in my stomach."

"You used to love being a copywriter. You have such a lovely way with words."

Sadie released her grandmother's hand and dropped her chin to her chest. "Yeah, well, that was before the fiasco at Sternwood."

"Oh, honey. I'm so sorry you got caught up in that mess. Garrett was a cheating snake who had no business getting involved with you. He had all of us fooled."

"Especially his wife. When she stormed into the office and, in front of everyone, accused me of sleeping with her husband . . . well, I just wanted to die." Sadie's face heated as the memory from six months ago surfaced.

"Well, I'm glad you didn't. I know it hurt at the time, but you're moving through the pain, and you will be that much stronger for it."

"Strong enough not to give my heart away again."

"With the right man, you'll find it's easier than you think."

"Yeah, well, that's not going to happen. I learned my lesson."

Gran reached up and tucked a stray piece of hair behind Sadie's ear. "I heard you singing in the kitchen. It's been a while. I've missed it. Remember the concerts you and your sister used to do on the front porch for Gramps and me when you were little?"

"Lauren had the voice. I just gave her the words to sing." Her heart squeezed as more memories flooded her mind. Sadie blinked back the sudden rush of tears as she edged off the bed and moved toward the door. "I'll leave you to eat in peace. I'm going to tidy the kitchen before Dani and Lily arrive."

"Dani Sullivan and Lily Hart? They're coming here?"

"Yes, I ran into them at Martha's last night when I picked up dinner. They asked if we could get together today because Dani has an idea she wants to discuss, so I suggested breakfast here. You don't remember me mentioning it when I came back last night?"

Gran waved a hand as she picked up her fork. "Right, right. I remember now. These pain pills Doc has me on give me foggy thinking."

"You just had your hip replaced, Gran. Healing takes time. Isn't that what you just told me?" Sadie left the door open, then returned to the kitchen.

She wiped spilled milk off the counter, put the cobalt blue mixing bowl in the dishwasher, and slid a tray of French toast and sausage in the oven to stay warm. As she set the skillet in the sink of soapy water, she heard a nickering from somewhere close by.

She peered through the blue and white checked curtains and found a gray horse staring at her through Gran's open kitchen window. The skillet slipped from her hands and splashed into the water, soaking the front of her tank top.

"Uh, Gran." Sadie grabbed a dish towel as she backed away from the sink, then hurried down the hall. "There's a horse in the window."

Gran looked up from the devotional book in one hand,

her teacup in the other. She set it back on the tray. "A horse? Gray, dappled coat with a black muzzle?"

"I didn't get a great look, but that sounds about right."

"That's probably Gus. He's an escape artist who lives next door. He likes my apple trees. I'll give Asher a call to come and get him."

"Who?"

"Asher Quinn, Terry and Angie Quinn's nephew who's managing their ranch while they're RVing around the country."

"Right—the one who rang the doorbell at three this morning." The image of the soaked guy with dark hair, dark beard, and even darker eyes swam into focus. In her sleep-fogged brain, the details were a little fuzzy.

"He's always looking out for me." Gran patted the white top sheet with lavender flowers rumpled around her. "My phone's around here somewhere."

Sadie lifted the quilted lavender bedspread. The phone tumbled from the folds. She caught it and handed it to Gran.

"Thanks, love." Gran scrolled down her screen, found the number, and called. When he didn't answer, she left a message and set her phone on the tray. "Maybe you should take Gus back to the barn."

Stepping back, Sadie pressed a hand to her chest. "Me? I don't know anything about horses. And that thing was huge."

Gran waved away her words. "Aww, he's a gentle giant. Grab an apple from the kitchen, talk softly as you approach, then hold out your hand. Direct him across the lawn to the Quinn property."

She made it sound so simple. As if an apple was going to lure the horse home.

Gran raised her eyebrows and lifted her chin. "You may want to change first."

Sadie glanced at the wet, gray tank and navy running shorts she wore as pajamas. She blew out a breath and headed for the guest room down the hall, calling over her shoulder, "If I'm not back soon, you'll know that beast got the best of me."

Sadie exchanged the wet clothes for tan shorts and a red T-shirt. She pulled her hair into a ponytail and threaded it through a navy hat to help shade her eyes from the rising sun. Sliding on her sunglasses, she headed to the backyard.

The morning air chilled her arms as the wet grass soaked her flip-flops. Maybe she should've borrowed Gran's rain boots.

She rounded the side of the white cottage and stopped, a gasp whooshing from her lungs as her eyes widened.

A large tree sprawled across the patio. Splintered wood, shattered glass, broken pots, spilled dirt, and decapitated flowers littered the concrete. She followed the length of the tree and found the fractured base on the other side of the damaged split-rail fence that separated Gran's property from the Quinn ranch.

The gaping hole explained how the horse had escaped.

Sadie eyed the large animal grazing under the apple tree. Without any kind of rope, she had no clue how to get Gus back to his owners. And she'd forgotten to grab an apple out of Gran's fruit bowl. Sadie shielded her eyes and glanced at the large stone house next door.

Was it too early to knock and ask Asher to fetch the horse? It wasn't safe for the animal to be roaming free.

The sound of a chain saw whined across the yard. Okay, so someone *was* awake.

Sadie plodded through the wet grass, climbed over the fence, and headed for the neighbor's property.

She passed the dark stone house and headed down the dirt path that led to the large, white-washed building with a forest green metal roof. Scents of hay and fresh wood wafted in the morning air.

Chips of wood flew around a man bent at the waist as he sliced through the thick trunk of a different downed tree. Sawdust blanketed his cargo shorts, bare legs, and grimy work boots.

Apparently more than one tree suffered in last night's storm.

The man cut the power to the saw and straightened, pressing a hand to his lower back.

"Excuse me."

He turned. Dark sunglasses shielded his eyes, and a black ball cap covered his dark hair, shadowing his face. Stray wood chips clung to his dark beard. Faded, puckered scars ran down the left side of his neck and disappeared into the collar of his T-shirt. "Yeah?"

"Are you Asher?"

"Who wants to know?"

Feeling a sense of déjà vu, she cleared her throat and removed her sunglasses. Squinting against the morning rays shining toward her, she jerked a thumb toward Gran's house. "I'm Sadie, Henrietta's granddaughter. I believe we met early this morning when you checked on us during the storm."

"Right." He lifted two large pieces of wood and chucked them toward the growing pile next to the building.

Okay, then.

She took another step toward him. "Your horse is in Gran's backyard, and I need you to get it."

Straightening again, Asher turned and dragged the back of his wrist across his forehead, dislodging his hat. Then he reached for a half-full water bottle sitting on the ground and chugged the rest. As his head tipped back, she caught the lines and angles of his profile—straight nose, high cheekbones, and squared jaw covered in scruff. Something about him seemed familiar, but she couldn't place it.

Without a word, he headed into the large open door that led to the stable.

Sadie exhaled and followed him. "Well?"

"Well, what?" He pulled some sort of equipment off a hook near one of the empty stall doors.

"Are you going to get the horse?"

He held up his full hand. "Had to get his harness and lead rope."

"You could've mentioned that."

"I just did." He strode out of the stable.

She hurried after him. "Whatever. There's also a tree across Gran's back patio. It came from this property. You'll need to get it removed."

He started for the yard, then faced her. "Are you always this bossy?"

She swallowed the words blistering her tongue. "Would you please get your horse and remove the tree?"

He snapped a salute that would've made her father proud. "Ma'am, yes, ma'am."

Rolling her eyes, she jammed her sunglasses back on her face and headed back to Gran's.

Jerk.

What did Gran see in him?

Wasn't Sadie's problem. She didn't do mysterious. Since Asher had it practically tattooed on his skin, she planned to stay as far away as possible.

She'd been gullible once, and that was enough for a lifetime.

Trudging into the house, Sadie headed down the hall to her grandma's room. She heard talking and paused. Something in Gran's tone kept Sadie from returning to the kitchen and giving her privacy.

"Thank you, Mia. I'll have to think about it, then let you know what I decide." Gran let out a sigh.

Sadie knocked on the doorframe and stepped into the room. "Everything okay?"

Chin trembling, Gran fingered the quilt, then looked at Sadie with watery eyes. She waved a hand over the room. "The cottage needs some work if I'm going to stay here. Aging in place, I think your father called it during our phone conversation last week. My only option is to sell the bakery, so I contacted Mia Franklin. She called with the appraisal, but it's much lower than I expected. Maybe it's time to sell this place too and move into an apartment complex off island."

Sadie moved into the room and sat on the edge of the bed. "Gran, no. You love this place. It's been your home for decades. You can't leave the island. What would you do without your daily visits with Doris and Annabelle?"

"I don't want to leave, love." She waved a hand over her room. "The cottage needs a new roof, new windows . . . It's too much for one person, especially on a limited income. And the bakery's just sitting there. Seb Jonathon offered to buy it after Gramps passed away, but I couldn't part with it, sentimental fool that I was. With your father stationed in Hawaii, he's not going to want it." She shook her head. "I don't know what to do."

Sadie leaned forward and gathered her in her arms. "Don't make a rash decision based on how you're feeling right now. After Dani and Lily stop by, I'll call Mia and talk to her about the appraisal. We'll figure it out."

"Promise me one thing, love?"

"Anything, Gran."

"Don't tell your parents about me needing to sell the bakery. I'll tell them when I'm ready. Your dad's already questioning my decision to stay here. I don't want to give him more ammo to ship me off to a retirement home."

Sadie hated secrets, especially keeping things from her parents, but she also didn't want Gran to worry needlessly. "I won't say anything, Gran, but you know Dad would never do that. He's just concerned, especially after your recent fall. With them being in Hawaii, it's challenging for him to be here when you need him. I think that's what's bothering him more than anything—they aren't here for you."

Having lived around the world as an Air Force brat, Sadie always found security in her grandparents' home on Jonathon Island, and she'd do whatever she could to keep Gran in the cottage she loved so much. Even if it meant paying for the repairs herself.

But that meant taking on more SEO remote work until she could find a better job.

She'd do it for Gran. She'd been so supportive after Sadie's life had fallen apart and she'd spent the last six months treading water.

She'd figure it out.

Somehow.

Two

SADIE WANTED TO SAY YES AND HELP her friends. So what was holding her back?

She refilled Dani's and Lily's cups and then her own with coffee from the small pot she'd made before her friends arrived. "I'll be honest, Dani, I didn't expect this."

Dani Sullivan, her friend on the island since they were kids, tossed her long blonde ponytail over her shoulder, tapped the screen on her iPad, and handed the tablet to Sadie. "I know it's a big ask, especially since you just arrived and you're caring for your grandma. Even though we just celebrated the arts-and-crafts festival over Labor Day weekend, Liam and I came up with the idea of an end-of-summer music festival, and your name popped into my head. Since we started the season late, we're ending a little later than usual. Problem is, with everything else on my plate, I don't have a lot of extra time for marketing and advertising."

Dani added two more teaspoons of sugar to her coffee and nodded to Lily, who sat across the table from her. "Lily raves about your skills, so I was hoping I could talk you into helping. Or at least getting us pointed in the right direction. The Tourism Bureau doesn't have much money right now, so we can't pay you. But I'll give you free advertising for your freelancing business. Maybe you could gain more clients while you're here."

"I've already said I could use help with marketing the fudge shop. I'm sure other businesses could use some on-line exposure as well." Lily swirled a bite of French toast through a puddle of syrup on her plate. "I heard Patrick and Martha Kelley arguing about social media the other day. Patrick muttered something about the only thing he knew about reels were the ones attached to his fishing pole. I didn't mean to, but I couldn't help but laugh."

A smile tugged at her lips as Sadie glanced at her best friend and former roommate of ten years from when they both lived in Florida. Lily's blonde hair streaked with lavender had been piled in an artistically styled messy bun that probably took her less than five minutes to accomplish. If Sadie tried with her own hair, she'd look like she'd just crawled out of bed.

As she surveyed her friends watching her with hopeful eyes, she found herself nodding. "Maybe. If I did reach out to local businesses with an offer to help build up their online presence, then I could build my clientele, especially if they'd be willing to give me positive references."

Sadie turned her attention back to the tablet and scrolled down the page, taking in the header showcasing the island and a couple of basic pages advertising the big draw for the festival—a free concert at the park on Blueberry Hill. She looked up at Dani with wide eyes. "How did you get Ariel Sullivan and Dahlia Denton to be your concert headliners? And Drake Hamilton? Seriously?"

She grinned as she stirred cream into her coffee. "Umm, quite easily. Ariel's my cousin, remember? Her dad Bryan is my dad's younger brother. After my grandparents passed away, Dad got the hotel, and Uncle Bryan got the pumpkin farm. Unfortunately, it's been vacant for the past few years, but Dad mentioned Uncle Bryan, Aunt Mary, and my cousin Ethan are planning to return to the farm next year. Anyway, after Liam and I brainstormed, I texted Ariel and asked if she'd headline. Of course she said yes. She's pretty awesome that way. Drake's lead guitarist is Caleb Kennedy. His grandfather owns the Island House Inn. Even though Drake is touring, he agreed to come to the island for the festival."

"Oh, that's right. Caleb's great-aunt Annabelle is one of Gran's best friends. I'd forgotten you had cousins on island too."

"Yes, Ariel, her brother Ethan, and her sister Charlotte. Ariel was born on island, but she grew up in Nashville with her great-aunt, Dahlia Denton."

"I love their music." Lily picked up her coffee mug and hummed a few bars of Miss Dahlia and Ariel's latest single, "The Long Way."

"Me too." Sadie tapped another page on the tablet. "You're doing a talent show the day before the concert?"

"Yes, and that's another thing I wanted to mention."

Dani grabbed Sadie's wrist. "You should enter. I contacted a few local businesses this morning and plan to ask more, but there will be a cash prize for first place as well as a chance to sing with Ariel and Dahlia on their next album."

The idea of the cash prize held some appeal, especially to help Gran, and to sing with Dahlia Denton and Ariel Sullivan . . . well, that would be pretty incredible, but Sadie couldn't shake her head fast enough. She slid the tablet across the table to her friend. "No way. I'm not risking humiliation by singing in front of a crowd. I'm not that good anyway."

Dani dropped her hand, reached for her vintage Hudson Bakery coffee mug, and leaned back in her chair, her gaze unwavering. "Sade, your lyrics need to be heard."

Sadie bit the inside of her lip, then speared the last bite of her now-cold French toast with her fork. "I haven't written a word since Lauren died. My sister was the talent in the family."

"I disagree, but I will try to respect your wishes." Dani stood, carried her empty plate to the sink, rinsed it and stacked it in the dishwasher. "I hate to eat and run, but I need to meet Liam at the hotel."

"Did downtown receive much storm damage?"

"A few downed limbs and scattered leaves, but nothing major. The hotel's fine. Liam's crews are busy enough with renovations. They don't need to add storm damage on top of that. What about you guys?"

"Actually, I'll walk you out and show you." Sadie left her breakfast dishes on the table and headed for the back door where she slid her feet into her flip-flops. She held the door for Dani and Lily, then followed them outside.

They rounded the side of the house, and her friends gasped.

Lily's hands flew to her mouth. "Oh, my."

"Yeah, quite the surprise this morning. After I made breakfast for Gran, I found a visitor staring at me through the kitchen window." Sadie picked up a flowerpot that managed to survive the storm.

"That's kind of creepy." Lily slid her sunglasses on her face. "Who was it?"

"A horse named Gus."

"Gus! I love him. He's one of the Quinns' horses. Apparently, he looks for any opportunity to slip through the fence. He's a sweetheart though." Dani started picking up sticks and dropped them in a pile.

"More than I can say for his owner." Sadie eyed the Quinn property.

"Terry? I'm surprised." Dani straightened and brushed dirt off her hands. "He and his wife Angela are so kind. But I thought they were still traveling."

"Not him. Their nephew, I guess, according to Gran."

"Asher." Dani and Lily said in unison.

"Yeah, him." Sadie jerked a thumb toward the Quinn property. "What's up with that guy anyway?"

Dani looked away. "Why? You like him?"

Sadie made a face. "Hardly. He's rude."

"Come on, Sade." Dani added more sticks to the growing pile. "He's not that bad."

"You know him?"

She lifted a shoulder. "He used to visit his aunt and uncle when he was a kid, so I'd hang out with him, his younger sister, and his cousins, even though they were older than I was."

Sadie shaded her eyes and glanced at the ranch. "I didn't see anyone else at the house. Looked like he was alone."

Lily picked up a decapitated gerbera daisy head and smoothed out the petals. "You've been there?"

Sadie explained about going to the Quinn ranch to get someone to retrieve Gus.

"Ahh, yes. Makes sense now." Dani wiped her hands on her jeans, then eyed Sadie. "You know, Asher is pretty good with a hammer, from what I hear. Maybe he'd be willing to help us with the stage construction for the concert."

"Gran talked highly of him, but he didn't come off as the kind of guy who wanted to lend a hand." Sadie surveyed the mess in the backyard. "He was a little gruff when I asked for help in getting Gus back where he belonged and getting the tree off Gran's patio."

"Maybe you could give him a second chance." Lily straightened one of the spilled pots, scooped the soil, and patted it in place around the red geraniums.

Sadie righted one of Gran's patio chairs and set the cushions back in place. "Second chance for what?"

"To change your opinion of him."

Shading her eyes, Sadie squinted at her. "Why would I want to do that?"

Lily laughed as she rescued a pot of pink and white striped petunias. "Well, you'll be neighbors as long as you're on island."

"And I'm perfectly content staying on my side of the fence." Sadie eyed the property line.

Dani folded her arms over her chest. "Okay, then, but would you do it for me?"

Sadie swiveled on her heel and faced Dani. "Do what?"

"Ask him to help with the stage construction?" Dani pushed to her feet and rubbed dirt off her fingers.

"Why me? You're the one who's friends with him."

"I mentioned it in passing, and he just laughed. I don't think he took me too seriously." Dani looked away but not before Sadie caught the flash of hurt in her large green eyes.

"You mean he knows how to crack a smile? I find that hard to believe."

Holding pieces of broken glass in her hands, Lily frowned. "Wow, Sade. It's not like you to be this judgmental."

Her friend's words poked at her heart. Lily was right. She did her best to try and not pass judgment. She lifted her hands, then dropped them to her sides. "Sorry. The guy got under my skin."

"Oh, did he now?" Dani winked.

Sadie rolled her eyes and made a face. "Nothing like that. Maybe I did come off as a little bossy. He just annoyed me when I asked for help."

"Maybe if you get to know him, then you'll see he's not that bad."

"But I don't want to get to know him. I came to care for Gran after Mom came down with the flu. And to see you guys, of course. While I'm here, I need to figure out what's next. After leaving Sternwood, I haven't found a job that's worked out. And doing remote work is fine, but it feels a bit isolating. At least, it was until I came to the island." Flashing her friends a smile, she opened the outside basement door and retrieved a broom off a hook on the wall. "And that definitely doesn't involve getting to know some guy. I'm not the best judge of character when it comes to choosing men."

"Just because that last guy was a jerk doesn't mean they all are. After all, we ended up with good ones." Dani waved a finger between her and Lily, then took the broom from Sadie and started sweeping the storm debris off the patio. "Now it's your turn."

Sadie glanced at the diamond glinting in the morning sunshine on Lily's left hand. "You're right—Liam and Declan are great. But most of them are less than honorable."

Lily slung an arm over Sadie's shoulders. "That's your broken heart talking. Give it time, and you'll be ready for romance again."

"Spoken like someone in love. And engaged." Sadie snatched one of the outdoor throw pillows. Water dripped from the corner. She tossed it near the back door to the kitchen so she could wash it. "Seriously though. I just can't take it again. I thought Garrett was the one. We were together for over a year. A year of me being duped by his lies."

"Dani's right—he's a jerk." Lily fisted her hands on her hips. "I never cared for him anyway. Forget him. It's been six months since you guys broke up. It's time to move on. He's not worth your emotional energy."

"He's the reason why marketing is a bit tainted for me right now."

Dani stopped sweeping and leaned on the broom. "And here I am asking for your help. I'm sorry. Please forget I asked. I'll figure out something else."

Sadie grabbed her arm. "No, it's okay. Working with you is going to be much different. Besides it's only short-term. Once the festival is over, I can go back to reinventing myself."

"Why mess with perfection? There's nothing wrong with you, Sadie. You just need the right guy to prove it to you." The kindness in Lily's eyes warmed the hollow in Sadie's heart.

"I don't need any guy. Especially not a grump who can't say more than two syllables."

"And now we're back to Asher. Interesting." Dani crossed her arms over her chest and shot Sadie a sly smile. "I think you like the guy more than you're letting on."

"And I think you're becoming annoying."

Dani laughed, apparently not taking offense to Sadie's words. "And with that, I'll head to the Grand for my meeting. If I can find time, I'll call Asher and ask for his help . . . for real this time. Unless you want to do it."

Sadie folded her arms over her chest and eyed her friends standing shoulder to shoulder. Their solidarity put her as the odd person out. She released a sigh as she shot Dani a mock glare. "Yep, definitely annoying. If it gets you to drop it, then I'll ask him. But be prepared for him to say no."

"What if he says yes? Then what will you do?" Lily waggled her eyebrows.

Sadie lifted a shoulder. "Nothing? If he agrees, it will be to work on the stage. That has nothing to do with me."

Lily shot her a sly smile. "Maybe so, but if he's a part of the festival, your paths may cross more often."

Sadie looped an arm through Lily's. "Lil, I love you, but don't start playing matchmaker."

As Lily and Dani headed toward Sugar Maple Lane that ran in front of Gran's cottage and would take them downtown, Sadie waved goodbye and shook her head over Lily's ridiculousness.

Sadie was perfectly content to care for Gran and help her friends. That was it. She didn't return to Jonathon Island to fall in love. She didn't have room in her life for a man, especially someone like grumpy Asher Quinn.

Asher rarely had visitors at the ranch. Now Sadie Hudson made a second appearance in the same day.

He shut off the chain saw and set it on the ground next to the downed tree. "Ms. Hudson, to what do I owe the pleasure?"

She stood several feet from him and clasped her hands in front of her. "Ms. Hudson? A little formal isn't it?"

"With the way you barked orders earlier, I felt like it was a little fitting."

Her face reddened. "Yeah, sorry about that. I'm not usually so bossy."

Her eyes drifted to his bare chest, then she looked away, her face turning almost crimson.

He grabbed his T-shirt slung over the split-rail fence and tugged it back over his head. No need to invite any more distaste over the scars that lined the left side of his neck, shoulder, and back.

Dog-tired from not sleeping well, he squeezed his gritty eyes shut for a moment, then looked at her again. "How can I help you?"

"Gran would like to invite you over for lunch." She jerked a thumb over her shoulder toward the white cottage.

His stomach growled, reminding him he hadn't eaten yet. But as much as he enjoyed lunch with Hetty, he found himself shaking his head. "Can't today. Too much to do. But tell her thanks for the invite."

She nodded but didn't move.

He reached for the chain saw and restarted it. Maybe she'd take the hint and walk away. But she remained in the same spot as if rooted in the ground. Swallowing a sigh, he turned off the chain saw and set it back on the ground. "Was there something else you needed?"

She removed her sunglasses and twirled them in her fingers. "There's a festival coming up toward the end of September. A summer send-off, if you will. Food vendors. Talent show. A concert in the park. I met with Lily Hart and Dani Sullivan this morning, and Dani asked if you'd help."

He froze. "Help? In what way? Does she want me to . . . sing?" He could barely get the word out.

"Sing?" Sadie frowned. "No, why? That never came up. She wondered if you'd be willing to help construct the stage. Ariel Sullivan and Dahlia Denton are headlining the concert."

"Dani's cousin? The country singer?"

"Yeah, she's the one." Sadie lifted a shoulder. "You know her?"

"Dani's mentioned her a time or two." He used the hem of his T-shirt and wiped the sweat off his face.

"Drake Hamilton will be there too. He's a contemporary Christian artist."

"Yes, I'm aware."

"So, you'll do it? Help with the stage construction?"

The last thing Asher wanted was to hang out in town. He'd heard enough whispers to know he was the island mystery. What was it Sadie had called him last night? The reclusive neighbor.

And he liked it that way.

He was better off alone.

"No." He picked up the saw again.

She frowned. "No?"

He shook his head. "No."

"No." Her repeated word sounded more resigned.

"What part of that confuses you?"

"Wow, rude much?"

Asher waved a hand over his family's property. "Listen, I have plenty here to keep me busy. I don't have the time or the inclination to build a stage."

"Not even to help Dani?"

Asher pinched the bridge of his nose. Sure, toss in his kryptonite.

Dani Sullivan, who'd become more like a kid sister, was one of the few people he could trust on the island. When she learned he'd be looking after his aunt and uncle's place while they traveled, she'd showed him nothing but kindness.

Maybe he owed her a chance to hear her out.

He glanced over his shoulder and found Sadie still standing there with her arms folded over her chest as she watched his every movement.

"Dani will understand." Not caring if he was being as rude as Sadie claimed, he turned his back to the pretty intruder and started the chain saw once again.

When he looked up again, he saw her marching across the grass and returning to her grandmother's property.

Good. He didn't need her to become a regular visitor.

While he was glad Hetty had someone looking after her since her daughter-in-law had to cancel her trip, his visits to her place would be less frequent now. The fewer people he got to know, the better.

With the tree finally cut into manageable chunks, he headed back into the barn for the log splitter. As he moved equipment and dug out the splitter, his shoulder bumped against the hulking frame covered in a dusty tarp.

Asher straightened and gave the tarp a tug. Dust motes exploded as the worn plastic fell to the ground.

The skeleton of the surrey sat in the corner of the barn, cast in the shadows, almost abandoned and forgotten.

The open four-wheeled carriage with the two bench

seats for passengers and rigid canopy had been one of the first that his grandparents had used when they opened their tour business over seventy years ago.

Now the aged beauty was nothing more than a relic of the past.

But what if it didn't have to be?

His eyes roved over the solid lines and curves of the body as an idea took shape. If he could get his family's carriage business up and running again, then maybe he could pay his aunt and uncle back for their kindness of the past year and give them a reason to want to return to the island.

That would mean he'd have to find a new place to crash, but he'd worry about that later.

His phone chimed, signaling a video call.

He groaned and fished it out of his front pocket. His cousin's face appeared on the screen. He accepted the call. "What up, Busy Lizzie?"

She made a face as she twisted her dark brown hair into some sort of knot on the top of her head and jammed a pencil to hold it in place. "Ugh, don't call me that. You're the only one who could get away with it, you know. You and . . . well, you."

The catch in her voice did little to settle the tightening in Asher's gut.

She'd been about to say Jared.

"Sorry, hello, Eliza Jo Quinn. How may I be of service?" He rolled his hand and bowed at the waist.

"Weirdo." She stuck her tongue out at him. "To be honest, I can't believe you actually answered the phone."

"Maybe I missed you and wanted to hear your voice."

"Missed me like a hangnail, maybe. More like you're tired of listening to yourself talk to Gus and Ginger." She folded her arms on the desk. Behind her, the city skyline lay in the shadows of the late morning sunshine.

"Did you just call to bust my chops?" He strode out of the barn and grabbed his water bottle off the chopping block. "I have work to do."

"Yes, you do lead a very busy life these days."

"Not all of us can sit in cushy offices and create social media memes for a living." He guzzled half the bottle, wiped a hand across his mouth, then turned his attention back to his cousin. "How's life being an assistant to our world-famous author auntie these days?"

"Aunt Sally works very hard, and you know it. She deserves everything she's achieved."

"I never said she didn't. She's just a bit . . . opinionated about it."

"That's because you don't like anyone telling you what to do."

To do."

There was that.

"Where were you, by the way? Looked as dark as a tomb."

"I was in the barn." Squinting against the sun, Asher jerked a thumb over his shoulder, then rested an elbow on the split-rail fence. "So, what's up? Seriously. You don't call to chat."

She paused a moment, which wasn't like his chatty cousin. "Mom called."

"Okay . . ."

"She and Dad are heading home."

Asher straightened and glanced back at the barn where the carriage sat shrouded in shadows. "Home? As in back on island?"

"Of course. Not all of us have houses on three continents."

He let the dig slide. "Do you know when?"

"I think they plan to be home by the end of the month or something like that. Mom doesn't want to miss some concert in the park. Know what she's talking about?"

"I just learned about it. How'd she hear about it so quickly?"

Eliza shrugged. "Gossip on island spreads faster than the flu."

"From what I understand, Ariel Sullivan and her great-aunt Dahlia are coming back to headline."

Eliza's face brightened. She picked up a pen and tapped it against the top of her desk. "Seriously? I haven't seen them in forever. We tried to connect when Aunt Sally had a book signing in Nashville last year, but it didn't work out. Maybe I'll plan to come home too."

"Did your mom say why they were returning?"

"No. But I think something's wrong." The tapping stopped as Eliza rested her elbow on the desk and cradled her chin in her cupped palm.

"Like what?"

"I don't know. But Mom didn't sound like herself. Too happy. The same way she was after Jared's funeral."

Hearing his cousin's name sliced through Asher's chest.

Jared should've been on island instead of Asher. If he

was still alive, then maybe Uncle Terry and Aunt Angela would have stayed.

"Don't jump to conclusions."

"I'm trying not to, but even Aunt Sally noticed something was off when they talked."

Asher laughed. "Aunt Sally has a flair for drama."

"Whatever." Eliza leaned back in her chair and folded her arms over her chest. "Listen, Ash, if Dad calls, don't mention I said anything about Mom, okay?"

"Yes, ma'am." He touched his fingertips to his forehead and gave her a quick salute.

"Oh, by the way, I talked to Abi the other day."

Asher smacked the heel of his work boot against the chopping block and dislodged a chunk of mud. "How is my little sister doing?"

"How about calling her yourself and finding out? She mentioned she hadn't talked to you in a while." Eliza shoved her glasses to the top of her head and raised an eyebrow.

"I've been busy. Plus, the phone works both ways."

Truth was, he did miss his sister, who was three years younger. And his mom. He needed to be better about calling home. Problem was, his mom would want him to visit, and that wasn't happening. The more distance he put between him and his dad, the better for everyone. Holing up on island and caring for Gus and Ginger kept the peace.

They ended the call, and a million thoughts swirled through Asher's head.

Eliza's news about her parents created a pit in his gut.

He hoped she was overreacting. The last thing their family needed was to lose someone else they loved.

But Asher wasn't going to jump to conclusions. He had a lot of work to do if he wanted to make up for past mistakes, to prove he could be more than the family screwup.

So, for now, he'd focus on what needed to be done and keep those necessary secrets buried.

Three

A SHER HATED SURPRISES.

From his experience, nothing good came out of them. So he appreciated the heads-up from his cousin, which gave him time to put his strategy in place.

If he could revive the family's carriage tour business, then his aunt and uncle would have a reason to stay on island.

And maybe, just maybe, they wouldn't mind keeping him around too.

Eliza was right—he did have places on three different continents, but they didn't bring him the same peace and satisfaction the ranch and Jonathon Island had over the last year.

He stacked the last log from the tree he'd cut and dragged an arm covered in wood shavings across his sweaty forehead.

His phone vibrated on the chopping block. He snatched

it up and answered on the first ring. "Hey, Uncle T. How's it going?"

"Hey, Asher. I kind of expected to get your voicemail."

"Didn't realize that was a thing with me. Sorry about that."

"No worries. How's everything at the ranch?"

"Busy. A storm blew across the island last night. Downed a couple of trees. Unfortunately, one of them landed on Henrietta's house."

"She okay?"

"Yes, there's some damage to her back patio and side porch, but the house is intact."

His uncle murmured something, then let out a deep sigh. "Be sure to let her know we'll take care of it. And any damages."

"Already planned to. I'm sure her insurance company will send out someone to do a property assessment. I can talk to the agent and then remove the tree, if she wants me to. A large limb landed on her porch railing, so I'm going to remove that and repair the porch as well."

"You're a good man, Ash."

With the way Asher and his dad had butted heads through the years, those weren't words he'd heard too often. So, not sure he truly believed them. If he was a good man, he wouldn't be hiding on Jonathon Island.

No, he was a coward. Plain and simple.

Asher cleared his throat. "Dani Sullivan came up with a major project to revitalize the island, beginning with repairing and renovating the hotel."

"I heard something about that. Think she'll make a go of it?"

"Already has. Plus, she's pretty persistent. She and Mia Franklin worked with the town council, sold houses for a dollar, and rented storefronts at cheap rates to bring back businesses."

"You know, I think Eliza mentioned that. Couldn't believe ole Seb went along with it."

"He did more than that. He backed his niece and daughter."

"Yeah, that's what I heard." Uncle Terry chuckled. "I really didn't think there was much hope for the island anymore after the hotel fire and pandemic pretty much shut down the businesses."

"Well, you know how Dani can be about rallying the troops." Asher ran a hand over his chin and combed chips from his beard. "With that in mind, I wanted to run something by you."

"What's that?"

"I'd like to restore Grandpa's carriages and revive the carriage tour business."

His uncle didn't say anything for a moment. "You?"

"I know I don't know the business very well, but I'm a fast learner. In my spare time, I can begin stripping the old surrey."

"Man, that thing's pretty much ready for the burn pile."

"I think it can be restored—revive its purpose. The frame's pretty solid. I can scrape the wheels and repaint the metal. The canopy's pretty beat-up from age and years of sunshine. I'll buy a new hard top. The carriages at the livery are newer and just need cleaned up."

"You'd be investing a lot of time into that old thing. Why?"

Asher lifted a shoulder, then realized his uncle couldn't see him. "I'm sure I can find some time and put it to good use."

"You could try picking up a guitar."

Although his uncle's words were spoken low and without judgment, that didn't stop the tightening in Asher's gut. He squeezed his eyes tightly to blacken out the images that filtered through his head.

Images best kept buried.

"That's in the past." His voice cracked on the last word, and he swallowed hard.

"Doesn't have to be, Ash. God gave you a gift."

"What good is a gift if it destroys others?"

"We've talked about that. Wasn't your fault."

Asher wasn't going to argue with his uncle, but he knew the truth. The craving that came from hearing his name being chanted and the thunderous applause at the end of each set had become an addiction. One that drove him to put others' lives at risk. If he'd forced his drivers to take a break and not drive through the storm, then they'd be alive today.

No, he didn't deserve to pick up a guitar or to set foot on stage. His pride and inflated self-importance had become his downfall.

Asher blinked rapidly and ground his teeth. His fingers curled into a fist, but punching something wouldn't solve his problem. It would give him nothing more than a broken hand. He swallowed hard. "So, about reviving the family business . . ."

"Yeah, I don't know if this is the best time." His uncle's drawn-out sigh nearly vibrated through the phone.

"Why? What's going on?"

"Your aunt and I are heading home." He sounded more resigned than hopeful.

"You're cutting your trip short?"

"Not really short. We've been gone nearly ten months. Angela hasn't been feeling well lately, so we decided to head back to the island. We have some decisions to make."

Asher tightened his grip on his phone. "Like what?"

"To be honest, we're thinking of selling the ranch."

The air leaked out of Asher's lungs. That was the last thing he'd expected to hear. And Eliza hadn't mentioned it, so maybe she didn't know either. "Seriously? Why?"

"It's kind of big for two people. We wanted to leave it to our kids, but with Jared gone and Eliza traveling the world with Sally, it's time to downsize. And to be honest, we didn't think there was much to return to on island."

"But there will be. Like I said, Dani's working hard to revive things around here. We can restore the carriages and get the tour company back up and running."

"Sounds good, Ash, but adding a business on top of the ranch is way too much work for two people. Especially two people who are getting older. And if there is something going on with Ang . . ."

"I'll help, if you'll let me." The words tumbled out in a rush. He just needed a yes.

"I appreciate it. You have a home on the ranch for as long as you wish. Or for as long as we own it. You know that. But you have your own life to lead. You can't remain holed up with a bunch of horses. I believe the Lord led you to a higher calling."

Asher lifted a foot to the lower rung of the fence and gazed over the pasture where Gus and Ginger grazed in the rich, sun-warmed grass. "Uncle Terry, I appreciate your wisdom, but I need to disagree with you. That life is over. It's time to find something new."

"Don't underestimate the Lord, son."

Son.

A title he didn't deserve. At least, not from Uncle Terry.

"Promise me something?"

"What's that?"

"If you decide to sell, then I'll be given first chance to buy the ranch."

"With a flat in London, a house in Australia, and a place out in L.A., why would you want a run-down old ranch?"

"This is home."

Those three words were the most real he'd been in a long time.

He'd sell those other places in a heartbeat—and maybe he would—if it meant being able to keep the ranch in the family.

Until he'd come to the ranch, he hadn't had a real home since leaving his hometown near Flint after graduation. When his fight with his dad over pursuing music instead of joining the family construction business had nearly come to blows, Asher knew it was time to strike out on his own.

Uncle Terry released another sigh, and Asher could imagine him rubbing his forehead as he always did when trying to make a decision. "Well, okay then. If we do decide to sell, then you will have first option."

"Thanks, Uncle T." Asher couldn't contain the smile that creased his face.

"See you at the end of the month. When we get home, we'll talk about the carriage business and see if the idea has merit."

"Sounds good."

"Oh, and Ash?"

"Yeah?"

"Don't mention our call to Eliza. I don't want her to worry until we know more about Angela and the decisions about our future."

"Your secret is safe with me."

They ended the call, and Asher stared at the black screen, shaking his head. His family and their need to keep secrets . . . Well, he understood that too well, but the irony was, the information he was being asked to keep secret was something they both knew but didn't realize the other person already suspected.

He pocketed his phone and headed back to the barn.

He surveyed the carriage, still in disrepair but showing promise.

Then he left the barn and faced Hetty's cottage.

Dani wanted an end-of-season music festival to give tourists a reason to return to the island next year. If he could have the carriage ready by the time the festival began and offer discounted trial tours, then he could show his family reopening the tour business for next season was more than an idea.

But if he wanted this idea to take shape, he needed to put himself out there. Maybe helping with the stage construction could bridge the gap between reclusive neighbor to spreading the word about the potential business.

Before he could change his mind, he headed across the yard to see if Sadie's offer was still available.

To say Sadie was surprised to find Asher standing on her grandmother's front porch would be an understatement.

But more than that, hearing him saying yes made her question her own auditory abilities. "What did you just say?"

"I think you heard me." He raised an eyebrow as he pressed a hand against the doorframe. "I'll help with the festival. Stage construction or whatever it was that you and Dani cooked up for me."

Sadie folded her arms over her chest. "We didn't cook up anything for you. This was Dani's idea. *She's* the one who thinks you can do it."

He lifted a brow. "And you don't?"

She shrugged. "I don't know you. Except that you're a bit surly and rude."

He chuckled, a rich sound that rumbled in his chest.

"Well, at least you're not offended." She gave him the barest of smiles.

"You're not the first person to call me rude, and I'm sure you won't be the last. Haven't heard surly in a while though." He shook his head and stuck out a hand. "What do you say to a truce?"

Eyeing him, she took his hand. His fingers were warm and rough. Working man hands. Not smooth and polished like . . . Nope, not going there. "Why the change of heart?"

"I want to bring my family back together." His face softened as the words escaped in a quieter tone.

Before Sadie could respond to that, the door opened behind her. She turned and found Gran standing behind her, leaning heavily on her walker.

"Gran, the doctor said no weight bearing on your left side, remember?" Sadie reached for her grandmother's arm.

Gran shook off her hand. "Sadie, I'm fine. Stop treating me like a fragile flower."

Sadie's cheeks heated at Gran's unusual brusqueness. Her independent grandma hated being hampered by the walker.

Practically elbowing Sadie out of the doorway, Gran moved past her. Her eyes warmed as she smiled at Asher. "Asher Quinn, what are you doing standing on the front porch? You know you don't need an invitation to come into my home."

He directed a look at Sadie as if to imply she was being the gatekeeper. She stepped back and waved him inside.

She followed them into the living room, where Gran lowered herself into the dark gray lift chair Sadie's parents had delivered the day before her surgery . . . under great protest, but Gran didn't seem to mind it now.

A light breeze fluttered the lace curtains at the open window next to Gran's chair, which overlooked the side of the porch with the damaged railing. Family photos of Gramps and Gran at the bakery, Sadie's parents on their wedding day, and Sadie and Lauren through the years lined the light-gray walls.

Soft music drifted from the kitchen where Gran must've been puttering before going out to the porch to see Asher.

"So, what's this I hear about you helping with stage construction?"

Asher's face softened as he sat on the gray couch and leaned against one of the gray and white Buffalo checked pillows. Georgie jumped up next to him and pawed at Asher's faded black T-shirt with a guitar stretched across the chest.

Asher picked up the dog gently, and Georgie settled on Asher's legs as if he'd done it many times in the past.

"Dani is putting together a crew to build a stage for a music festival that will be held at the end of September. Apparently, she thinks I'm handy with a hammer and sent your granddaughter to ask me to help."

"Well, I concur. I've seen your work. You'd be an asset to the stage construction crew."

"Speaking of construction, sorry about the tree." Asher jerked his head toward the front door. "I'll get it moved and your porch railing fixed as quickly as I can."

Gran waved away his words. "Don't worry yourself over

it. Sadie called the insurance company, and we're waiting to hear back from them."

"Still, I don't want it to cause more problems." He glanced at Sadie. "Have you taken pictures?"

She gave him a blank stare, then shifted her eyes to the phone on the coffee table. She swiped it and tapped on her camera. "No, I didn't think about it. I'll do it now."

As she headed outside, the phone vibrated in her hand. Not recognizing the number, she nearly let it go to voicemail, then remembered waiting for the insurance company to return her call.

"Hello?"

"This is Blue Lake Insurance calling for Henrietta Hudson."

"Henrietta is my grandmother. One moment, please." As Sadie reached for the screen door, warm laughter met her. She stepped into the living room and found Gran laughing and a genuine smile on Asher's face.

She tried not to stare, but his whole demeanor changed. He seemed so at ease around Gran. But that wasn't surprising. Gran had a way of making everyone feel at home.

She handed the phone to Gran. "The insurance company."

Gran nodded and took the phone. "Hello?"

Sadie turned back to Asher. "Would you like something to drink?"

"No, thanks. I'm good." Pushing to his feet, Asher nodded toward the door. "I'm going to take a look at the railing and see how much damage was done."

As he pushed through the door, Sadie wavered between following him and staying put in case Gran needed her.

"Sadie."

Sadie turned and found Gran looking out the window next to her chair with a hand covering her mouth as a tear drifted down her cheek.

Gran seldom cried. And now Sadie had witnessed tears twice in the same day. Could she still blame the pain meds, or was there a deeper issue?

She hurried over to her. "Gran, what's wrong?"

Gran sucked in her lips and shook her head. She dropped her gaze to her hands still curled around Sadie's phone. "I screwed up."

"Screwed up? How?"

She lifted a shoulder. "Apparently, I missed a payment and my homeowner's insurance lapsed. I don't know how it happened. I'm so careful about paying all of my bills on time."

"Oh, Gran." Sadie knelt in front of her chair and wrapped her arms around her. "Don't worry about this for another minute. We will get it figured out."

"But without the insurance, I can't afford to get the railing and patio fixed."

"Again, don't worry about it. We'll figure something out."

A soft knock sounded on the screen door.

Sadie turned and found Asher in the doorway, watching them.

How much had he heard?

Without waiting for an invitation, he opened the door

and stepped inside. He glanced at Sadie, then his eyes lingered on Gran. His mouth downturned. "I'm sorry for eavesdropping—your window was open—but I heard about your insurance, Hetty. I promise, you don't have a thing to worry about. Since the tree came from Quinn property, my uncle's insurance will cover any damages. And I'll fix your railing. You won't have to pay a penny."

Gran lifted her head, her eyes much brighter than a moment ago. "Asher Quinn, you are a godsend." She pressed a hand against her chest. "I don't know what I'd do without you. I can pay for the materials and give you a little for your time."

He made a face and waved a hand. "No, absolutely not. I want to do this for you. We have plenty of lumber at the ranch, so I'll find something that works. Won't cost you a cent."

Gran reached for her chair remote, pushed herself to a standing position, and grabbed her walker. "Come here and let me hug you."

Asher crossed over to her in two long strides and gathered her in his arms. He held on a little longer than Sadie expected. Then he released Gran and looked at her with such a gentle expression that Sadie's heart panged.

Gran gripped his muscled forearms. "What's your favorite pie?"

He gave her a mock scowl. "Well, Michigan blueberry, of course."

Gran laughed, a beautiful sound that appeased Sadie's soul and loosened the tightness in her chest. "Blueberry, it is."

Behind them, the music switched to a song that sent chills skittering along Sadie's spine. She turned toward the kitchen and raised her voice. "Ugh. Alexa, stop the music."

Gran frowned at her. "Sadie, what in the world is going on with you?"

Sadie jerked a thumb over her shoulder. "The music. In the kitchen. I hate the song that just came on."

"What one was it?"

"'Dark Side of Midnight' by Phoenix."

Gran's mouth formed an O as she glanced between Sadie and Asher. "Oh, Phoenix . . ."

Asher shot her a look she couldn't quite read. "You don't like that band, I take it?"

"Can't stand them." Sadie wrapped her arms around her waist.

His mouth tightening, he gave her a curt nod as he disengaged himself from Gran's arms, straightened his ball cap, and headed for the door. He looked at Gran. "I'll see you later."

He headed out the door, and Sadie stared after him. "He's one difficult guy to understand. That's so nice about him fixing your railing though."

Gran hobbled over to her, leaning heavily on her walker. "Love, it's the little things that show us who a person really is."

Yeah, she was beginning to see that. The Asher she'd met that morning was much different from the guy around her grandma.

Which one was the real one?

She couldn't spend much time thinking about their

mysterious neighbor. She had to focus on selling the bakery. And that began by meeting with Mia Franklin and seeing what needed to be done so they could fetch a higher price.

Four

ASHER OWED IT TO HETTY TO MAKE nice with her granddaughter.

Even though she didn't know him very well, Sadie didn't seem to care for him, if her attitude from yesterday was anything to go by.

Somehow, they'd gotten off on the wrong foot, but he didn't have time to lose sleep over it. Truth was, he wasn't that crazy about her either. But he'd act like an adult and put his feelings aside regarding the bossy brunette and focus on what needed to be done to help Hetty.

It was better that way.

He preferred his solitude and his privacy.

Removing the branch and repairing Hetty's porch railing was going to take more time than Asher had expected. He'd looked closer and realized the rotting wood needed to be replaced. In fact, the railing all the way around the porch needed to be replaced rather than repaired.

He adjusted his grip on the pry bar and wedged it under the top rail. He gave it small but steady smacks with the mallet and loosened it from the damaged balusters—the vertical slats that supported the top and bottom railings. He knocked the balusters as well. With the condition of the deteriorated wood, he didn't need to smack them that hard. He removed the broken railing and tossed it on the pile behind him.

Swiping an arm across his sweaty forehead, he dropped the mallet on the ground and studied the remaining pieces. Was it more for function or aesthetic? Hetty's answer would determine the direction he took for repairs.

He rounded the porch and took the steps two at a time. The front door opened, and Sadie stood in the doorway. Her dark hair fell in loose waves around her face and hung down her back. Her blue eyes connected with his, then she lowered them to the tray in her hands. She held the door open with her left shoulder. He grabbed the door and held it for her. Stepping onto the porch, she flashed him a brief smile, then set the tray on the small round table between the vintage wicker furniture.

Turning to him, she wiped her hands on her cuffed denim shorts, which, once again, showcased what nice legs she had, then pointed to the tray. "Gran thought you'd need some lemonade. She added peanut butter chocolate chip cookies she'd made before her surgery too."

He glanced at the small table. One glass. She wasn't planning to join him. Fine by him. "Thanks. I appreciate her thoughtfulness. Is she busy? I have a few questions about the railing."

Sadie glanced at the gaping hole along the side of the porch, then returned her attention to him. "Actually, she just went to rest for a bit. She's been getting tired much quicker since her surgery."

He nodded, and Sadie turned toward the house.

"Wait." He didn't mean for his word to come out so sharply.

Sadie spun around and wiped her hands on the edge of her light-blue T-shirt. "What?"

Asher jerked his head toward the railing. "Mind giving me your opinion about something?"

She eyed him. A bit warily, perhaps. Crossed her arms over her chest, then shrugged. "Sure. What's up?"

Asher strode across the porch, jumped down, and headed to the pile of balusters he'd removed. He picked up one and pointed the jagged end toward her. "These are rotted, which is why the branch created so much damage."

Sadie crossed the porch and knelt on the floor. She ran a finger over the bottom railing where the balusters had been. "I'm not surprised, considering how long ago the porch was built."

"When was that?"

Sadie looked off in the distance as she gnawed on her bottom lip. "I was eight, I think, when my dad and grandpa built it, so about twenty years ago. Dad was on leave, and he and Grandpa Hank surprised my grandma with the porch of her dreams. Gran wanted a peaceful place where she could sit with some shade but still enjoy being outside."

"Leave? Your dad was in the military?"

"Still is. He's a general in the Air Force, stationed at Hickam on Oahu."

"Gorgeous island."

"You've been there, I take it?"

"Several times. I to—traveled there with some friends." He needed to watch his words. "How about you?"

"I went a couple of years ago after he and Mom arrived on base. I plan to visit in the next month or so once Gran is moving around on her own."

"It's good that you're here for her."

"With my grandpa gone and my dad being an only child, I'm all she has now. Well, not all—I mean my parents would've been here if they could. Mom planned to come and care for her, but she ended up getting sick. Just worked out that I was able to come and stay with her."

"Only child too, I take it."

"I am now." A shadow passed over her eyes as her mouth took a downturn.

"Sorry."

He needed to be careful. Conversations like this one tended to reveal more than a person anticipated. Getting comfortable and opening up led to friendships he couldn't afford right now. He needed to focus on fixing the porch.

"Do you think Hetty will want just this railing replaced, or should I consider removing all of it for a more open aesthetic?" He waved a hand over the whole porch.

Sadie stood and ran one of her hands down the vertical columns. "I'm sure she wants the railing. She likes to decorate it for the holidays."

The wistfulness in her voice made him wonder if she

wanted the porch restored for Hetty's sake . . . or for her own?

Asher riffled through his canvas tool bag, grabbed the tape measure, and measured the opening on the side of the porch. He typed the measurements into a note on his phone, then went to the small wagon filled with tools and lumber he'd pulled so he could manage everything in one trip. He grabbed a chunk of treated 2 x 4 and returned to the porch.

She shielded her eyes and squinted as she watched. "What are you doing with that?"

"I'll cut new railings to fit in place and make new balusters—these vertical pieces." He pointed to the undamaged ones on the next section of railing. "But I need to see if this piece is thick enough or if I need to find another one. Maybe Hetty should consider changing out the whole railing from wood to vinyl. It would be much more durable for Michigan winters."

Sadie shook her head. "Maybe in the future. She can't afford it right now."

"I'm sorry about the insurance problems."

Sadie shrugged. "I'll call and get it straightened out. Gran's a little more emotional than usual due to her surgery and pain meds. It's quite possible she misunderstood what the agent was telling her."

Still, he didn't like the idea of his friend having money problems. If he could, he'd replace the whole thing with weather-resistant vinyl at no cost to her, but he knew she wouldn't go for that.

"Mind holding this for me?" He pointed to the end of the wood.

She did as directed. And without complaint.

"So, this music festival—what's that all about?"

"Dani and Liam came up with the idea as an end-of-season celebration. Hopefully it will become a yearly thing, and it will draw people back to the island. She's doing a talent show too. Have any talents you want to share?"

His hand slipped and he chipped the end of the wood. He bit back a word.

Not in a million years.

Reaching down, he grabbed the mallet off the ground. "Does tree removal work?"

She cracked another rare smile. "I don't think that will score you the grand prize."

"Which is?"

She sighed. "Five grand. Dani asked the local businesses to donate in exchange for more free advertising."

He raised an eyebrow and whistled. "That's a lot of bacon."

Still holding on to the end of the lumber, Sadie shifted off her knees and sat on the porch. "Dani's hoping it will encourage people to sign up."

"What about you?" He shot a look at her. "Any talents you want to share?"

She shook her head. "I don't do well in front of crowds."

"Stage fright, huh?"

"Something like that." She made a face.

"Performing with others helps. Reminds you that you're not alone on stage. Plus, controlling your breathing—pulling from your diaphragm—gives you more control and power over your voice."

"Sounds like you have more experience than just tree removal."

"I can saddle a horse too." He flashed her a grin. "What else does Dani have up her sleeve for this end-of-summer celebration?"

"In addition to the concert and talent show, she wants games on the lawn of the Grand, a parade showcasing the island businesses, and plenty of food. She asked me for more ideas, including a name for the festival, but I'm kind of stuck. I haven't been on island in almost five years."

Satisfied the piece of lumber would work, he marked it, set the longer end on the edge of the porch for stability, and lopped it off at the penciled mark with his uncle's battery-operated circular saw.

"You could call it Summer Sunset MusicFest." Asher picked up the cut-up chunk of wood and tossed it into the wagon. "What about a battle of the bands? Local performers could battle against one another."

She looked at him a moment as if pondering his words. "Maybe you should be doing the advertising for the festival. I like that name. I'll share it with Dani. As for the battle of the bands, isn't that what the talent show would do?"

He shrugged. "Maybe. But I feel like a talent show highlights one individual or a small group of people, whereas a battle of the bands could bring in bands from the surrounding areas. You could sell tickets and raise even more money for the revitalization of the island."

Sadie stayed quiet as she cupped a hand around her face and tapped a finger against her slightly turned-up nose. Was that respectful pause or did she hate his idea?

He really needed to keep his mouth shut, but there was something about Sadie that had him opening up more than he had to anyone else in a long time.

He wasn't sure what to think about that.

If someone told her a year ago that she'd be living out of boxes right now while crashing with Gran, Sadie would've laughed.

A year ago, she had her life mapped out. She had a plan and loved working the plan.

That was before her faith and trust in humanity were shattered. Now there were very few people she believed.

She could trust her gran. And her parents. And Dani and Lily.

Her friends wouldn't let her down.

Maybe it was their belief in her that sparked the urge to dig into the past.

And her recent conversation with Gran's neighbor, who didn't seem as grumpy as she'd first expected.

Maybe she'd misjudged him.

Maybe.

Time would tell.

Once her eyes adjusted to the dimness in the musty garage, she lifted another box off the towering stack she'd put in place only a week ago and set it on the floor at her feet. She opened it, and a familiar fragrance wafted from the cardboard.

Her heart seized as she breathed in the subtle scent that reminded her of her late sister. A hammered metal photo frame of Lauren's face smiled at her from underneath the box flap.

Sadie pulled it out and pressed it against her chest. "I miss you, sissy."

She turned the photo upside down and set it on the shelf next to the stack of boxes, then dug out assorted journals decorated with doodles and stickers, gathering them in her arms.

"Sadie." A deep voice sounded behind her.

She yelped, sounding more like someone had stepped on a duck. Sadie spun around and lost her hold on the journals. They splayed at her feet, spines up.

As she reached for them, she found Asher in the doorway.

"What?" Then she cringed at her own harshness and held up a hand. "Sorry, you startled me."

Leaning against the doorframe, he folded his arms over his chest. His navy T-shirt stretched across his broad chest. His jeans clung to his muscled thighs. He radiated strength.

Get a grip.

She forced her attention back to his face, hidden by dark sunglasses and a worn Q3 Ranch ball cap. "What can I help you with?"

Asher straightened, then jerked a thumb over his shoulder toward the house. "Hetty wants your opinion about the railing. If we go with wood, I can replace it and have it fixed by tomorrow. If we go with vinyl, then it's going to cost more, and we'll need to replace the whole thing."

Sadie frowned and fought to keep the snark from her voice. "I thought we discussed this already. Gran doesn't have that kind of money. Why'd you even ask her?"

Asher held up his hands. "Whoa. I don't know what I did to become the bad guy, but I didn't ask her anything. She came out on the porch while I was working and asked me for my input. I wasn't going to lie to her."

Sadie crouched and picked up the journals. She stood and held them against her chest. "Sorry. Again. I'm not usually this prickly."

He lifted an eyebrow but remained quiet.

Probably a good thing.

He strode into the garage and leaned down in front of her. He swiped something off the floor and then held it out to her. "Looks like you missed something."

She took the paper and turned it over, then her chest tightened again. A picture of her and Lauren making cheesy grins at the camera while wearing rhinestone sunglasses, Gran's vintage hats, and boas from the dress-up chest that was probably now buried somewhere in the attic.

It had been five years. When would she get over this awful feeling of loss?

Probably never.

She flashed the photo to him. "Thanks. A picture of my sister and me when we were kids."

He took it, glanced at it, then handed it back to her. "You guys look cute. How old were you?"

Sadie tucked it inside the cover of one of the journals. She didn't need the picture to remind her of one of her favorite memories.

"I was ten, and Lauren was twelve. We'd just put on a concert for my grandparents on the front porch. Gran presented trophies she and Grandpa Hank had won during an island bake-off. They declared us the winning team."

"Who'd you compete against?"

Sadie grinned. "No one. Not much competition when you're the only ones performing. We didn't care about the trophy either. The pride in our grandparents' voices was enough."

"Sounds like a great memory. Do you and Lauren still sing together?"

Sadie tried to swallow, not surprised by the thickening in her throat. She'd never get over losing her best friend. "No. Lauren passed away. Tragic accident."

He winced. "Right. You mentioned you were an only child now. I'm sorry. I understand that kind of pain."

"You lost a sibling too?"

He shook his head. "Not a sibling."

"Then how can you understand?"

"I have a younger sister—Abi, short for Abigail—but my cousin Jared and I were close like brothers. He's been gone for a few years now. I miss him."

A shadow passed over his eyes, and Sadie frowned. "I'm sorry for your loss." She tightened her hold on the notebooks. "You know, I used to spend my summers here.

Some of the best moments of my life I've been on this island. I'm surprised I didn't run into you. Especially since you and Dani were friends. She said she used to hang out with your sister and cousins. Did they leave the island too?"

"Your grandma hasn't mentioned them?" He glanced toward the house.

"Not that I remember. Why?"

"My cousin Eliza left the island several years ago to work for our aunt."

"What does she do?"

"My cousin or my aunt?"

Sadie lifted a shoulder. "Either one."

"Well, my aunt writes books, and my cousin works as her assistant."

"That's pretty cool. Is she someone I may have heard of?"

"Depends on if you like to read." Asher shoved a hand in his front pocket and wandered around the garage.

"I used to read all the time. The past couple months, well, I really haven't had the time or the energy."

"Sally Jo Wilson."

Sadie reached out and grabbed his arm, his skin warm under her touch. "Shut up. Are you serious? Sally Jo Wilson, *The New York Times* bestselling author, is your aunt?"

He laughed. "For thirty-three years now. You're not the first person to have that kind of reaction. She's the baby of the family but the bossiest one if you ask me. Doesn't need an invitation to share her opinion. Dad and Uncle

Terry call her Pipsqueak, which annoys her, so she said she had to learn to stand up for herself."

Sadie set the journals in the box on the floor next to her feet and closed up the flaps. She hefted it in her arms. "She comes across so friendly in the interviews and podcasts that I've listened to."

Asher took the box from her and added it to the stack. His T-shirt slid up, offering her a glimpse of a muscled stomach. "She is very friendly. Pretty great, actually. I've been around my share of divas, and she doesn't even compare. Besides, she's family, and I love her."

"She has a new book coming out, doesn't she?" She gathered the journals in her arms once again and headed for the open garage door. She needed a little air.

Asher shrugged. "Don't know. Can't keep up. Seems like she's putting one out every six months now."

"Do you read them?"

"Chick books? No way." Asher laughed, a rich sound that bounced off the ceiling and pinged her heart. "I'm more of a Lee Child or David Baldacci fan."

If she wasn't careful, she could get used to hearing him laugh pretty quickly.

"So, family saga romances aren't your thing, eh?"

"I prefer suspense novels. Or even psychological thrillers. I like knowing what makes a person tick."

"I'm not a very good judge of character these days." She muttered the words to herself.

He took a step closer. "Why not?"

She stepped back and knocked her shoulder against the

metal door track. "Let's just say I had trouble discerning between who a person seems and who they really are."

Now they were venturing into territory she didn't want to explore.

Sadie eyed the open door that gave her an angled look at the front porch. "Regarding the railing, would you mind replacing it with wood for now? Then we can look into doing vinyl a little down the road."

"Works for me." Asher turned and headed back to the porch.

As if her feet had a mind of their own, she walked out of the garage and stood in the driveway, watching him jog across the grass to where his tools glimmered in the yard.

At first, she'd thought Asher was a bit mysterious, and she didn't do mysterious.

Not anymore.

Now, he was more like an enigma. A puzzle with a missing piece.

But she didn't have the time or the desire to put it together. Meeting Gran's needs and keeping her on island was her highest priority.

Five

ASHER HAD BETTER THINGS TO DO than to hang out at Martha's on Main to discuss what needed to be done for the upcoming festival. But he had given his word to Dani a few days ago that he'd be there, so he showed up.

With his baseball cap tugged low and sitting in the back corner, Asher hoped to be as unobtrusive as possible. Around him, other people filed into the dining room that closed half an hour earlier for tonight's meeting.

Despite the dark wood-paneled walls, pendant lighting, and wooden booths lining the wall across from the bar, the room vibed with a warm and homey atmosphere. Sounds of clinking glassware and utensils came from the kitchen separated from the dining room by a swinging door.

Scents of seafood mingled with grilled steak, which had been the evening special according to the chalkboard easel next to the hostess station.

His mouth watered. He hadn't had a decent meal in ages, preferring to grab a quick sandwich over actually cooking for himself.

The door opened again, and Sadie held it for Hetty, who moved slowly with a walker. Then Seb Jonathon, the mayor of the island and Dani's uncle, grabbed the door from Sadie and followed them inside the diner.

Seb's presence nearly filled the room. Tall with wide shoulders, the man could wrestle a bull and win. His deep voice boomed over the din of conversation as he greeted others sitting on the green vinyl stools lining the bar.

Dani and her boyfriend, Liam Stone, who'd finally learned to shed his California suits for casual shorts and a T-shirt, headed for the hostess podium turned toward the dining room.

Sadie left Hetty seated at one of the front tables closest to the door and joined them, giving Asher ample opportunity to observe his new neighbor.

Her dark hair had been twisted and clamped with a colorful clip at the back of her head with a few loose hairs framing her face. She didn't need to turn for him to remember the blueness of her eyes or the dimple in her cheek when she shot him one of her rare smiles.

He'd met her three days ago or so, and already he spent more time thinking about her than he had any other woman in the past eighteen months.

Liam moved to the front of the dining room and lifted both hands. "Hey, everyone. If you could find a seat, then we'll get started. We don't want to take up too much of your time, but we wanted to get some plans in place so we could move forward with the festival."

Chairs scraped across the floor as people found places to sit.

Pete Graves, the prop plane pilot, nodded to Asher as he pulled out the chair next to the booth Asher had claimed. "Evening."

"Pete." Asher returned the nod and pressed closer to the wall.

Pete's bulk overflowed the chair. He smelled of fuel and sunshine. Sunspots dotted the man's large hands. He spent plenty of time outside with very little—if any—regard for sunscreen.

Once people settled in their seats, they quieted as Dani and Liam exchanged places.

Dani Sullivan, the island sweetheart who wanted to make the island a better place and bring it back to its former glory, stood quietly with her hands clasped in front of her.

She flicked her blonde braid over her shoulder and smiled at the crowd. "Thank you for coming on such short notice. Tonight, I want to share more about Summer Sunset MusicFest. We've been working hard to revitalize the island to draw in tourists." She paused and waved a hand toward the large front window that overlooked Main Street where guests crowded the sidewalks. "Now, let's send them off with a musical celebration and give them a reason to return."

Dani rattled off her ideas for the music festival—the

same ones Sadie had shared with him. But then she included his idea about the battle of the bands.

Huh.

Sadie actually listened to him. Asher tuned Dani out while his eyes drifted to Sadie, who laughed at something Hetty had said.

She looked up and caught his gaze. Held it a moment. Then she returned her attention to Dani, but not before she gave him a quick look over her shoulder.

"Asher?"

He jerked his attention to Dani, who grinned at him with her eyebrow raised. "Yes?"

"I asked if you had any input about the stage you wanted to share?"

"Stage?" He searched his brain, trying to recall what she was referring to.

Wait a minute … stage. That's right. He'd said he'd help with the stage construction.

He lifted a shoulder. "What do you want to know?"

"Well, I—"

"Wait a minute." Russell Smith, the owner of Smith's Hardware, cut her off as he pushed to his feet. He waved a hand toward Asher. "What does he know about stage construction?"

Quite a lot, actually. But, of course, he remained quiet. He didn't need to start answering nosy questions.

"He works with horses. You need a professional. I can donate lumber from the hardware store in exchange for advertising and construct a stage in no time." Russell hitched up his belted jeans already nearly to his armpits.

Asher slid out of the booth and planted his feet on the wooden floor. Hands on his hips, he faced the older man with a graying comb-over who had at least thirty years and fifty pounds on Asher. "With all due respect, I don't think a wooden stage is the best answer."

Russell swiveled and glared at him. "And again, I ask—what experience do you have?"

Ignoring him, Asher focused on Dani. "A modular stage made of aluminum would be lightweight, movable, yet sturdy enough for performers. They're compact and portable, so you could store it effortlessly and reuse it again if you'd like to have another concert in the future. Plus, we could have a non-skid surface that remains safe for the performers."

Dani eyed him and bit the corner of her lip as if processing his words.

Russell, on the other hand, waved a hand. "Aluminum? A wooden stage would be much stronger."

"And heavier." Asher cut in. He turned back to Dani. "Talk to Ariel—see which type she'd prefer. I can almost guarantee she'll take an aluminum stage over a wooden one."

Russell rolled his eyes and didn't attempt to mask his disdain. "You talk like you know what performers want."

"That's because I—" Asher clamped his lips shut. He lifted his hands, then dropped them at his sides. "I'm not going to argue about this. Dani, you decide, and I'll help out whenever I can."

He needed to keep the peace if he wanted the islanders' support in getting his family's touring company going again.

He slid back into his booth and pressed a shoulder against the wall.

Dani's lips thinned as she twisted her hands in front of her. She caught his gaze, then looked at Liam, who leaned against the bar with his hands tucked under his arms. "That sounds great, and maybe eventually, we could do that. Right now, though, I'm not sure we will have the funds to invest in a stage of that caliber."

Russell flashed him a triumphant grin, then took his own seat.

Asher's hands curled into fists. Another time, and he wouldn't have hesitated decking the jerk and wiping the smarmy smile off his face. But Asher's brawling days were behind him. He couldn't react every time someone annoyed him.

The meeting continued for another forty-five minutes, but Asher paid more attention to the bottle labels on the glass shelves behind the bar.

The desire for a shot of Jack made his teeth itch.

He needed to get out of there, but he couldn't leave without anyone noticing.

Thankfully, Dani and Liam wrapped things up with the promise of another meeting.

One he'd most likely skip.

He slid out of his seat a second time and tried to skirt between the booths and the rows of tables. A hand clamped on his upper arm.

He turned and found Dani looking at him with an imploring look. "Hey, you got a minute?"

He jerked his head toward the door. "Not in here. I need some air. The walls feel like they're closing in."

She nodded, then turned toward the door. He followed her outside.

The bright streetlamp haloed over her, stripping her blonde hair to platinum. She glanced at him, dropped her gaze to her feet, then refocused her attention on him. "Sorry for Russell in there."

Asher lifted a shoulder. "No need to apologize. You're not responsible for that jerk."

"He's not a bad guy—just opinionated."

"That's one word for it."

Dani's mouth twitched. "I do appreciate your input, Ash. To be honest, I'm sure Ariel would agree with you. Problem is the money."

"Then I'll buy it."

She shook her head. "No, I can't have you do that."

"Why not? I offered." Asher dragged a hand over his face. "Listen, Dani, I respect wanting to keep business on island, but a wooden stage will be heavy and cumbersome. And slick if there's the slightest bit of rain. How will you store it when the concert's over? Take it apart and rebuild the next time?"

"If there is a next time."

He lifted her chin. "Hey, it's a great idea. I'm sure it will be the first of many concerts."

"Thanks for the name, by the way. And the idea for

the battle of the bands. Sadie mentioned you came up with them."

Heat warmed his neck as he shoved his hands in the front pockets of his frayed jeans.

"You know, there's still room on our schedule for another act. I was serious before when I asked if you'd be willing to sing."

He couldn't shake his head fast enough. "No, that part of my life is over. Went up in flames, remember? Literally."

She pressed a hand against his arm. "But it doesn't have to be. God has given you an incredible talent."

"Oh, yeah? I seem to be more talented in destroying the lives of those I love." His voice rose as he shook off her arm. A band cinched around his chest, creating a vise around his lungs. "Where was God then? Huh? God doesn't care about people like me. I deserve to be alone."

With that, he pushed past her and strode down the sidewalk.

"You're wrong, Asher." She called after him.

He stopped at the pain in Dani's voice and turned.

Her eyes glistened as her eyebrows furrowed. "I hope you can realize that someday, before it's too late."

He closed his eyes as her words socked him in the chest. He rubbed a hand over his sternum, his gut on fire, and kept walking. He strode past the door as Sadie stepped onto the sidewalk.

"Asher, you okay?"

He lifted a hand but didn't stop. Couldn't. If he did, then she'd see the pain on his face. And nobody needed to witness his silent torture. And he didn't want anyone else's pity.

He should've stayed home. He should've stayed with the 'no' he'd given Sadie after she asked for his help with the stage. Getting involved with the island and anyone here was only going to lead to trouble.

Was something going on between Dani and Asher?

Asher retreated into the darkness, his form becoming nothing but a shadow under the streetlights. And leaving Sadie with more questions.

She stepped onto the sidewalk and hurried over to Dani, who stood against the restaurant wall with a hand covering her face.

"Hey, you okay?"

Dani jumped. Seeing Sadie, she nodded. She pasted on a smile that Sadie knew was fake.

"Everything okay between you and Asher?"

Frowning, Dani waved away Sadie's question. "Yes, it's fine. Just a difference of opinions, that's all. I wanted to remind him of his value to the island. We didn't see eye to eye on something I said."

"About the stage?"

Dani shook her head. "Not directly." Then she flashed another overly bright smile at Sadie. "So, what did you think about the meeting?"

"You and Liam were clear with your plans, and I think people are getting excited about your cousin and Miss Dahlia putting on a show for the island." Sadie pressed her back against the brick next to Dani. "For what it's worth, I agree with Asher about the stage. A modular unit would be a lot less clunky."

"But much more expensive." Dani turned and leaned her shoulder against the building. "How's the ad copy coming along? Will you have it ready to go to the printer by Monday?"

Sadie nodded as the pressure of her looming deadline weighed on her. "Somehow, I'll find a way to capture the essence of the island in order to stir up excitement for the festival."

Dani grabbed her hand and gave it a squeeze. "See, that's why I knew you were the right person. I wouldn't have come up with the idea of 'capturing the essence of the island.'"

"I don't know about that. I'll have it to you soon." Sadie returned the squeeze, then nodded to the business next door. "I'm going to check things in the bakery while Gran's still chatting with Doris and Annabelle. If she asks, will you tell her I'll be back shortly?"

Dani nodded, then held up a finger. "Wait. Mind if I tag along?"

"Not at all."

"Great, I just need a few minutes to clear my head. I'll pop inside and let Liam know where I'm going."

Sadie remained where she was while Dani headed back into Martha's.

A moment later, Dani joined her, slinging her cross-body bag over her chest. "I told them. Your grandma's laughing with Annabelle over Doris's latest stories from manning the desk at the airport. Liam's deep in conversation with Uncle Seb about something regarding the hotel renovations. I'm not even sure they paid attention to anything I said."

"I'm glad Gran came tonight. It was good for her to get out and see her friends. She loves the island." Sadie moved down a few squares on the sidewalk and stood in front of the once-thriving storefront that now sat dark and abandoned.

Her stomach tightened as she stared at the faded and torn blue-and-white canopy that fluttered in the breeze. The dusty window, with the words *Hudson Bakery* curved over a loaf of bread, appeared lifeless and forgotten.

She sighed. "Gramps used to throw open the windows every morning so scents of fresh bread and cinnamon rolls would waft down the block and entice customers to come into the store. He'd be so sad to see the state of this place now."

"He knew how to grow his business."

"And he did it through word of mouth. Refused to let me create a website or put them on social media." Gramps's deep voice echoed faintly through her head as he disagreed with her marketing ideas.

"No website can capture the smell of fresh-baked bread, Sadie girl."

Dani sighed along with her. "I miss this place. Your grandma made the best cookies. And your grandpa's Italian herb bread always sold out within hours of being put on the shelf."

Sadie blinked back unexpected tears as memories resurfaced of her and Lauren racing down the sidewalk ahead of their parents to be the first one inside to claim the first cookie from Gran. "This was one of my favorite places on the island. So much love and laughter spilled out of here. I wish we didn't have to sell it."

Dani grabbed her arm. "Wait a minute. What do you mean? Your grandma's selling the bakery?"

Gnawing on the corner of her lip, Sadie nodded. "Her cottage needs repairs she can't afford. She doesn't want to sell, but by doing so, she'll have money to improve her home so she can stay on island. Otherwise, she's considering moving to a senior complex in Port Joseph."

"I can't imagine the island without her."

Sadie used Gran's key and unlocked the front door. As she turned the doorknob, tarnished bells jingled against the glass. She flung it open, stepped inside, waited for Dani to enter, then closed the door behind them.

Stretching on her tiptoes, Sadie unhooked the bells from the top of the window and curled her fingers around the faded blue ribbon. "Lauren and I saved up our money and bought these for Gran and Gramps for Christmas one year. I was eight and she was ten. They've been hanging here ever since."

Dani slung an arm over her shoulder and gave her a gentle squeeze. "Take them home and give them a good polish. You can rehang them in Henrietta's kitchen."

Sadie reached for the light switch. No matter how many times she flipped the switch, the room remained dark. "I guess Gran had the utilities shut off when she closed up the place."

"Many owners did the same thing after closing their doors." Dani's words held a thread of wistfulness.

They pulled out their phones and tapped on their flashlights. Sadie shined her light over the dust-covered, round tables where guests used to sit as they chatted over coffee and Gran's baked goods.

Faint scents of vanilla and sugar mingled with the mustiness from being closed up. More than anything, she wanted to throw open a window like Gramps used to and allow the fresh air to circulate once again.

If only . . .

Oversized, intricate cobwebs hung from the corners. Sadie suppressed a shudder as she walked behind the counter and pushed through the swinging door into the kitchen. She held it for Dani.

"Man, this brings back memories. Remember when your grandpa let us frost doughnuts and we dropped that huge container of sprinkles into the frosting?"

Sadie laughed. "The kids on the island loved the one-day special on confetti doughnuts."

She trailed her fingers over the empty racks that used to hold trays of raised glazed doughnuts. Now all they held were memories.

Shafts of light from the streetlamps strayed through gaps between the boards nailed over the window. She shined her light over the industrial ovens that sat cold and unused. The commercial mixers remained silent. The stainless counters that used to be lined with trays of cookies waiting to be frosted, muffins to be boxed, and pies to be sliced were blanketed in a thick layer of dust and cobwebs.

Sadie left the kitchen and returned to the dining room where Dani stood in front of the large chalkboard. Gran's script had been smudged by time, but Sadie could still make out a few faded, chalky letters on the specials board.

"You know, if I close my eyes, I can almost see this wonderful place coming back to life."

"Me too." Sadie's words came out almost hushed, as if she were afraid to disturb the memories.

Dani turned to her. "What would it take to restore its former glory?"

"Money. And time. Two things we have very little of these days." Sadie lifted her shoulders, then dropped them. "Reopening it doesn't make sense with my parents in Hawaii. Selling will keep Gran on island. Problem is, the place didn't assess very high. Mia and I did a walk-through two days ago. She suggested doing some minor repairs, repainting walls, and putting down new flooring to see if it would fetch a higher price. Any idea who I could ask?"

"Cody Hart has been the town handyman for years and helped get the one-dollar houses ready, but he's also trying to revive the fishing business he's taken over for his dad." Dani pointed to the ceiling. "Hunter Barrett lives in the upstairs apartment with his brother Waylen, who is one of the island police officers. The Barretts used to have a construction company on island, but Hunter's dad left several years ago and moved his construction business to Port Joseph. I think Hunter goes off island to help his dad. Let me text Liam and see if he knows of anyone working at the hotel who could do it." Her head lowered to her screen as she tapped a message.

Almost immediately, Dani's phone chimed. She looked at Sadie with a frown. "Liam says the only ones he knows are booked."

"Bummer." Sadie turned slowly, phone held up in her hand, and shined the light over the walls painted a soft blue. "This was more than a bakery. At least to me. I'd love for it to be that again to someone else."

Dani moved next to her, her shirt brushing Sadie's shoulder. "What about Asher?"

"What *about* Asher?"

"He knows construction. His dad has a thriving business near Flint, and Asher worked with his dad until—" Dani's words died suddenly as she bit her lips.

"Until what?"

Dani shook her head. "Nothing. Until he quit to do something else. I think he and his dad had a falling out."

"You know a lot about him."

"We're friends. Like I told you before, I used to hang out with his cousins, even though Eliza was a couple of years older than me. Do you remember her? Dark hair, serious eyes."

"Asher mentioned her the other day, but I'd have to see a picture to know if I'd recognize her again."

"Asher knows his way around a hammer, which is why I wanted him to be a part of the stage construction. Wouldn't hurt to talk to him."

"He helped fix Gran's railing. I'd hate to impose on his time for this."

"Seems like he has a soft spot for Henrietta. Drop her name and see what happens. Or have her ask him."

"See, that's the thing. She doesn't know I talked with Mia about what it would take to up the price. I want to do it as a surprise."

"Won't she notice people in and out of the bakery?"

Sadie lifted a shoulder. "Maybe. I'll figure out something if she asks."

Dani was right—Asher did have a soft spot for Gran.

Maybe it wouldn't hurt to talk to him. Maybe he could just inspect the place and give her a general idea of how much it would cost to fix.

Somehow, Sadie would get the money, even if it meant going against her word and calling her parents. Anything to give Gran the peace she deserved.

Six

THE HAUNTING IMAGES FROM HIS dreams were becoming too real.

Asher sat up in bed, the darkness surrounding him, as he pulled himself from the dregs of sleep and tried to make out shapes in his room.

His chest heaved as sweat slicked his skin.

Instead of the past bus crash that changed his life, his present life intervened.

Dani was in the middle of the lake. No matter how fast he swam, he couldn't reach her. She'd gone under, screaming his name.

He untangled his legs from the twisted sheet and tossed it aside. Moving to the edge of the bed, he buried his clammy face in his shaking hands.

Must've been the argument with the guy about the stage and his conversation with Dani outside of Martha's that triggered it.

Asher hadn't had a nightmare in a while, and now he'd had two in the same month.

Check that, the same week.

He needed to get out of his room. Do something to clear his head. Maybe a walk would help. No one was around to judge him. He did plenty of that on his own.

He threw on a pair of running shorts and yanked a T-shirt over his head. He slid his feet into his flip-flops, grabbed his phone and keys, and headed out to the hall and down the stairs.

As he stepped outside, he sucked in a breath of chilly night air and filled his lungs. Goosebumps prickled his skin as he jammed his hands in the pockets of his shorts. Gravel crunched beneath his feet as he headed down the driveway, then turned onto Sugar Maple Lane, which ran past Hetty's house.

Wings flapped and owls hooted from their perches in the branches hanging over his head.

As he passed Hetty's darkened cottage, someone coughed softly.

He paused.

Was that from inside the house with the window open, or was someone awake and sitting outside?

He crept closer, trying not to come across as a stalker. He just didn't want to startle whoever could be on the porch.

He took another step.

"Hello?" Someone called from the porch.

Sounded more like Sadie than Hetty. Besides, he couldn't imagine the older woman still being awake at this hour. He trudged through the yard, the wet grass soaking his feet.

He rounded the corner of the house and stopped.

Sadie sat on one of the wicker chairs with her knees close to her chest and her arms wrapped around her legs.

"Sadie?" Even though he knew it was her, speaking her name hopefully let her know he wasn't some stranger.

She pushed to her feet and moved to the railing. "Asher?"

He came into the glow of the porch light and lifted a hand. "Hey."

"What are you doing here? Especially this late at night?"

He waved a hand toward the road. "Just out for a walk, trying to clear my thoughts."

"You too, huh?"

He edged closer to the porch, then jerked his head toward the path separating the two properties. "Wanna go for a walk?"

She glanced around. "Is it safe?"

"Anyone with common sense is in bed." He grinned, showing he was teasing. "You'll be safe with me. We might run into a deer or a squirrel, but we'll be fine. I walk this path all the time."

"Do you have a lot of late nights where you can't sleep?"

"More than I'd like." Asher stabbed a toe against a clump of grass at the edge of Hetty's sidewalk. He jerked his head toward the path. "Come on. A walk will be good for both of us."

She eyed him a moment, then grabbed a sweatshirt off the chair and pulled it over her head. Then she pocketed her phone, slid her feet into her flip-flops, and joined him in the grass. She shivered. "I'd forgotten how chilly the island can be in the evenings."

"Feels good. So much fresh air." As they headed down the narrow path, the wind rustled through the trees, stirring the leaves.

Next to him, Sadie stopped and grabbed his arm. "Is that an animal?"

"Where?" Asher scanned the nearby foliage. "I don't see anything."

"I don't know. I thought I heard something." She removed her hand from his arm and shoved it in the front pocket of her hoodie. "Must be my overactive imagination."

"So, what has you awake at this hour?"

She didn't speak for a moment.

Maybe she didn't trust him, not that he blamed her. Even though they'd gotten along better lately, they weren't exactly BFFs or anything.

"You knew my grandmother owned the bakery in town, right?"

"Yes, I used to go there all the time when I visited the island as a kid."

"She's considering selling the bakery so she has money for much needed updates on her cottage." She explained about the problem with the appraisal.

"How does she feel about selling?"

"I think she's sad. She and my grandpa ran it for over fifty years. After the hotel burned, the seasonal workers didn't have places to stay. Then the pandemic hit, and businesses pretty much shut down. Then Gramps had a heart attack one morning before the bakery opened and passed away. I'm sure Gran would love to see it reopened for business, but I don't know anything about running a bakery. And my dad can't do anything from Hawaii. Dani made a couple of inquiries about getting someone to help with bakery repairs, but they're booked out for the rest of the summer. I'm not sure who else I can ask."

"What about me?"

"What about you?" She lifted a shoulder. "Have a cool half a million sitting around that you want to invest in a defunct property?"

Asher laughed. If she only knew ... "I could lend a hand and help get things spruced up."

"Thanks. That's kind of you, but you're busy enough as it is."

"I'm busy by choice. I can make time to help you."

She looked down at her feet, then glanced at him, her eyes soft and a bit vulnerable. "Again, thanks, but I can't pay you."

"I'm not looking to be paid. I love Hetty, and she's a great neighbor. I'll do what I can to help her stay in her home. I can meet you at the bakery first thing in the morning." Asher rolled around a sudden idea in his head, then stopped and faced Sadie. He tried not to be distracted by the way the moonlight captured her beauty. "What if we trade services?"

"What kind of services?"

"I'm restoring one of the carriages my grandfather built before starting his own touring company over seventy years ago. With more and more people coming back to the island, I want to revive our family's tour company. That means an online presence, but I'm not good with that sort of thing. You have such fond memories of the island and knowledge that I don't have."

"You spent time here as a kid too. What about your fond memories?"

"Yes, but we didn't visit every year like you did. Would you be willing to help me get the business online, then conduct a few trial tours? I could drive the team, and you could narrate for the guests."

"Narrate? Like talk in front of people?" She swallowed, then shook her head, her eyes wide. "I'm sorry, Asher. I can't. While I'm grateful for your offer of help, I don't think I could return the favor, at least the touring part of it. I don't do well speaking in public. I'd be willing to give you free marketing advice about how you can advertise and grow your business online though. I can write copy in my sleep." She scoffed. "Except where the festival is concerned."

"Why's that?"

She lifted a shoulder. "No clue. I'm working with some clients remotely, and I'm not having an issue with their stuff. But when Dani asked for my help, I kind of froze. Doesn't make sense."

"What do you have so far?"

Sadie pulled out her phone and opened her app where she'd written out her notes. She handed it to him. "Read for yourself, but it's pretty blah."

He took the phone and scrolled through her words. "I

don't know, Sadie. You have some pretty cool stuff here. I like the description of the music festival—'Set against the background of the lake, the first annual Jonathon Island Summer Sunset MusicFest combines the sounds of nature with talented performances under the open star-studded sky. From sunrise to sunset, enjoy warm breezes blowing across the tranquil shores and soak in the last rays of summer while enjoying fare from local businesses. As the sun dips into the horizon, gather in the park for an unforgettable concert as vibrant voices come together in a kaleidoscope of music to bid farewell to another fabulous summer on our enchanted island.'"

She groaned and covered her face with her hands. "Hearing it read out loud makes it sound even cheesier."

"Cheesy? No way. You've brought the island to life with your description."

She peered at him through parted fingers. "Seriously?"

"Yes, seriously." He held her phone out to her.

She took it and returned it to her hoodie pocket. "Thanks for being nice about it."

He nudged her with his shoulder. "Believe it or not, I am a nice guy."

"I'm learning that."

"You have a way with words, Sadie."

"Now you're just trying harder to be a nice guy."

"No, I'm dead serious." He stopped and turned her to face him. Behind her, the glow of the moon cast a halo in her hair. "You're very talented. Your words evoke emotion, and that's not always easy to do. I think you'd be an asset as a tour guide for my family's company."

"If only it weren't for that whole speaking in public thing."

"What if you didn't think about it as speaking in public? What if you were having coffee with friends and wanted to share your love of the island with them?"

"Are you going to offer free coffee with your tours?"

"If that's what it takes to get you to relax, then sure."

"Why me? Why not someone else, like Dani? She has plenty of experience with doing tours."

"Dani has enough to do. You know as well as I do if I ask her, she will say yes. But I don't want to add more to her already full plate. You want help with your bakery, and I can do that. I need help with my tour company. It's a great opportunity for you to step out of your own comfort zone and do something new. Who knows—you may even surprise yourself and enjoy it."

"Gran calls you the reclusive neighbor for a reason. Are you willing to step out of your zone to get to know the people on the tours?"

"I'll drive the team. No one cares about me. They'll be too busy staring at the pretty lady telling them about the history of the island."

She laughed, a musical sound that wound its way around his heart.

"Pretty lady? Now I know you're full of it."

Asher laughed along with her, but Sadie's words touched a chord. She was right—if he wanted to pull off having the tours in place for the festival, then he needed to put himself out there a little more. Even if it meant dealing with people like Russell Smith. But with someone like Sadie by his side, he'd give it a shot.

A week on island and Sadie's personal and professional paths were at a crossroads. She needed to figure out a way to navigate both without losing herself in the process.

Her gritty eyes burned from lack of sleep. After returning from the midnight stroll with Asher, her brain refused to settle into a necessary slumber. Instead, she wrote copy in her head for Asher's touring company, imagining his strong arms guiding a team of horses around the island.

Despite what he thought, he *was* part of the package. Female guests would appreciate his presence.

His very handsome presence.

As she studied the dining room in the dusty bakery, she took a sip of the caramel swirl cappuccino she'd picked up from Jill Kelley's Good Day Coffee Shop and nearly dropped it when the scalding liquid seared her tongue. Tears pricked her eyes as she searched for her water bottle to cool her mouth.

Gramps's old radio played the oldies station from the kitchen, just like it did every day that the shop was open. She'd convinced Gran to turn the utilities back on so prospective buyers could have a better look at the interior.

A mellow tenor with perfect pitch sang along with the music.

Sadie's hand loosened on the water bottle as she lowered it to the counter. Slowly, she moved to the swinging door and peered through the circular window.

Asher lay on his back under the deep sink, replacing a leaky pipe that left a slimy green puddle on the tile floor. His foot tapped in time to the beat of the music.

She pushed the door open. "You should enter the talent show."

A metal tool clattered to the floor, followed by a soft *thunk* and an "Ow!"

Sadie winced. "Sorry."

"What did you say?" Asher pushed himself out from under the sink, scowling as he rubbed a reddening spot on his forehead.

Folding her arms over her chest, Sadie leaned against a dusty table and forced a lightness in her tone. "You should enter the talent show. You have a really nice voice."

The lines around Asher's mouth deepened. "I'm not much for the spotlight. Reclusive, remember?" He reached for the wrench. "Almost done with this drain."

"Thanks, I appreciate it." She pushed away from the table and moved to the sink. She tapped her flip-flop against the side of his work boot. "I think you're being modest. With your voice, you're sure to win."

Asher paused. "I'm more of a behind-the-scenes kind of guy. I'd rather muck out stalls and fix leaky drains than stand in front of a microphone." He slid out from under the sink, stood, and turned on the water. Then he shut it off and dipped below the sink. "Good, no more leaks."

"One thing to check off the growing list."

"Growing?"

"Um, yeah. The toilet is running in the women's restroom."

"It doesn't end, does it?" Asher gripped the sink, straightened his arms, and blew out a breath. "How old is the plumbing?"

Sadie shrugged. "I don't know. I could ask Gran. If you can't do it, I'll find someone else . . ."

He held up a hand and smiled. A real one that reached his eyes . . . and tripped her pulse. "No need to do that. I'm not complaining. Just making a comment."

"If you're sure—"

"I am. I want to be here, to help Hetty any way I can."

"You're very sweet to her."

"She makes it easy. One of the nicest people I've ever met." He crouched and dropped his tools in his beat-up canvas bag.

"How long have you known her?"

"Just since I came to the island about eighteen months ago."

"Where'd you live before that?"

He looked up at her, his eyebrows drawn together. "Why all the questions?"

"All the questions? I asked two." She studied him, but he wouldn't meet her eyes.

She was so over men keeping secrets.

She leaned against the counter, arms crossed, trying to remain cool. "You always manage to steer the conversation away from yourself. Is there something you're not telling me?"

Asher's mouth tightened. "What's next on your list?"

Sadie frowned. He deflected smoother than Garrett had when he didn't want her digging too deep.

She wanted to press him, but clenching in Asher's jaw told her she would be wasting her breath.

He cleared his throat. "By the way, I've been thinking about what you said regarding my need to put myself out there for the tour."

"Oh, yeah? So, you want to sign up for the talent show, after all?"

His face twisted. "Would you let that go? I'm not singing."

Sadie's eyes widened at Asher's sharp tone. She wrapped her arms around her waist. "Sorry. Won't mention it again."

Asher took a step toward her. "Sorry, I didn't mean to sound so harsh. It's just . . . a touchy subject."

Sadie backed up and bumped the table. She cleared her throat and forced a neutral tone. "About putting yourself out there . . . with the tour, I mean."

"Right." He opened his mouth to say something, but her ringing phone cut off his words.

She pulled it out, looked at the screen, and saw her mother's name and number. She glanced at Asher. "Excuse me a moment. It's my mom."

Moving into the dining room, she answered, "Hey, Mom. What's up?"

"Hey, honey. I was at the commissary when you called. It was packed and tough enough to maneuver a cart with two hands. I'm home now and putting away groceries. How are things on island? How's Gran doing?"

"Both are going well." Sadie filled her in on the events of the past couple of days. Well, minus her walk with Asher. And the work on the bakery. "Have you and Dad made a decision about the festival? It's coming up in a couple of weeks. I know Gran would love to see you. And me too, of course."

Mom paused, and Sadie's shoulders slumped. She knew that pause all too well. Too often through the years, Mom had paused before giving bad news. Her tell.

Sadie forced enthusiasm into her voice. "I knew it was a long shot since you and Dad are super busy. Don't worry about it."

"Honey, we really want to. Your dad put in leave, but you know how those things go. Depends on his schedule."

"Right." How many times had she heard that through the years?

"You okay, honey?"

Sadie leaned forward and rested her elbows on the front counter and balanced the phone between her ear and her shoulder. "Yes. I guess."

The heaviness of her burdens pressed her elbows harder onto the table. She couldn't share about Gran's finances. Or the bakery. Keeping such a significant decision from her parents felt almost deceitful, but she'd given Gran her word. And that had to mean something.

She was out of a job and living in Gran's guest room. She had only her integrity to hold on to right now.

"Any ideas of what you plan to do once Gran is up and around?"

Sadie hesitated, glancing around the bakery etched in cobwebs and memories. "Not really. Now that my lease is up in Florida, I don't have an apartment anymore. My furniture is in storage in Port Joseph. Once I figure out where I'm going next, I'll have to move everything again. I've got enough savings to last another month or so. After that, who knows what's next?"

"Take it to the Lord, honey. He'll provide. Your dad and I really appreciate you caring for Gran. I'm sure she loves having you there."

"I'll do anything for her."

Even including lying by omission to her parents.

After a little more chitchat, they ended the call.

Even though Sadie talked to her parents almost daily, she hadn't seen them in person since they arrived at Hickam. And that seemed like half a lifetime ago now.

Her shoulders sagged as a wave of homesickness swept over her.

But how could she be homesick without a home?

More like she missed her parents. Simple as that.

Noise from the women's restroom reminded her she wasn't alone in the store.

Asher.

Working steadily down the to-do list they'd constructed together. Even though he seemed to be busy at the ranch and helping with driving people around the island, he'd made time to help with repairs at the bakery and figured they could have everything done within the next two weeks.

She didn't get him. Hadn't from the moment they met.

Even though they'd spent plenty of time together in the last week or so, she knew very little about him. He was good with his hands, just as Dani and Gran claimed.

And he had an aversion to being in the public eye. And talking about himself.

Something about him still tugged at her, and it bugged her that she couldn't figure it out. She needed to let it go. None of her business.

Or would learning more about him create even more of a tangle of her emotions?

Seven

ASHER QUINN WAS GETTING UNDER her skin. And that wasn't a good thing.

Sadie would deny it if asked, but she was actually a little disappointed to step out onto the front porch and find the railing securely in place and repainted.

Not only that, but Asher had scraped and repainted the remaining railing that lined the other side of the porch so that everything matched.

The permanent smile that spread across Gran's face had been worth it.

The man deserved more than lemonade and treats from Gran's kitchen, but that's all she could afford.

"Looks like Gran owes you more cookies." Sadie set a tray on the small wicker table with a plate of Gran's sliced chocolate chip banana bread and a small ramekin of whipped honey butter she used to sell in the bakery.

Scents of sugar and chocolate rose from the warm bread

and tickled Sadie's nose, making her mouth water. She lifted the plate and handed it to Asher.

Asher lifted the corner of his faded T-shirt, giving her a glance at his trim waist, and wiped his face. Then he reached for the plate. "Thanks."

He took a slice and bit off a corner. Asher patted his flat stomach. "Not sure I can afford to keep working for her if she's paying me with baked goods."

"Right. Like you have anything to worry about." Sadie cringed the moment the words escaped her mouth. Heat fanned across her cheeks. Could she blame her fire-engine cheeks on the sun?

Probably not.

Chalk it up to another awkward encounter in the life of Sadie Hudson.

She set the plate on the tray, then brushed her hands together and faced him as if she hadn't just complimented his muscular physique. "Thanks again. The railing looks great. I know Gran—"

The front door opened, cutting off Sadie's words. The leg of Gran's walker appeared, then she made her way onto the porch, one clunking step at a time.

Sadie hurried over and held the door.

Gran clutched a white envelope in her hand as she made her way across the porch to where Asher stood in the grass next to a nearly empty can of white paint and a used paintbrush. She held the envelope out to him. "It's not much, and you certainly deserve more, but this is a little something to say thank you."

Asher held up his hand. "Hetty, no. I didn't do this for the money."

"I know you didn't. And that's why I wish I could pay more."

Raising both hands this time, Asher shook his head as he took a step back. "I'm not taking your money."

"Young man, you saved me hours of trying to find someone who would repair my porch railing. Not only that, but you made it look good as new. When I sit out here, I can enjoy it without stressing about who I could get to repaint it. Take the money. Please."

Asher's shoulders sagged as he stepped forward and took the envelope. He tapped it against his other palm. "I'm not keeping this. Some way, I'm going to sneak it back to you."

"If you do, that will hurt my feelings."

Asher lifted his hands, then dropped them back at his sides. "Okay, Hetty. You win. I don't want to hurt your feelings."

Gran shot him a victorious grin.

Sadie turned away and lowered her voice for her grandmother's ears only. "Gran, you manipulator, you."

Gran winked at her. "I told you Asher was a good man."

Yes, she was learning that.

Asher shoved the envelope in his back pocket. "I'll get this paint cleaned up. Let me know if there's anything else you need done."

Gran eyed him, looked at Sadie, then tapped her chin. "Come to think of it, my bedroom closet door keeps getting stuck. I have to yank on it to get it open at times."

Sadie's eyes narrowed. "Gran, it was fine yesterday when I put away your laundry."

Gran shrugged. "Maybe it's temperamental."

The closet door wasn't the only thing . . .

"Sure thing, Hetty. I'll take a look. It may need rehung."

Shooting him what looked like another triumphant grin, Gran turned and headed for the front door.

Sadie grabbed it and held it while Gran made her way back into the house. Sadie followed her inside.

"Gran, what are you doing?"

Gran paused and looked at Sadie over her shoulder. "Walking to the kitchen."

"That's not what I meant, and you know it." Sadie jerked a thumb over her shoulder. "There's nothing wrong with your closet door."

"Oh, love, I know that." Gran pressed a hand against Sadie's cheek.

"Then why did you ask him to look at it?"

"That wasn't about me." Gran chuckled and shook her head. "I've seen the way Asher looks at you. Wouldn't hurt to have him around a bit."

Sadie followed Gran into the kitchen. "That's ridiculous. We barely tolerate each other."

Again, memories from the walk the other night and being together at the bakery rolled into her head.

His closeness. The easy way she could talk to him. His quickness in helping Gran.

Resting a hip against the counter, Sadie crossed her arms over her chest and blinked away the rogue thoughts.

"He's not my type, remember? He doesn't open up, and I'm done with secrets."

"He will." Gran smeared honey butter on a slice of bread and handed it to her. "When the time is right."

She took the still-warm bread and tore off a corner. "Yeah, well, I may not be here when that happens. I need to find a job, remember? I can't stay on island forever."

"Love, you can stay here as long as you like." Gran lowered herself in a chair, trying not to wince. "In fact, I quite like the company. This place gets too quiet for one person. Start your own copywriting business until you can find your dream job."

"My heart's not really in copywriting these days." Sadie opened the fridge and reached for the milk. She moved to the cupboard and pulled out two glasses. "But it does pay more than my non-existent songwriting career."

"Don't give up hope on that."

Sadie set one of the glasses in front of Gran and gave her a slice of bread. Then she pulled out a chair across from her. "It's not the same without Lauren. We were going to do it together."

"I know, love. I miss her too." Gran covered her hand with one of her own.

Sadie blinked back tears, then forced a smile in place. "Speaking of copywriting, I need to head to Dani's office so we can get flyers printed for the festival. Can you believe Ariel and Miss Dahlia are going to be performing?"

"It will be a great concert." Gran gave Sadie's hand a gentle squeeze. "I've known Ariel since she was a child.

Sweetest little girl with the voice of an angel. Maybe she could give you some songwriting tips."

"Maybe. We'll see. If you're going to be fine for a while, I'll meet Dani now and be back before lunch."

Pushing to her feet, Gran waved her away. "Take your time and enjoy Dani's company. I'm going to read. Sally Jo Wilson sent me a signed copy of her newest release. I helped her with research when she decided her heroine's family needed to own a bakery. And maybe I'll rest my eyes."

Once Gran was settled in her favorite chair, Sadie made sure her water cup was full and that she had her phone.

"Call me if you need anything." Sadie lifted her small sling bag off the hook by the door and draped it over her chest. Grabbing her reusable water bottle, she blew Gran a kiss and headed back out the front door.

Asher was gone. And he cleaned up all the painting tools.

It was as if he'd never been there.

Except the newly repainted railing testified to his presence.

She really needed to get a grip. She didn't have the time or the emotional bandwidth to be interested in another guy.

She opened the side garage door and wheeled out Gran's mint-green retro cruiser bike. She dropped her water bottle in the front wicker basket, closed the door behind her, and headed for the narrow dirt road.

As she pedaled down Sugar Maple Lane past Gran's cottage, she turned toward the Quinn property. Gus and

Ginger grazed in the pasture behind the barn, their tails swishing.

No sign of Asher . . . that she could tell from the road.

Why did she even care?

He was becoming more intrusive in her thoughts.

She needed to keep her focus on the festival. And caring for Gran, which also included getting the bakery ready to go back on the market.

Sadie returned her attention back to the road as a gray rabbit darted in her path. She jammed the pedals backward to lock the coaster brakes.

Instead of stopping, the rear end of the bike started skidding. Sadie jerked the handlebars to veer around the animal that stopped in front of her and stared.

The bike wobbled. Sadie tried to regain control. Before she could counter-steer, the bike toppled sideways, pitching her into the grass along the side of the road.

She face-planted in a patch of white and purple clover. She came eye to eye with a yellow jacket.

Sadie pressed a hand against the ground and pushed herself up. A sharp, sudden pain lanced the side of her thumb. A dark, sliver-like splinter protruded from her left hand, which started to throb.

"Sadie! Are you okay?"

She turned her head. Asher raced across the grass toward her.

"Perfect. Just perfect." Wasn't it every girl's dream to have a hot guy view her misfortune?

Sadie tried to push herself up again, but her left hand burned, and her right shoulder ached.

Asher dropped to his knees in the grass next to her. "Hey, you okay?"

Sadie closed her eyes. Partly to avoid staring into his and partly hoping the earth would develop a sudden sinkhole and swallow her so Asher wouldn't witness her humiliation.

He braced her shoulders gently. "Can you stand?"

She nodded, not trusting her voice.

With his strong hands gripping her, Sadie pushed against him and made it to her feet.

She brushed bits of dried grass and decapitated wildflowers from her cutoff shorts and pale pink T-shirt. She found her right flip-flop that had flown off when she landed in the grass.

"Anything hurt?"

She lifted a shoulder, then winced. "My right shoulder hurts a little, but I'm sure it will be fine." She lifted her left hand. "I think I angered a bee and it stung me."

He reached for her hand. "Let me see."

Sadie held out her hand, and he took it. He ran a rough, calloused finger over the growing red spot.

"Are you allergic to bee stings?"

Sadie shrugged, then winced again. When would she learn? "I don't know. I don't remember being stung before."

Asher lifted his sunglasses, then brought her hand closer to his face. He touched the swollen flesh, and Sadie sucked in a breath. "We need to get that stinger out."

"I have a tiny sewing kit in my bag." She nodded toward the spilled bike where her bag lay in the grass.

Asher lifted a brow. "Seriously?"

Sadie shrugged her left shoulder. "A gift from Gran."

Pulling her hand away and missing the warmth of his touch almost immediately, Sadie swiped the bag off the ground and unzipped it. She pulled out a small blue cloth pouch that held her sewing kit and a few Band-aids. After finding a needle, she handed it to him.

His eyebrows furrowed and his mouth tightened as he focused and removed the stinger from her hand. He brushed his index finger over the wound. "Feel anything?"

"Just your finger."

"Good." Asher handed her the needle, then peered at her hand again. His calloused finger traveled slowly over the reddened spot then across her palm. "It may itch for a while, but if it starts to hurt, or if the pain and itching travel up your arm, you may want to get it checked out."

"Thanks." She stifled a shiver at his tender touch, then pulled her hand away and tucked it in her front pocket. Then she looked at the bike still lying on the ground. Releasing a sigh, she reached down and righted it. Holding on to the handlebars, she turned back to him. "Thanks for your help. I appreciate it."

He shot her one of his rare smiles that sent a jolt straight to her stomach. "Sure thing. Anytime."

As she moved the bike back to the road and balanced herself on the seat, Sadie pondered his words. While she was sure he meant it, she couldn't risk leaning on him on a regular basis.

Seeing that he was a nicer guy than she thought originally played a risky game with her heart. One she couldn't afford to lose, so it was better to keep her distance.

With her opinion changing about Asher, that may be easier said than done.

Asher needed to focus on fixing Hetty's closet door rather than remembering the feel of her granddaughter's soft skin.

When he'd come out of the stable and had seen Sadie fall off her bike, he didn't think. He just ran.

And running to her constantly was going to get him into trouble.

But he couldn't . . . he wouldn't walk away from someone in need.

Somehow, he had to shut off his brain to keep rewinding that moment like an old movie.

Asher forced his attention back to the closet. He dragged a finger over the faint spot on the wooden frame where the door had rubbed a time or two while being opened and closed.

He pushed it open as wide as it would go and peered at the hinges. One of the screw heads appeared bent, as if it had drifted out of the hole. Asher braced the hinge with his thumb and forefinger and gave it a little jiggle. It shifted slightly. He closed the door and headed for the living room.

He crouched next to the chair where Hetty had been reading his aunt's latest novel. "Hetty, looks like one of the screws may be stripped and that's causing the door to rub against the frame. I'm going to remove the door from the hinges so I can check the other holes, maybe fill them in and realign everything."

She turned the book upside down and set it on the table. "Well, aren't you just the sweetest."

Asher gave her a stern look. "Now, remember our promise."

Hetty sighed and waved her hand. "Fine. You can fix my closet."

"And?"

"And I promise not to pay you."

Asher stood and dropped a kiss to the top of her silver head. "Thanks for listening."

As he started past, she reached for his arm. "Why are you so stubborn?"

He let out a laugh. "Oh, that's rich coming from you."

Hetty sniffed. "I'm not stubborn. Just strong-willed. My Hank always said so."

"I'll let you in on a secret, Ms. Hetty." He leaned closer to her ear and whispered, "They're both the same thing."

She laughed and batted at his arm. "Some lucky lady's going to have her hands full with you."

Asher sobered. "Yeah, no worries about that."

Hetty turned and looked up at him. "Asher Quinn, one day, when you least expect it, some young woman is going to come along and snatch that big heart of yours right out of your chest and claim it for her own."

Visions of Sadie lying on the ground next to her toppled bike looped through his mind. "I need a heart for someone to steal. My chest is empty."

Even though he tried to make it a joke, the idea of falling for someone sent a chill through him. Once she learned his secret and the reason for his scars, she'd run in the opposite direction.

Not that he blamed her.

No one wanted to carry the baggage of his past.

Without another word, Asher returned to the bedroom and dug through his uncle's canvas tool bag for his battery-powered drill. He attached the right bit and backed the flush screws out of the hinge. Grabbing a pair of pliers, he caught hold of the bent screw and pulled it out. He stooped and did the same thing to the bottom hinge. Then he leaned the door gently against the wall so it wouldn't fall or chip the paint.

He dropped the screws into a magnetic bowl so they wouldn't get lost and then ran a hand over the carved-out section of the frame where the hinge had been.

Hetty's walker thumped against the wooden hall floor. He turned as she appeared in the doorway. "Need something, Hetty?"

She made her way into the room and lowered herself onto the wingback chair in the corner of her room. "Just thought you might like some company, that's all."

Where'd she get that idea?

But Asher wasn't about to argue with her. Maybe she was the one who was feeling lonely.

"I'm pretty boring company."

She waved away his words. "Now, I'll be the judge of that. Sadie mentioned you're restoring your grandfather's carriage?"

"That's right." He sanded the wood lightly, then rubbed away the dust with a microfiber rag. "If I can get it up and running, I'd like to do a trial tour during the festival and see how that goes. Then I can give them a stronger reason to return home."

"You know why they left, don't you?" Hetty's soft voice floated over him.

He lifted a shoulder. "I figured losing my cousin had a lot to do with it."

"Partially, yes. Everyone grieves in their own way. But you showed up."

"Yeah, and they couldn't wait to escape me." Asher laughed, but his voice sounded more like a croak.

"No, they trusted you. For the first time, Terry had someone who could watch over the ranch so he could take Angela on a getaway."

"Don't they travel during the winter months?"

"Sometimes. Winters are pretty cold on the island. And quiet, as you saw. When the season wraps up, there will be about five hundred of us who remain year-round." She gave him a pointed look. "You've been a godsend to them."

Oh, if she only knew how much literal grief he'd actually caused them.

"What do you remember of my grandfather's touring company?" Maybe a change in topic would ease the burning in his chest.

"Oh, quite a bit, actually. Walt and Alice used to dress up in these wonderful Edwardian era costumes and give fascinating historical tours of the island. Your grandfather drove Hank and me around the island on our wedding day. I was new to the island, and the narrated tour helped me to love it even more. A lot of history here, you know."

Asher dug his putty knife into the container of filler and spread it across the holes. "You wouldn't happen to have any pictures, would you?"

"Oh, my lands, yes! Of course I do." She pointed to the closet area. "Grab that faded floral box off the top shelf, would ya?"

Asher did as instructed, then carried it to her.

Hetty removed the lid and lifted out a worn, black photo album with a tied binding and paper pages. "Hank's parents gave us this album as a wedding present. I keep it in the box to protect it. Sadie and her sister Lauren used to lay on my bed and turn each page so carefully. Sadie said she wanted to wear my wedding dress someday and have a carriage ride like Gramps and mine. I'm sure she's grown out of her silly ideas by now."

"I don't think they're silly."

Hetty eyed him. "That's because you're a romantic."

Romantic?

He raised an eyebrow. No one had called him that before.

The word rolled around in his head as he turned the brittle pages aged by time. A young Hetty, who looked so much like Sadie, wore a white lacy dress that showed off her slender neck. Sleeves came to her wrists as a full skirt took up much of the black leather carriage bench. A short veil sat on her dark hair. Next to her, a slimmer Hank than Asher remembered from his childhood visits to the island wore a black suit with a skinny black tie. His short hair had been slicked back, and he had nothing but love in his eyes for his new bride.

"You guys looked great."

Hetty ran her finger over the picture. "Hank was my everything." She looked at him and blinked rapidly a few times. "Falling in love means giving pieces of your heart away. When those you love leave you, then those pieces of your heart are gone forever. I miss him daily, but I'm glad he didn't suffer."

"What happened? How did he die?"

"A heart attack. At work. Went into the bakery at four in the morning like he did six days a week. When I arrived an hour later, he was on the floor next to the mixer, an open bag of flour spilled all around him. I hold on to the peace that he went quickly and didn't suffer."

Asher took her wrinkled hand in his and gave it a squeeze. "I'm sorry for your loss."

"We'll all leave this world someday. And time on this earth is temporary. I'll see my Hank again in Heaven where we'll be together for eternity." Sniffing, she covered his hand with her other one and gave it a pat. "Do you have pictures of the carriage?"

"It's not finished yet. I need to replace the top." Asher pulled his hand away from hers, then fished his phone out of his front pocket. He scrolled through his photos and found the images he'd sent his cousin for her input. He tapped on one and enlarged it, then turned the screen so Hetty could see his work.

She took the phone in both hands and brought it closer to her face. A smile drifted across her lips as she looked at him. "This is beautiful. You're an excellent craftsman, Asher. Your grandfather would be so proud."

Her words, spoken with sincerity, wove through him and filled in those empty spaces in his chest. "Thanks, Hetty. That means a lot."

He'd stripped the old paint, repaired the wood, and reinforced the joints before adding a coat of primer and an oil-based paint to help the carriage endure the weather better.

Hetty returned his phone to him, and he set it on the edge of her bed. She reached for her walker and pulled herself out of her chair. Her face twisted as she got her balance. "I'll be so glad when I'm done with this old thing."

"It's to help you. Remember that."

"It reminds me just how old I'm getting."

"But you're not losing your spunk."

"You're right, kiddo. We all need spunk, don't we?" She flashed him a smile and winked as she shuffled toward the door.

As Hetty moved out of her bedroom, Asher filled in the rest of the holes. He'd hoped to be done already, but taking the time to talk with Hetty seemed like a higher priority. He snapped the lid on the small tub of wood filler, tossed it in his tool bag, then tucked everything inside her closet.

He headed for the hall. "Hetty, I'll come back later once the wood filler is set—"

A thump and a yell from the other room cut off his words.

He raced into the living room and found Hetty lying on the floor next to her favorite chair. The walker lay on its side next to her, one of the wheels still spinning. "Hetty! Are you okay? Can I help you up?"

Her face twisted in pain, she shook her head and pushed away his hands. "Call 9-1-1. I can't move my leg."

Asher reached for his phone only to realize it wasn't in his pocket.

Hetty's bed.

He raced back to her room and snatched it off the corner of her bed and called 9-1-1 as he hurried back to his friend. After giving his identity and relaying what had happened to the dispatcher, he remained on the line as he knelt next to Hetty and reached for her hand.

Her face twisted with pain as he tried to keep her calm. He pressed two fingers to the inside of her wrist and felt her thundering pulse.

Within minutes, the ambulance siren—one of the few vehicles allowed on island—split the air. He left her and opened the door as two EMTs guided a stretcher into the house.

While a female EMT named Emily talked to Hetty, Asher shared what little he knew with the paramedic, Simon, a broad-shouldered guy with tattooed sleeves on his arms.

Hetty sucked in a breath as the two EMTs worked together and lifted her onto the lowered stretcher. She reached for Asher's hand. "Call Sadie. Tell her I'm fine. I don't want her to worry when she comes back and finds me gone."

He stroked the older woman's silver hair off her forehead and pressed a kiss to her temple. "I'll call her from the medical center. I'm not leaving your side."

Hetty made a face. "Asher, that's not necessary. You have work to do."

"My work can wait. You are more important."

Fifteen minutes later, Asher stood in the tiny waiting room of the medical center's emergency department. He pulled out his phone, texted Dani for Sadie's number, and then made the call that tightened his gut.

Sadie answered on the first ring. "Hello?"

"Sadie, I'm at the medical center with Hetty. There's been an accident—"

"On my way." She cut him off before he could finish.

The line dropped and Asher stared at the black screen, then stowed his phone in his pocket. Arms crossed over his chest, he stared out the window that overlooked Blueberry Boulevard and watched for Sadie.

Thank God he'd been there when Hetty fell, but he couldn't shake the sinking feeling that Sadie would blame him.

Eight

SADIE SHOULDN'T HAVE LEFT GRAN alone.

Maybe if she'd been there, she could've kept Gran from falling. Then she wouldn't have needed to be airlifted off the island and returned to Port Joseph where she'd had the initial hip replacement.

With the ferries done running for the night, Sadie had no choice but to remain where she was. First thing tomorrow, though, she'd get herself to the mainland, even if she had to hitch a ride on Cody Hart's fishing boat or ask Pete to fly her to the hospital.

Arms wrapped around her waist, Sadie eyed Gran's bike shoved into the rack in front of the medical center. She didn't want to ride it back to the cottage and spend the night by herself. She wasn't afraid of being alone, but she didn't expect to get much sleep until she heard how Gran was doing.

A strong hand rested on her upper back. "Come on, let's get something to eat."

"I'm not hungry." She didn't need to turn to know Asher was behind her. Not only was his distinctive voice on a regular loop in her head, but her skin tingled every time he came near.

That needed to stop.

"Then keep me company while I scarf down a burger at Martha's. I haven't eaten yet today." Asher's hands moved from her back to rest on her shoulders. "Besides, you don't need to sit alone at the cottage and beat yourself up."

"I should've been there." She turned and pressed her forehead against his chest.

His arms wrapped around her. "Well, I was there, and she still fell. Do you blame me for her accident?"

She lifted her face. He looked at her with a softened, almost pleading, expression. More than anything she wanted to blame someone, but Asher was right. She lowered her chin and shook her head. "No. It wasn't your fault."

"Mind if we get that printed on a T-shirt for the next time you disagree with me?"

She laughed and punched him playfully in the side. "You know there will be a next time."

Asher grabbed her hand and rubbed his thumb over her knuckles. "I'm looking forward to it."

His voice, low and husky, melted over her. He locked her in a stare, and she didn't want to look away. His calming presence did much to settle the rising anxiety in her chest.

She'd been so wrong about Asher Quinn. He wasn't the jerk she'd first met. He truly cared. The way he helped Gran was evidence of that.

"Thank you. For everything. Helping Gran. Calling me."

He touched her chin. "Hey, what are friends for?"

She looked at him again. "Is that what we are? Friends?"

"I'd like to think so. I know we got off on the wrong foot somehow, but I'm an okay guy. Most of the time." He shot her a wink that caused her heart to stutter.

Without taking the time to weigh out the consequences, Sadie wrapped her arms around his waist and rested her cheek against his chest. "I think you're more than okay."

The sliding doors to the island emergency department opened, and Sadie jumped. Realizing she was still wrapped in Asher's arms, she stepped back, needing the distance to find some sort of coherent thought.

Being near Asher was dangerous. She could find herself falling for him. Or at the very least try to get him to open up and share some of those secrets he was keeping. Maybe they could be real friends, someone she could count on.

Clearing her throat, she eyed the bike again. "Let's walk to Martha's. I'll come back tomorrow and get Gran's bike."

Ten minutes later, they stepped inside the restaurant. Pendant lights hanging from the ceiling cast a peaceful glow over the woodwork. They found a booth near the back and settled in with menus.

Even though Sadie wasn't hungry, she scanned the lists of sandwiches and salads, deciding on a strawberry salad with grilled chicken. Maybe if she picked at a few berries, then Asher wouldn't fuss about her needing to eat something.

She closed the menu and left it on the end of the table. "At the medical center, you mentioned you and Gran were talking about your grandparents running the carriage tours."

Asher closed his menu and set it on top of hers. Then he pulled out his phone, scrolled down the screen, found the picture he'd taken of Hetty's wedding photo, then turned it to Sadie. "Yes, she showed me a picture of my grandfather's carriage on her wedding day."

Sadie took the phone, her fingers brushing his. "I remember this picture from Gran's wedding album. She looked so gorgeous. When I was little, I said I wanted to wear her wedding dress and have a carriage ride after my ceremony. But that's not going to happen now." She handed the device back to him.

"Why not?"

"Because I won't be getting married."

"How do you know that?"

"Well, for one thing, most men are liars and can't be trusted." Her words came out a little sharper and louder than she'd expected. Several heads turned toward them.

Sadie slid lower in the booth. Before she could apologize for her tone, their server Vera Graves, former Sunday school teacher at the Little Stone Bible Church, appeared with their drinks. She wore a black Martha's on Main T-shirt tucked into her jeans. Her dark hair streaked with gray had been pulled back into a low bun at the base of her neck. Wire-rimmed glasses sat low on the bridge of her nose.

She set a glass in front of Sadie. "Good to see you, hon. How's your grandma doing?"

Not ready to share about Gran's recent fall until she had more information, Sadie smiled at her. "Getting better every day."

Or at least, she hoped today's fall didn't set Gran back in her progress.

"Glad to hear it. Let her know we're praying for her." Vera set a cup in front of Asher and filled it from the pot on her tray.

"Thanks, Vera. She'll appreciate that."

As the older woman bustled away, Sadie unwrapped the straw and shoved it in her water.

Asher's mouth tightened as he took a sip of his black coffee. "Most men."

"Excuse me?"

"You said most men are liars and can't be trusted."

She lifted a shoulder. "Some men."

"Bad experience, I take it."

"Something like that. I fell for a guy who lied about who he was. I didn't discover it until his wife showed up at my job and made a scene in front of everyone. I got blamed for being the home-wrecker when I didn't even know the jerk was married."

Asher let out a low whistle. "Man, that's tough. I'm sorry that happened to you."

She lifted a shoulder. "It is what it is. I don't trust people who can't be real with me." Tired of talking about her past heartache, even for a few minutes, Sadie pointed to Asher's phone, face down on the table. "Your grandfather looked very handsome in that photo. You look a lot like him."

The lines around Asher's eyes deepened as a smile tugged on the corner of his lips. "So you think I'm handsome too?"

Instead of replying, Sadie rolled her eyes and reached for her drink. She took a sip, needing the iciness to chill the warmth climbing up her throat.

Asher drummed his fingers on the phone case. "Hetty gave me an idea. What if we were to dress in period costumes and offer historical tours like my grandparents did as one of our packages?"

"We?"

"I'm still hoping to convince you to help me with the tours. Pretend you're playing a role."

"I'm a terrible actress. In third grade, I was a tree and couldn't stop shaking. My leaves kept falling off. People laughed and I wanted to cry. My friend said I ruined the whole play and stopped wanting to hang out with me."

"People won't laugh at you now."

Absorbing the gentleness of Asher's voice, Sadie closed her eyes a moment, then reopened them and peered at him over the rim of her glass. She found him watching her with a serious expression on his face. She set her nearly empty glass on the table and folded her hands in her lap. "After the way you helped Gran tonight, I don't think I can tell you no again. If you hadn't been there . . ."

He reached for her hand. "Hey, don't go there. I was right there, and she got the help she needed. She's going to be fine. Sending her to Port Joseph where she had her original surgery is a precautionary measure to ensure she's healing properly and didn't reinjure her hip."

Their server arrived with her salad and his steaming black and blue burger—a mix of blue cheese and blackening seasoning—and fries. For the next few minutes, she toyed with her lettuce while Asher practically inhaled half of his burger.

"Something wrong with your salad?"

She shook her head and set her fork on the side of her barely-touched food. "The salad's fine. I'm not hungry. I'll ask for a box and take it home."

Asher lifted a hand and signaled their server. She came to their table, and he asked for two boxes and the check.

"We don't have to leave. Stay and enjoy the rest of your food."

He pushed his plate away. "I ate enough. I can have the rest for a snack later if I get hungry."

Their server returned with the white take-out boxes and set the check face down on the table. Sadie reached for it, but Asher was faster.

"Hey!"

Grinning, he dumped his half-eaten burger and the rest of his fries in his box. "Not my fault you have slow reflexes."

"I have cash to cover my share of the bill. You don't need to buy me dinner." Sadie reached for her purse, but the bench was empty next to her.

"Need to—no. Maybe I wanted to."

She peered under the table to see if it had fallen on the

floor. Nothing was there except for the table leg. She slid out of the booth and looked all around her.

"I was with Lily and Dani when I got the call and must've left my purse at Lily's. I left in such a hurry . . ." Sighing, she texted a quick message to her friend. Within seconds, three dots appeared to show Lily responding. Then she replied with the answer Sadie expected. She turned the screen toward Asher. "It's at Lily's."

Standing next to their booth, Asher picked up their check and grinned. "I get to buy you dinner after all."

"I'll pick up the check next time."

"Next time?" Asher raised an eyebrow. "I'll look forward to that." Then he patted his back pockets and his eyes widened. "I don't have my wallet either."

"Are you serious?" Sadie darted a look at Martha Kelley, who was talking to a table of women near the bar. "Gran and Martha are longtime friends. Maybe she'll let me run to get my purse and come back and pay the check."

Another grin split Asher's face as he lifted out a brown leather wallet. "Just kidding."

Sadie fished an ice cube out of her water and threw it at him. "You're a jerk."

He hooked an arm around her neck and pulled her playfully toward him. "Just wanted to lighten the mood. You're too serious, Sadie."

Asher removed a credit card and slid it into the pocket of the folder that held their bill. He handed it to Vera as she passed.

She took it and shot him a smile. "I'll be right back."

A moment later, she returned with a copy for Asher to sign, a pen, and his credit card.

A matte black card had a gold guitar in the corner.

How on earth did Asher qualify for a premium luxury card?

They weren't uncommon on the island, but they were usually reserved for the wealthy and not the average consumer.

Just *what* was Asher hiding?

The question dogged Sadie as they left the restaurant and headed down the sidewalk.

"I need to run to Lily's and grab my purse."

"I'll walk with you."

As they passed the bakery, Sadie stopped and returned to the dark window. She traced over the faded *Hudson Bakery* letters. "I don't think I'll get used to having this closed. I spent so much time here as a kid."

"Why don't you reopen it?"

Taken aback, Sadie looked at him and pressed a hand to her chest. "Me?" Then she shook her head. "Well, for one thing, I can barely cook. Even though I worked at the bakery during the summer, I didn't have to do the actual baking. When we lived together, Lily kept me fed. I can barely pay my bills these days, let alone run a business. If I could afford it, though, I'd buy it from Gran and hire people to run it. That way, Gran's legacy lives on, and she gets to remain in her home."

Feeling drained, Sadie pushed away from the window then wrapped her arms around her waist. She turned around and faced the direction back to Gran's cottage. "I think I'll grab my purse tomorrow. I have my phone, and I know where Gran keeps her emergency key, so I'm going to head back to her house."

"Well, that's the direction I'm heading anyway, so I'll walk with you. By the way, I didn't think to lock Hetty's door after the EMTs loaded her into the ambulance."

"No worries. No one's going to bother her place."

They turned and headed up Main Street. As they reached Blueberry Boulevard, Sadie paused at the edge of the park. She shielded her eyes as she gazed at the construction happening in the corner where Pinnacle Drive met with Lake Shore Drive. "Looks like the stage is coming together."

Asher inhaled, then exhaled slowly as he shook his head. "I think it's a waste to build the stage out of wood only to tear it back down after the concert is over. I tried to convince Dani to go with a modular set up, but since Russell Smith donated the materials, she couldn't really argue. At least for this year."

"How does a guy who cares for horses know so much about stages?"

Asher was quiet a moment, then he pulled out his phone and waved it to her. "There's this thing called the internet. You click a button, and you have a wealth of information at your fingertips."

Hands on her hips, Sadie eyed him. "You're a smart-mouth tonight. I'm seeing a new side of you."

"How would you like to see another side of me?"

Sadie's eyes narrowed as her arms slid back around her waist. "What do you mean?"

Shaking his head, Asher ran a hand over his face. "Don't look at me so suspiciously. I'm talking about my crafty side."

"Like with sequins and a glue gun?"

"More like wood stain and elbow grease."

"I'm listening."

"Come with me, and I'll show you."

As they walked back, Sadie picked up her pace to match Asher's long-legged stride.

At the ranch, Asher slid open one of the large barn doors, then flicked on a light. He stepped aside and waved a hand, ushering her into the building.

Rays of the sinking sun shot through dusty windows, illuminating dust motes floating in the air.

Asher moved in front of her and gestured for her to follow him. He moved deeper into the building until he came to something large and bulky in the corner. He tugged on the faded blue tarp and revealed an antique touring carriage.

"This was my grandfather's carriage." Asher stepped back and flicked a switch.

Rows of utility work lights brightened the room and cast a glow over the gleaming carriage.

Sadie moved closer and ran a hand over the carriage's glossy black side panels.

Between helping with the stage construction, repairing Gran's porch, doing repairs at the bakery, and maintaining the ranch, he still found time to refurbish his grandparents' carriage. Was there anything he couldn't do?

She turned to Asher. "This is simply beautiful. It's more

than that—it's incredible. You brought your grandfather's carriage back to life. He'd be so proud."

Asher lifted a shoulder. "I don't know about that."

"You're being modest."

"We used to visit the island when I was a kid. After my grandma passed away, my grandfather declined rapidly. He had dementia. But on a particularly lucid day, I remember him telling the story of how he bought this beat-up carriage and restored it to start a company so he could impress my grandma's father enough to give his daughter's hand in marriage. He spent most of his life building up the touring company. Now I want to resurrect it to give my aunt and uncle a reason to stay on island."

"That's really sweet. I love how you want to continue your grandfather's legacy."

"We'll see."

"Maybe it's something *you* could do—restart the company and create your own legacy for your future family to carry forward."

"Yeah, well, I don't see myself getting married."

"Did you have a bad experience too?"

"Something like that." Asher pulled the tarp back over the carriage. "Tomorrow, I'm hitching Gus and Ginger to the carriage and driving around the ranch to see how well they handle it. You're welcome to join me, if you'd like."

More alone time with Asher?

She wanted to say yes, but she needed to check on Gran. Besides, spending time with him was risky. Did she have enough strength to shield herself against his growing charm?

Ignoring the nagging tug in her head, Sadie found herself nodding. And prayed she didn't regret it.

Asher was used to pretending to be someone he was not. So playing the role of carriage driver should be a piece of cake.

With Sadie narrating, no one would be paying attention to him anyway.

And that was how he liked it.

As the early morning sun rose over the island, Asher led Gus and Ginger to the carriage he'd managed to haul out of the corner of the barn where it had been abandoned for too many years. He didn't doubt their strength or abilities. More like he needed to be sure the carriage drove the way it was supposed to.

Comforting scents of hay and warm animals breezed over him. Gus eyed him and flicked a tail as Asher slid the bridle in place and adjusted the bit so it sat comfortably in the Percheron's mouth.

"Good morning."

Asher turned at the sweet sound and smiled as Sadie approached him, carrying a foil-covered plate. "Good morning. I was beginning to wonder if you changed your mind."

She shook her head and bit the edge of her lip, which he found endearing. "Not at all. Doris Poe dropped off some fresh Michigan blueberries, so I made a batch of muffins for our trial run."

Asher shook his head and patted his stomach. "You

Hudson women really do know the way to a man's heart, don't you?"

Sadie lifted a shoulder. "Worked for Gran."

He didn't want to take time and ponder what she meant by that because he had a feeling it would lead to nothing but heartache. Instead, he focused on a safer subject. "How is Hetty? Did you see her this morning?"

Sadie shook her head. "I'm going after our ride. I called first thing this morning, and she was doing physical therapy. I talked to the nurse who said Gran had a good night. Thankfully her fall didn't cause more injury to her hip. She's just a little sore. By the time I get there, she may be allowed to leave."

"I hope so. I'm glad to hear she's okay." He lifted a head toward Ginger. "I'm tacking the horses. Care to learn something new?"

Sadie eyed the large animals and took a step back. "Only if it's a demonstration and not a hands-on learning experience."

Asher waved her closer. "Come on. They're gentle giants. Besides, I won't let anything happen to you. Promise."

Sadie set her foil-covered plate on a vintage barrel sitting outside the door of the stable and inched closer, staying behind Asher.

He picked up the matching leather harness. "I just put this on Gus, but I'll show you how I put it on Ginger." He slipped the straps over the horse's head. "This is the noseband and this metal piece is the bit, which helps me control their heads."

Sadie moved a little closer as he picked up one of the collars. "This padded piece fits around their neck."

"It looks pretty thick."

"It needs to be. It helps to distribute the weight so they can pull the carriage better."

For the next five minutes, Asher demonstrated how to harness the horses and couldn't help the pleasure he felt at Sadie's attention to what he was doing.

Confident the horses were comfortable, Asher moved to the side of the carriage and held out a hand to Sadie. "Your chariot, m'lady."

She put her hand in his and shot him another one of those dazzling smiles.

Oh, man. This ride was going to take more out of him than he'd expected. She'd be sitting inches from him. Hopefully, he didn't screw up too badly and look like an idiot in front of her.

Once she was settled on the coachman's box, he climbed up next to her and reached for the reins. His phone vibrated in his front pocket. He pulled it out, found his mom's number on the screen, and shot an apologetic look at Sadie.

"Hello?"

"Hey, honey. I'm sure you're busy, so I'll make this brief. I'm finalizing the guest list for your dad's sixtieth birthday party and wanted to see if you planned to come."

Asher glanced at Sadie, who had her head turned. Kind of hard to have any privacy when they were only inches apart.

"Hey, Mom. Now's not a great time. I'll give you a call later, okay?"

"Okay. Love you."

"Love you too." He ended the call and gripped the phone. He forced a smile in place and glanced at Sadie. "Ready?" At her nod, he flicked the reins. "Giddyap."

Next to him, Sadie giggled.

He shot her a look. "What's so funny?"

"Sounds like something from an old black and white western."

He grinned and took a second to take in the way her laughter lit up her blue eyes. "If it ain't broke, don't fix it."

Gus and Ginger pulled the carriage down the road past Hetty's cottage and rounded the corner toward the state park. Asher let them plod, not in any hurry, especially with Sadie at his side and occasionally brushing against him as they bumped over a rut. He wanted to be sure the horses could handle the vintage wagon without any difficulty.

Sadie leaned back in the seat and lifted her face to the sun. "It's so beautiful out here. I can't imagine why anyone would want to leave."

He glanced at her again. "Does that mean you're planning to stick around after the festival?"

She lifted a shoulder. "Depends."

"On?"

"What I can figure out to do with my life."

"If money was no object, what would you like to do? No overthinking. Tell me the first thing that pops into your head."

Sadie started to speak, then shook her head. "Nope.

We always talk about me. This time, it's your turn. What brought you to the island?"

Asher blew out a breath and ran a hand over his face. More than anything he wanted to spill the secrets of his past, but if he did, he could almost guarantee she'd hop off the carriage and sprint all the way back to Hetty's.

Keep it simple.

"I was going through a tough time, and my aunt and uncle gave me a safe place to land."

"I'm sorry about the tough time." She sat quietly for a moment. "I heard you refer to the caller on your phone as Mom. Your parents are still alive, I take it?"

"Yes, very much so. My dad has a construction business outside of Flint, and my mom is his office manager. They've been married for thirty-five years. To be honest, I'm surprised. I don't know how she puts up with him." As soon as the words left his mouth, Asher wanted to snatch them back.

"Him being your dad?"

He nodded.

"You guys don't get along?"

"We had a falling out nearly fifteen years ago when I didn't want to go into the family business after high school. Even though I worked with him during summers while in school, I didn't want to follow in the family footsteps. Since then, things have been . . . tense, with Mom caught in the middle."

"What did you want to do?"

Her questions were nothing more than conversation, but the more he shared and the more she knew, the closer they would become. Asher really needed to fight harder to keep his distance.

He shrugged. "Not construction."

She made a sound next to him, and he glanced at her. "What was that?"

"For someone who doesn't want to do construction, you're pretty great at it."

"I pick things up quickly. Always have."

"That day in Gran's garage, you mentioned a sister. Do you get along with her?"

"Abi? Yeah, she's great. She teaches preschool in the same town where we grew up." He pulled gently on the reins and turned Gus and Ginger back toward the ranch. "I'm happy with the way they've handled the carriage. Now I'm even more encouraged to offer a tour or two during the festival."

"Dani will love that, especially when we tell her about the period costumes. Speaking of which, we need to order those right away so they'll be here in time." She pulled out her phone and typed something in the search bar, then lifted the screen to him. "I've been thinking about what you said since last night. What do you think about something like this?"

Asher took her phone and glanced at a woman wearing a mint-green dress and a man dressed in decorative threads, complete with a morning coat. "Looks pretty fancy to me."

"The outfits were worn during the early 1900s—the Edwardian era. Reminds me of that Christopher Reeve and Jane Seymour movie, *Somewhere in Time*, set on Mackinac Island."

"I don't know if I've seen it, but I'll take your word for it. That's not what my grandparents wore, but we don't have to be matchy-matchy to them."

A few minutes later, Asher commanded the horses to stop in front of the barn. He jumped out of the carriage and helped Sadie down.

She held up a hand. "Wait. Don't move." Then she lifted her phone and snapped a few pictures.

He glanced down at his grubby jeans, navy T-shirt with a tear at the hem, and grimy work boots.

Not exactly GQ.

"What was that for?"

"Posterity."

He reached over and swiped her phone, still open on the camera app, and flipped it to selfie mode. Then he slipped an arm around her waist, lowered his head so they were both in the frame with Gus and Ginger in the background, and snapped a couple more shots. "There. Now you're a part of history too."

She reached up for her phone and her fingers brushed against his. Instead of releasing the device, he pinned her fingers with his. She frowned at him while his eyes skated over her face, taking in the gentle curve of her cheek, the slightest upturn of her nose, and the barest of gloss on her perfect lips.

He released her fingers and slid a hand up her arm until he could curve it around the hollow in her neck. As he stepped closer, her eyes widened and she swallowed.

Behind him, Gus nickered. He nudged Asher's back, pushing him closer to Sadie. Asher stumbled over his other foot and nearly plowed her over. He caught Sadie before she fell back into a shallow puddle.

She cleared her throat, glanced at the ground, and took a step back, widening the distance between them. She tucked a loose strand of hair behind her ear. "I, uh, should head to the ferry and check on Gran." She lifted a hand, then turned and raced for the fence.

Once she disappeared, Asher turned back to the horses. "Thanks, pal. Way to ruin the moment."

Even though every inch of Asher was disappointed he hadn't kissed Sadie, maybe it was for the best. If she knew the truth about him, she'd be running anyway, so no sense in leading her on when there was no hope for a relationship between them.

And that was even more disappointing than the missed kiss.

Nine

SADIE COULDN'T FIGURE OUT WHAT IT was about Asher that seemed so familiar, and it was bugging her.

His refusal to talk about his past did little to assuage the nagging feeling that pricked the back of her neck. What was she missing?

Despite her hesitancy, there was something about Asher that continued to draw her to him. And that was dangerous.

With her feet tucked under her, she sat in Gran's comfy chair with a knitted blanket tossed over her legs. Rain pattered gently against the roof, lulling her into a state of contentment, especially now that Gran had come home that afternoon and was resting in her own bed.

Sadie lifted her mug and took a sip of hot tea as she continued to thumb through the photos in her camera roll.

The man could be a model.

No doubt about it.

Even the scarring on his neck could be airbrushed, but it didn't bother her or detract from who he was.

A thump sounded from Gran's room down the hall.

Sadie set her mug on the side table, tossed the blanket aside, and hurried to the bedroom. She braced the doorway. Gran sat on the edge of her bed. "Gran, you okay?"

"Yes, love. Just trying to get comfortable and knocked into my nightstand. A picture fell to the floor."

Sadie spied the frame face down on the floor, crossed the room, and picked it up. She ran a finger over her sister's face, her lips lined with red. "I remember this day. We'd returned from making doughnuts at the bakery. You let Lauren and me frost our own. She chose strawberry and I had lemon."

Her grandparents, with hair more brown than silver, sat on Gramps's old glider on the front porch. Dad stood behind them, his hand on Gran's shoulder, while Mom leaned into him, her cheek resting against his upper arm. Eight-year-old Lauren looped her arms around Gramps's neck, her blonde hair in two ponytails, while six-year-old Sadie sat on Gran's lap, head against her chest.

"That was a good day." Gran sighed as she turned her head toward the window. "We had so many good days as a family."

Sadie set the frame in place, then sat on the edge of the bed. She leaned against her grandmother and rested her head against her chest like she'd done in that photo. "I'm so glad you're home and nothing was broken. I was terrified when I saw you in the emergency department."

"Oh, love, I was in good hands." Gran ran a hand over Sadie's hair. "I just need to be more careful until this hip is healed. I'm glad Asher was here to help. He's a fine young man."

Sadie nodded, her hair rubbing against Gran's cotton nightdress. Then she straightened and scooted off the bed. "I'll let you get some rest. Call if you need anything."

"Okay, sweet girl. I'm tired. There's no sleeping in hospitals. My own bed feels so good tonight." Gran kissed her own fingertips, then pressed them against Sadie's cheek. "You get some rest too."

"I will. I'm going to do some work on my computer, then call it a night."

At least she'd given Dani the copy for the festival, which took one more thing off her plate. Thanks to Asher's encouragement, she found the confidence to turn it in. And thankfully, Dani liked it too.

After turning off the light and closing the door, Sadie headed back to the living room. The rain had stopped, and a cool breeze blew in through the open window, lifting the curtains in a spectacular waltz.

She drained her cup of tea and carried it into the kitchen. As she rinsed it and opened the dishwasher, a nickering sounded through the open window.

Sadie's head jerked up, and she found Gus staring at her. "Gus, Gran's going to be upset if you keep trampling her flowers."

This time, instead of freaking out, she reached for an apple from the fruit bowl and rubbed it against her T-shirt as she returned to the chair. She pocketed her phone, slid her feet into her flip-flops, and headed out the front door, closing it quietly behind her. She sent a quick text to Gran.

Sadie

Gus got out. Returning him to the ranch. Be back soon.

Gran

Okay, love.

Sadie rounded the side of the house and shivered as a cool wind blew through the apple trees. She should've thrown on a sweatshirt and maybe a pair of jeans.

The Percheron stood sixteen hands high, or so Asher had said, and Sadie tried to swallow the mild panic that clawed up her chest as she reached the giant animal.

"Hey, Gus Gus. Want an apple?" She held the fruit out on her palm, and the horse bumped it. Then he opened his mouth and grabbed it with his large teeth, his lips barely grazing her skin. As he munched on the treat, she reached out a hand and touched the side of his muscled neck.

Gus remained where he was, so she ran her hand along his coat. He didn't have a bridle or anything on his head, so how was she going to get him back to the ranch?

She reached for a small handful of mane and tugged very gently. "Come on, Gus. Let's go home."

To her surprise, the animal turned toward the ranch and started walking.

Huh.

Okay, then.

As they walked through the wet grass, Sadie tapped the flashlight on her phone so she could see where they were headed. They reached the apple trees on Gran's side of the fence, and Sadie saw another light bobbing on the Quinn property, coming toward them.

Her heart picked up speed. "Asher?"

"Sadie? What are you doing out here?" He reached the fence, then shined his light over the escape artist. "Should've known you'd gone next door."

Water dripped from the branches of the apple trees and splattered her on the forehead. She tried to wipe it away, but several more joined. Soon, rain fell at a steady pace, soaking her clothes.

Thunder cracked and fingers of lightning crawled across the sky.

Beside her, Gus whinnied. Asher pocketed his flashlight and hopped over the fence. "Come on, boy, let's get you inside." He turned to Sadie. "Thanks. Head back to the cottage before you get soaked."

She lifted her arms, then dropped them at her sides. "I'm soaked already. Need a hand?"

"I don't know how he got out, and it's too dark to see tonight, but if you could get the gate, I'll lead him back to the stable." Asher reached for Gus's mane, then hurled himself onto the horse's back like some sort of modern-day superhero.

Sadie's eyes widened as her mouth dropped open. Was there anything this guy couldn't do?

She took a wide berth behind Gus to remain out of his kicking range and hurried to the gate. She unlatched it. As she yanked on it, her wet feet slid on the grass. Before she could catch herself, she ended up on her backside. Cold, wet mud oozed over her thighs.

"Gross." Curling up a lip, she hurried to her feet and opened the gate.

Asher guided Gus toward the stable. Sadie closed and latched the gate. But then she found herself on the Quinn side of the fence instead of on Gran's property.

She glanced at the cottage where a light shone in the kitchen and living room, then back at the stable that was illuminated in the darkness. Against her better judgment, she hurried toward the open door that beckoned like a beacon in the storm.

Stepping inside, she stopped and watched Asher rub a towel over Gus, then grab a stiff brush and run it down the horse's gray coat.

Asher didn't seem to notice her, and the cool night air coupled with her soaked clothes caused her to shiver. Maybe she should go.

She turned and eyed the rain.

"Stay."

The single word, spoken softly yet deeply, rooted her feet to the dusty floor. Slowly, she turned back and found Asher moving toward her with long, purposeful strides, a towel in hand.

She swallowed. Hard.

Her heart thundered in her ears as he ate up the distance between them.

He stood in front of her, and his gaze roamed over her wet hair plastered to her head. She crossed her arms over the front of her shirt.

Without a word, he turned on his heel, strode to a small room, then returned with a navy hoodie. Then he jerked his head toward the small room. "Go into the tack room and change into this sweatshirt. It will keep you dryer than what you have on right now."

She took the towel and hoodie and brushed past him, but he caught her arm. "Sadie."

Again, the single spoken word filled her with a warmth that chased away the cold.

She lifted her eyes to his face. "Yes?"

"Thanks." Then his mouth curved into the most alluring smile.

Oh, how she wanted nothing more than to close the distance between them, slide her arms around his neck, and press her lips to his.

Get a grip.

Nodding, she gently pulled her arm away from him, immediately missing the feel of his touch on her skin. Pressing the sweatshirt to her chest, she hurried into the tack room and closed the door. She pressed her back against the wood and shook her head.

What was she doing?

Rain or no rain, she needed to return to Gran's cottage where it was safe. Because the more time she spent in Asher's presence, the quicker her common sense flew out the window.

She struggled out of the soaked T-shirt and used it to clean the mud off her legs. Then, she dried herself with the towel and pulled the soft hoodie over her head. It smelled of hay, horses, and an essence she could only imagine came from Asher wearing it. She buried her nose deep into the collar and breathed deeply.

Even though she swam in the oversized sweatshirt, she appreciated being dry. She grabbed her filthy T-shirt and opened the door.

Asher used a wide broom and swept hay off the floor, the muscles in his back and arms cording with each movement.

She cleared her throat. "Uh, thanks."

He straightened and turned, a slow smile curving along his lips. Then he leaned the broom against one of the empty stalls and moved toward her. As he stood in front of her, he reached for the collar and straightened out the hood. "You look cute."

She scoffed. "I look like a drowned rat."

"Nah, I've seen drowned rats. There's nothing cute about them." One of his eyebrows lifted. "You, on the other hand . . ."

Her eyes widened as she swallowed again. "Asher . . ."

"Yes?" His voice, soft and caressing, melted over her.

She shook her head.

Asher's fingers left the collar of the sweatshirt and finger-combed her wet hair away from her face. His touch feathered over her skin as his thumb stroked her cheek. "I was wrong. You don't look cute."

She tried not to let his words deflate her. "I don't?"

He shook his head and drew her close to him. "You look amazing."

The three whispered words filled her with a longing she couldn't describe.

Asher cupped her face gently, then brought his lips to hers, softly, gently, caressing. Her arms made their way around his neck as she brought him closer against her.

Being in his embrace was better than she'd imagined.

The tenderness of his touch filled her heart to over-flowing.

As the kiss deepened, his hand moved over her back, pressing her against him.

Sadie's pulse thrummed. Despite what she truly wanted, her arms left his neck as her palms flattened against his chest. She pulled her mouth away from his and forced a little distance between them. "Asher, I . . ."

Shaking his head, he pressed a finger against her lips. "Don't say anything."

He pressed his forehead against hers. She cradled his cheek, her fingers touching the puckered skin at his jaw. She drew back and traced a finger over the left side of his neck. "What happened?"

"I was trapped in a fire and couldn't get out."

Suppressing a shiver at the agony he must've endured, she sucked in a breath at the pain that shadowed his eyes. "I can't even imagine that kind of trauma."

"Something I will never forget." He covered her hand with his and closed his fingers around hers. Then he opened her hand and pressed a kiss against her palm.

Frowning, his thumb traced the inside of her wrist. "What's this?"

She glanced at the faded white ink of a feather. Sadie took a step back and pulled her hand out of his grasp.

She rubbed a hand over her skin usually covered with her smart watch. "My only impulsive moment."

"Oh, I sense a story." A slow grin crawled across his face.

Sadie shook her head. "My sister loved this particular band. She was such a groupie and begged me to get a tattoo of a phoenix."

"Phoenix?" His voice croaked as he took a step back.

Turning away from him, she nodded. The warmth from their interaction dissipated as memories surfaced and crashed over her. "Yeah, that was the name of the band she loved. Lauren knew someone in the group—J.T. somebody—and started traveling with the band right before she died, hoping to sing backup. She used to share everything with me, but I didn't even know she was going with them. Five years ago next month, their tour bus was in a horrible accident. Everyone was killed except for the lead musician, Eli Noble. Not very noble, if you ask me." She scoffed and paced between them.

Asher lifted a hand. "Sadie, there's something—"

Her hand shot up, cutting him off. She needed to get the rest off her chest. Her throat thickened and tears warmed his eyes as she remembered the phone call that changed her life. "There were rumors of drugs and alcohol on the tour bus, and it makes me sick to think Lauren wanted to be caught up in that life. He tried to pay off my family, like money could erase our grief and bring my sister back, but my parents refused to take it."

Chest tight and her emotions battling to be free, Sadie faced him again. Asher stood in front of her, stiff, and stared at her with wide eyes. His skin took on a gray pallor.

"You okay?"

Instead of answering, he dragged a hand over his face. "Why do you think he was trying to pay your family off?"

"What?"

Asher waved a hand in the air. "The musician. Why do you think he was trying to pay you off? Maybe that wasn't his true intent."

Her eyes narrowed. "What else could it be?"

He lifted a shoulder and shoved his hands in the front pockets of his jeans.

Sadie's vision blurred as more memories surfaced. Lauren's service. Her parents' grief. She blinked back tears as resurrected sorrow carved a hole in her chest. She pressed a hand against her mouth. "My family was torn apart that night, our lives forever changed by Lauren's death. My parents lost a daughter. I lost my sister and my best friend. There's no amount of money in the world that could replace her."

A look of horror passed over Asher's face. He stretched out a hand—were his fingers trembling? "I'm so sorry, Sadie. So sorry."

The gruffness in his voice nearly unraveled her fraying emotions. He took a step toward her, then paused. Hands shoved in his front pockets, he shook his head and directed his attention to the floor. Then he looked at her with those dark eyes, but this time they had almost a haunted look.

He jerked a thumb toward the back door. "I, uh, need to go. Gotta take care of something in the house. And you need to check on Hetty."

A gentle hand rested on her shoulder, and he gave it a light squeeze. "Goodnight, Sadie."

Squeezing her eyes shut, Sadie dragged her fingers across her lashes and pulled herself together. Then she opened them as Asher headed out the back door of the stable.

"Asher?" She hurried after him, but with the rain and midnight sky, he'd disappeared into the darkness.

The cold rain pelted her in the face, and she backed into the stable.

Wait . . . what just happened?

She bared her soul, and the guy just . . . bolted?

She returned to the spot where Asher had kissed her, picked up her T-shirt that had fallen, and curled her fingers in the wet cloth.

Releasing a sigh, she walked out of the stable and headed into the storm.

Asher's past was catching up with him, and he had no place to run.

At least, not until his aunt and uncle returned.

Of all the girls on the island, he had to fall for the one whose family he'd destroyed by the choices he made.

Seeing that tattoo was like a punch in the gut.

Now he wanted to put his fist through something. Or grab a bottle and guzzle until the pain exploding across his chest was numbed.

Or just rage against the unfairness of it all.

He'd sent money to help cover funeral expenses, not

pay them off. He wanted to protest, to let her know that wasn't the intent.

But then he'd have to reveal who he was.

Sadie deserved to know the truth.

He tried, but she cut him off. But when he had the opportunity, instead of manning up, he took off and left her standing in the stable all alone.

She didn't need to witness him hurling his guts in the rain as he reacted to the bombshell she'd dropped on him.

Problem was, telling her not only risked their growing relationship, but if other people learned about his past, then he didn't stand a chance of revamping the tour company.

Asher ran a shaking hand over his clammy face and pressed his fist into his churning stomach that he'd just emptied behind the stable.

Rain assaulted his skin as he stumbled to the house. Without turning on lights, he headed upstairs to the shower.

Fifteen minutes later, and in dry clothes, he dropped on the edge of his bed and cradled his head in his hands.

Somehow, he needed to figure out a way to protect Sadie and his family from the sins of his past.

They didn't deserve it. Any of it.

Maybe it *was* time to leave the only place that had really felt like home.

He lay back on the bed and reached for his phone charging on his nightstand. He unplugged it and tapped on the name in his Favorites list. He stabbed the speaker button and listened to it ring.

"Asher, good to hear from you. It's been a couple of weeks." His counselor's voice boomed through the phone.

"Hey, man. Yeah. I've been busy." Asher shoved a hand in his back pocket and paced between the bed and the door.

"What's going on?" Corbin's voice mellowed into his usual counselor role.

Asher dropped on the edge of the bed once again and poured out what had just happened with Sadie.

"How will I be able to look at Hetty or Sadie again, knowing I'm the one who crushed their family? How could I not know her sister was on my own bus? And she thinks I was trying to pay off her family." Just saying it out loud made Asher want to smash his fist through the wall. Instead, he cradled his head in his hands.

"Your manager handled the aftermath while you spent months healing from the accident, right? Didn't you tell me he sent the money to the families as a way of saving face?"

"Yeah, but I didn't care about saving face. I cared more about the people's lives I wrecked. He could've given them all of my money—I wouldn't have cared. But now I learned the families—or at least one of them—felt I was paying them off. Like I was trying to cover something up."

"Come clean with Sadie. Her grandma too. Let them know who you are and that you had honorable intentions with the money."

Asher scrubbed a hand over his face. "I'm still helping her with her grandmother's bakery, and she agreed to help with the carriage tours during the festival. Maybe if I can prove she can trust me, then I can share about my past and she'll be a little more understanding. Especially when she hears my side of the story."

"As long as you're aware the longer you let it go, the harder it will be to receive the news."

"No matter when I do it, it's going to crush her anyway."

"Perhaps reading the police report will give you some insight into what to share with her, especially with the rumors. Put those to rest once and for all."

Asher's eyes shifted to the dresser. "Yeah, maybe."

Their call ended, and Corbin's advice echoed in Asher's ears. Asher fell back on his bed and dragged his wet hair off his face. His stomach rolled again.

He couldn't shake the feeling that no matter when he did it, though, it wasn't going to be enough. His confession was going to destroy anything between them.

He knew what he had to do. If only he could hold off for just a little longer until his aunt and uncle returned to the island.

Then Asher would leave before he caused any more pain.

And that made him sadder than he'd like to admit, because against his better judgment, he was falling for Sadie.

Ten

MAN, ASHER HADN'T EXPECTED TO hit so many roadblocks with trying to bring a few more horses back on island. But without his uncle's permission, written or verbal, Sawyer Hastings, owner of Hastings Horses where the horses wintered in the off-season, wouldn't release more horses to Asher, even though they belonged on the Quinn ranch.

While Asher appreciated the man's integrity, the setback led to frustration.

If he could bring a handful of horses onto the island for a few weeks, then they could offer more carriage rides during the music festival weekend. The extra money would help speed up the opening of the business next season.

He hated not being able to accomplish his goals.

If he wanted horses, he'd have to get his uncle involved instead of surprising him with the progress he'd made.

Now that the carriage was ready and the drive around

the ranch had been successful, Asher was eager to launch the family business once again.

The soft opening would show tourists one more perk of visiting the island.

Instead of going to his uncle, maybe Eliza would be able to help.

He pulled out his phone, scrolled through his recent calls, and tapped on her name. The call went to her voice-mail, and he bit back a groan. He ended the call without leaving a message.

He'd have to figure out something else.

But right now, he needed to meet Hunter Barrett at the bakery to get the equipment he needed to lay the new flooring.

Thoughts of the bakery reminded him of Sadie. And their kiss. And the way he bolted out of the stable.

He owed her an explanation.

His boots pounded against the cobblestone streets as he turned right off Blueberry Boulevard and headed up Main.

His eyes cut to the livery and darkened stables.

Soon, they'll be full again. Or so he hoped.

He missed the sounds of horse hooves and the clinking of harnesses.

His phone buzzed. He pulled it out of his pocket and read a text from Eliza.

Eliza

Sorry I missed your call. Need something? I have a few minutes.

Instead of responding, he tapped her name and held the phone to his ear.

"Hello?"

"Hey, Busy Lizzie. How's it going?" He sat on a bench and leaned back against the sun-warmed metal.

"Oh, you know, living up to the name. Another day in the life of being an industrious administrative assistant."

He couldn't stop the grin that spread across his face. "Where in the world is Aunt Sally this week?"

"We're in Pittsburgh, actually. She's teaching a workshop at a writing conference, so I took advantage of the beautiful weather, and I'm hanging out at Point Park."

"Isn't that where the three rivers come together in Pennsylvania?"

"Look who paid attention in geography class. Yes, the Allegheny, the Monongahela, and the Ohio. The park is lovely with this gorgeous fountain."

"I remember." He closed his eyes and allowed his memory to pull up an image of the park where he'd stolen away one afternoon for some peace and quiet.

"You've been here?"

"Yeah, I've been to the 'Burgh several times."

"Oh, right. For your con—"

"Listen, I called to ask—do you have any pull with Sawyer Hastings?" He leaned forward and rested an elbow on his knee.

"Sawyer? Absolutely. He's like a surrogate uncle. Why?"

Asher outlined his plan about offering tours during the festival.

"Ash, that's brilliant. Let me give him a call and see what I can do."

"Thanks, Eliza."

"Sure thing. I'll get back to you soon."

They ended the call, and Asher felt a bit more hopeful than he had ten minutes ago. He stood and stretched. As he turned toward Main Street, a familiar laugh drifted through the air.

Instead of heading to the bakery, he strode across the grass where the stage was being built in the park for the upcoming concert.

He still thought it was a waste of time and resources to do the wooden stage, but whatever.

A young couple walking a dog passed him. He gave them a quick nod and then side- stepped a toddler escaping from his mother.

Three children chased each other around the playground while a white-haired couple sat on a bench overlooking the water.

Community.

The park brought people together.

In front of the stage, he spotted Sadie laughing again at something Dani or Liam had said and gesturing with her hands. A trait she did often, and he found it to be endearing.

The sun, high in the sky, shone over her, burnishing her hair and bringing out the natural red glints.

A knot tightened in his chest as he took in the way her yellow and navy sundress swirled around her shapely legs.

He resurrected the memory of her kiss, the way her lips

felt against his, the way she felt in his arms. Then, the way his stomach dropped to his feet when he learned he was responsible for her family's deepest grief.

What was he doing?

He shouldn't be walking toward her. He needed to be running away. Far away.

But he wasn't a coward.

He needed to come clean with her. Even though he couldn't say anything to relieve her pain, he needed to confess and let things play out the way they were supposed to.

If she never wanted to speak to him again, he wouldn't blame her.

His fingers tightened into a fist.

"Hey, man. You okay? Saw you heading to the park, then you stopped."

Asher jerked at the sound of the deep voice next to him and found Hunter Barrett standing next to him.

He gave the man a quick nod, but that did little to soothe the tightening in his gut. "Just a lot on my mind."

For the first time in a long time, Asher longed to confide in someone who wasn't his counselor. To spill his guts and get wisdom about what to do. With Sadie. And his life.

But, while Hunter was an okay guy, Asher didn't know him well enough. He couldn't risk being exposed.

"Actually, I was heading for the bakery, but then I got distracted."

Standing next to him, Hunter laughed and folded his arms over his chest. "I wonder what could have distracted you . . ."

He wasn't wrong, but Asher couldn't really afford to allow Sadie to twist up his thoughts. He needed to focus.

Asher shook his head, then shot a look at Hunter. "You have time to head to the bakery now and show me how to use the machine to remove the old floor tile?"

"Sure thing, but I think someone else much cuter and way more interesting is about to take up your time." Hunter lifted his chin in the direction of the stage.

Asher's gaze swung around and found Sadie, Dani, and Liam walking toward them.

Sadie's eyes tangled with his, and the smile she'd shared with Dani disappeared as she approached them. She jerked a thumb over her shoulder. "Stage is coming together nicely, Hunter."

He ran a hand over the dark scruff covering his chin. "Thanks, Sadie. We're hoping to make up for time lost due to yesterday's storm."

"Everything will come together."

"Well, I better head back to work." He clapped a hand on Asher's shoulder. "Give me a buzz when you're ready to meet up."

Hunter left them, then paused to chat with Dani and Liam, leaving Asher alone with Sadie.

He turned his attention to her, forcing himself not to linger on the way the breeze toyed with her hair and blew it into her face. "What are you up to today?"

She turned slightly, shot him a cool look, then glanced at Dani and Liam still chatting with Hunter. "Working with Dani on some details for the festival. You?"

"Ran into some roadblocks with getting more horses

for the carriage tours, so I came into town to start remov-ing the floor tile at the bakery. Hunter is going to lend a hand."

Still holding hands with Liam, Dani hurried over to them. She dropped an arm around Sadie's shoulders and nodded to Asher.

Liam stuck out his free hand and Asher shook it. "Hey, guys. We're heading to the beach for a fire this evening with Mia, Cody, Lily, and Declan. You should join us."

Eyeing him, Sadie lifted a shoulder, then dropped it. "I don't know . . ."

Dani released Liam and grabbed Sadie's arm. "Come on. We've all been working so hard and need some down-time."

Sadie bit her lip and glanced at him before turning her attention to Dani. "I have to check on Gran. She may need me."

"Maybe you can get Doris and Annabelle to stay with her. You really do need a break, Sade." Dani turned to him. "What about you, Asher? You in?"

His gaze flickered to Sadie. Something unreadable crossed her face. Was she wanting him to join their group? He really did owe her an explanation for ditching her last night.

But he wasn't about to go into everything there in the park, especially not with an audience. Or should he make some excuse and bow out?

Then he thought back to his conversation with Corbin and his decision to show he could be trusted. Couldn't do that if they weren't together. He found himself nodding.

"Yeah, sure. Sounds great." He glanced at Sadie. "How about I pick you up, and we can walk to the beach together?"

Something sparked in Sadie's eyes, and she nodded. "Text when you leave the ranch, and I'll be ready."

Dani clapped her hands. "Great! We'll see you guys later." Then Liam slid an arm around Dani's shoulders and steered her toward Main, leaving Sadie and Asher alone.

Sadie shifted from foot to foot and wrapped an arm across her waist. "You don't have to go if you don't want to."

Asher took a step toward her and lifted her chin. "And miss out on spending time with the prettiest girl on the island? No way."

"Really? You had a chance to spend time with me last night, and you ditched me." Her cheeks turned pink, and she lowered her gaze, which forced him to drop his hand.

"I know. And I'm sorry."

Sadie pocketed her phone and folded her arms over her chest. "Did I do something wrong? Say something that upset you?"

Surveying the park, Asher dragged a hand over his face. This was not the place . . .

"No, you did nothing wrong."

"What happened? I thought we were having a good time, but then I shared about my sister and you bolted."

"All I can say right now is I'm sorry for the way I left you in the barn last night. Trust me when I say it wasn't you."

Her jaw tightened. "And the elusive Asher Quinn continues his quest of not divulging anything personal."

He slung an arm around her shoulders. "Believe me, Sadie, there's nothing special about me. I could share all of my secrets, and you'll be wondering why you even bothered trying to get me to open up."

"Whatever." Sadie stared over his shoulder, then looked back at him. "I'm heading back to Gran's. Want to walk with me? Or do you have other things to do in town?"

Hunter was waiting for him, but Asher would walk Sadie home, then backtrack. He reached for his phone and shot Hunter a quick text that he'd be a little later than expected, then he pivoted back toward Blueberry Boulevard that led the way to the ranch and Hetty's cottage.

As they walked, their shoulders brushed together. Choosing to ignore the voice in his head screaming, *Danger! Danger!*, Asher gently touched Sadie's palm until their fingers entwined.

Without saying a word, she shot him a smile and gave his hand a light squeeze.

Hope sparked in his chest, and more than anything, Asher wanted to fan that flame to see where it would lead. Maybe, just maybe, Sadie could see him for who he was now—the guy she could trust—and not the guy of his past.

Sadie made the right choice to go.

Knowing Gran was settled with her book with no plans to do much more than read gave her plenty of peace to enjoy the beautiful late summer evening.

The setting sun dipped low on the horizon, half hidden

by the water. The rays spread a coral sheen over the lake. A light breeze stirred the trees, a gentle rustling that soothed after the past few days of busyness and intense emotions.

Sadie tugged the light blanket around her shoulders. She pulled her knees up to her chest and braced her bare feet on the edge of the plastic Adirondack chair. The quiet, rocky beach behind, near the state park, gave them privacy and a great view of Lake Huron.

Liam crouched and blew on the slight spark he'd managed to coax to life. He added a little more tinder, and the flame caught. He jumped to his feet and pumped his arms in the air. "Victory is ours!"

Dani laughed. "Calm down, Warrior. It was a fire. You didn't take over a small country or anything."

"Kind of felt like it. I haven't built too many fires in my lifetime." He winked at her. "Besides, we need to celebrate the small achievements as well as the big ones. Right, Asher?"

"That's right, man." Asher lifted a fist and Liam bumped it.

"Too bad Declan and Lily bailed. Otherwise, you could've had more witnesses to your amazing feat."

Liam looped an arm around Dani's neck and pulled her close to him. "Listen, you. I'm a city boy, remember?"

Dani's face lit up as she playfully tried to disengage from the flirty neck lock. As she lifted her left hand, firelight reflected off her ring.

Sadie jumped to her feet and rushed over to her friend. She grabbed Dani's hand and gasped. "That's an engagement ring! When did this happen? Why didn't you say anything at the park?"

Her eyes volleyed between Dani and the man still holding on to her. Dani looked up at Liam with love in her eyes, then back at Sadie and nodded, a smile as wide as the island gracing her face.

"Because it just happened a little while ago." Laughing, she held up her hand and wiggled her fingers. "After we saw you at the park, Liam took me to the Grand where he'd set up a picnic on the community porch. We ate while looking at the water and talking about the island coming fully back to life after the repairs and renovations are complete on the Grand. Then Liam started talking about our future and what that would look like. As the sun started to set, he got down on one knee and proposed with the ring that used to belong to his mother. Of course, I said yes."

Squealing, Sadie threw her arms around her friend. "Congratulations. You two are perfect for each other."

Asher pushed to his feet, hugged Dani, then clapped Liam on the back. "Congrats, man."

"Thanks." Liam grinned, looking every bit the smitten fiancé. He waved a hand over the beach. "This was kind of supposed to be an impromptu celebration, but then the others couldn't make it. So you two are the first to know."

Blinking back tears of happiness for her friends, Sadie swallowed past the thickening in her throat as she returned to her chair. "We're thrilled to celebrate with you. Have you picked a date yet?"

Liam stoked the fire, sending a shower of sparks skyward. "We have a lot of details to work out—"

Dani clapped her hands together, cutting him off. "One thing's certain—we're getting married in the gazebo at the Grand."

As Dani shared some wedding ideas, Sadie wrapped herself back in the blanket. She was happy for her friend. Dani deserved someone in her life like Liam. But she couldn't quash her own feelings of envy.

She cast a side-eye at Asher, who kept his focus on the fire. What was he thinking? Did being around fire bother him after his accident? Or was he calculating how long he had to stay before he could retreat back into his reclusive self again?

But he had held her hand. And that kiss the other night... Wow. It meant something. At least to her. Asher had the ability to make her feel special. But she had no idea what he was thinking or feeling.

If only he'd let her in. Then she could get to know him better and see if he was the kind of guy she'd want in her life.

She wasn't going to spend the gorgeous evening wallowing in her thoughts. She glanced at the time on her phone, then back at Dani, who smoothed her blonde hair.

"Did Mia say how Finn's ear was?"

Dani reached for her phone and tapped on the screen. Then she frowned. "She and Cody are taking him to the clinic. His fever's gone up, and they suspect an infection. They wanted to try and stop by, but it looks like they're not going to make it after all. The four of us will enjoy the fire. And some music."

A moment later, music streamed from Dani's phone, and she set it on the wide arm of her chair.

With her chin tucked against her chest, Sadie hummed the chorus of a pop song, then sang the last few remaining words.

"I didn't know you could sing." Asher spoke softly next to her.

Sadie's head shot up, and her eyes connected with his. "I can't."

Dani gave her a playful swat on the shoulder. "That's not true. You have an amazing voice." Then she looked at Liam and Asher. "I'm trying to convince her to enter the talent show. We used to sing out here all summer long when you and Lauren visited. Remember? Maybe you should show off those singing chops again."

"I've had enough humiliation in my life. I don't need a stage to make it worse." Blurry memories of belting out tunes with Dani came into focus.

A deep V formed between Asher's brows, then a smile slid across his face. "I think you should do it."

"Do what?"

"Enter the talent show."

Sadie couldn't shake her head hard enough. "No way."

"Come on, Sade." Dani turned up the volume as "Here Comes the Sun" by the Beatles played on the streaming station. "Remember this one? We used to sing it on your grandparents' front porch." Pausing her phone, she threw off her blanket, stood in front of Sadie, and beckoned her to join her. "Sing with me."

Pulling in a deep breath, Sadie glanced at the guys who

watched her. She released the air slowly, then nodded. "One song, but I'm staying in my chair."

Dani plopped back in her seat and wrapped herself in the blanket, then she tapped on the phone screen and increased the volume.

Sadie listened a moment as the music competed with the water lapping against the shoreline. She closed her eyes and allowed the lyrics the feel-good song to wash over her.

Almost forgetting where she was, she sang softly at first, then she filled her lungs with air, engaged her diaphragm, and sang the bridge with the same intensity she'd done as a teenager. Back when time stood still and her talented sister partnered with her.

Sadie savored the final words, drawing out the last note. Feeling like she was awakening from her own long winter, she opened her eyes. To her surprise, a tear trailed down her cheek. She wiped it away slowly, then ducked her head in the security of her blanket as heat stole across her cheeks.

"Sadie." Asher's voice, soft and deep, beckoned. "Look at me."

She turned her face and peered at him with one eye. "I told you I couldn't sing."

Asher moved to the edge of his chair, reached under her blanket, and caught her hand. Then he shook his head as his mouth widened into a grin. Shadows danced across his face as the now-robust fire reflected in his eyes. "You were amazing."

Her head jerked up, and the blanket fell off her shoulders. Then she half-laughed and shook her head. "What do you know about music?"

Asher's face shuttered, and he released her hand. Pressing his back against the chair, he focused on the fire.

He did sing along to the song playing on Gramps's old radio while fixing the sink in the bakery kitchen and had a very nice voice and practically perfect pitch.

She reached over and touched his arm. "Sorry. That wasn't nice. Thank you for the compliment."

"You have a gift." His eyes, dark and serious, searched her face. "You got lost in the music. For a few minutes, none of us existed."

Sadie's face warmed again. Was it the fire, or the sincerity in Asher's words?

"Sadie's wanted to be a songwriter for as long as I've known her. Do you still have your journals of lyrics?"

Sadie's attention swiveled to her friend. She glared at her. "Dani! You promised!"

Dani clamped a hand over her mouth. "I'm sorry! That was so long ago, I just thought—"

"Promises don't have expiration dates." Sadie pushed to her feet and warmed her hands over the fire.

"I'm sorry, Sadie."

Sadie waved away her words. "Forget it. It's nothing but a dream, anyway. One that died when Lauren did."

The fire snapped and popped as silence shrouded them.

Asher joined her, his arm brushing hers. He bent his head low to her ear. "You okay?"

She nodded but didn't say anything more.

"That day in Hetty's garage—were those your journals that Dani just mentioned?"

"That was a long time ago. Ramblings from a starry-eyed dreamer, who thought she could change the music world."

Asher nudged her shoulder. "I once heard a quote that's stayed with me, but I don't remember who said it: 'Every great dream begins with a dreamer. Always remember, you have within you the strength, the patience, and the passion to reach for the stars to change the world.'"

"You're very kind, but I'm not a star reacher or a world changer."

"If you want to write music, do it. You never know whose life you will impact."

Sadie allowed his words to roll around in her head. On the other side of the fire, Dani snuggled deeper in her blanket and rested her head on Liam's shoulder. Her phone, still streaming, started playing a song that turned Sadie's veins to ice.

Next to her, Asher stiffened.

Throwing off the blanket, Dani jumped to her feet and fumbled for the phone but ended up knocking it on the ground. She snatched it and ended the song.

Liam reached for Dani's phone, but she tucked it in the back pocket of her jeans. "Hey, why'd you turn it off? I love that song. And the band. Whatever happened to the lead singer of Phoenix anyway? After the accident, he fell off the planet."

Sadie ground her jaw as she kept her eyes riveted to the red and blue flames licking the log, darkening it and turning it to ash. She shivered, despite the heat radiating off the fire.

"So, what songs do you think Ariel and Dahlia will sing at the con . . ."

Her words trailed off as Asher skirted the fire and stalked toward the woods at the edge of the beach.

"Asher." She frowned and started after him, but Dani jumped to her feet and caught her arm.

"Give him a minute." Dani looked at her, then glanced away, focusing on the inky-black water.

"Dani, what's going on?"

"Nothing's going on." Her voice hitched as she smiled widely and jerked her thumb toward the building near the edge of the woods, but Sadie knew when her friend was faking it. "Maybe he needs to use the restroom."

"Dani . . ." Sadie's stomach tightened. "What aren't you telling me?"

Dani waved a hand toward the trees. "Apparently, Asher needs a moment."

"But why?"

That question plagued her as he retreated into darkness.

She wasn't an idiot. Dani knew more than what she let on. And Sadie couldn't shake the feeling she wouldn't like what it was.

Eleven

ASHER GRIPPED THE EDGE OF THE sink and splashed cool water on his clammy skin. He glanced in the mirror and found his face drained of color. Water dripped off his wet beard and rolled down his scarred neck.

The scent of campfire smoke mingled with the industrial solution used to clean the public beach restroom sent another wave of nausea rolling up his throat. He swallowed several times as his eyes burned.

The door pushed open. Asher turned away and reached for a rough paper towel. He ran the sandpaper-like material over his face.

"Hey, man. You okay?"

At the sound of Liam's voice, Asher nodded. Then he turned and found his friend standing near the trash can, hands in the pockets of his expensive shorts.

Asher balled up the paper towel and tossed it into the

trash. It banked off the lip and bounced onto the floor, next to Liam's deck shoe. "I'm fine."

Liam snatched it and threw it away. Then he tucked his hands under his arms and leaned a shoulder against the doorway. "You don't look so hot."

"Something must not have agreed with me." Asher shrugged and darted a glance toward the door. "Nothing a good night's sleep won't fix."

Yeah, when was the last time he'd had one of those?

Liam continued to watch him, his brows furrowed. "If you say so. You seemed fine until a few minutes ago. Now Dani's acting strange."

"Strange? What do you mean?"

Liam lifted a shoulder. "I don't know. We were having a good time, then things got weird." He paused and his face scrunched. "As soon as that song came on . . . You know the one. What's the name?—that one that Phoenix sang."

"Dark Side of Midnight." The words sounded a bit strangled as Asher spit them out.

Liam snapped his fingers, then pointed at Asher. "Yes, that's it. It was almost as if Dani couldn't turn it off fast enough. We'd just listened to it a couple of days ago, and she knew how much I liked it."

Asher tuned out Liam's words as memories surfaced of writing his final song with Jared. Asher had sat at the baby grand at his flat in London, plinking out notes as Jared laid upside down on Asher's designer couch, his bare feet crossed on top of the back. Jared started singing words as Asher tapped the keys to eke out a few notes to match the lyrics. Then he'd left the piano bench, picked up his black and white electric Fender Stratocaster plugged into the Marshall amp, strummed a few chords, and allowed the music to speak to him.

Their last night together before flying back to the states for the final leg of the Dark Side of Midnight tour that stole Jared's life and ended Asher's career.

"Dude, you zoning out on me?"

Asher blinked several times as Liam's concerned face came into focus. "Sorry, man. Just not myself right now."

Liam laughed, the sound echoing off the tile walls. "I guess not. I was going on and on about this song, and your eyes glazed over. Sorry about that."

Shaking his head, Asher waved away the guy's words. "Don't worry about it."

The windowless room with its sickly yellow lighting and blue walls felt as if it was closing in on him. Asher removed his ball cap, dragged a hand over his hair, settled the hat backward on his head, then edged toward the door. As he turned, Liam sucked in a breath.

Asher's head jerked up. Liam looked at him with wide eyes. His mouth opened and closed like a trout struggling for air. "Oh, my—"

Asher knew that look. He'd seen it hundreds of times.

The need for recognition he used to crave like a drug. Being validated for who he was.

Now it caused his stomach to burn.

He held up a hand. "Listen, man . . ."

Liam pointed at him, then grinned. "I don't believe it. All this time, and you didn't say anything."

Asher took another step toward him and shook his head. "No, and you can't either."

Liam frowned. "Dude, you're Eli Noble. *The* Eli Noble. Your songs have dominated my playlists for years. You're a legend, man."

Asher shook his head. "I'm a nobody. Most definitely not a legend."

"If you sang at the festival, the island would be packed for your concert."

Just the thought spiked Asher's blood pressure. He couldn't shake his head hard enough. "No way. And you can't say anything. To anyone. If word gets out that I'm here, then I'll have to leave."

He hated the pleading tone that crept into his voice as he repeated the request, but he would do whatever it took to safeguard his privacy.

Liam shot him another dumbfounded look and shook his head. "But you're so stinkin' famous, yet you're holed up on island. What gives?"

The pain in Asher's chest expanded, threatening to tear his ribs apart. "What gives? How about the fact that I'm responsible for so many deaths, including my cousin's, who happened to be my best friend?"

Liam held up a hand. "But that was an accident. That wasn't your fault."

"My bus, my fault." Asher pressed a hand against the wall as his vision swirled and his head pounded.

Liam eyed him again. "You dyed your hair. It used to be blond and much longer. And you were clean-shaven."

"Actually, this is my natural hair color. I used to dye it

when I was on the road. Some dumb teen magazine did a poll about my hair color, and the blond won, so that's what I went with. Anything for the fans." Asher scoffed and rolled his eyes, then ran a hand over his beard that felt more like a mask. "When I'm off the ranch, I'm usually wearing sunglasses and a ball cap. Plus, the beard hides a lot of the scars, and I've filled out a bit more since being a punk kid. By keeping to myself, no one bothers me."

"So, who knows you're here?" Liam lowered his voice, almost resigned, as if the secret doused his enthusiasm. "Other than your aunt and uncle."

"Dani. That's it. She used to be friends with my sister and cousins, and Eliza told her about Jared and me forming Phoenix. But no one else knows, and I need to keep it that way to protect my family. They value their privacy. I don't want the paparazzi messing with the quiet island experience. And after losing my cousin . . ." Asher sent another pleading look to his friend.

Liam lifted his hands and stepped back. "No worries, man. Not my story to tell. I'm just saying, you could use this to your advantage."

"I'm done using things to my advantage. It's not about me anymore. Never should have been." An ache started at the base of Asher's skull. "I didn't like the guy I was becoming. Don't want to go back to him. After the accident . . . and being released from the hospital, I drowned my guilt, shame, and sorrow in alcohol. I was headed down a destructive road, and my aunt and uncle, of all people, were the ones who saved me and brought me to the ranch. Gave me a sense of purpose again."

"I'm sorry. I won't pretend to know what you went through. I do know what it's like to lose someone you love though. I lost my mom when I was a kid. Just know you don't have to go through this alone."

"Yeah, I kind of do."

"Why? For some sort of self-penance? Beating yourself up for an accident won't bring them back."

Asher's face hardened as he faced Liam. "Why do I get to have any sort of life when they don't?"

Liam shrugged. "I don't know the answer to that. God spared you for a reason. He has a plan for you, man."

"A pretty cruddy one, if you ask me."

"Only if you choose to look at it that way. The offer's there to talk if you want."

"Thanks."

"So, does Sadie know?"

Shaking his head, Asher moved and braced his hands on the edge of the sink. "Not yet. I just learned the other day that her sister died in the same crash. When I tell her who I am, she won't want anything to do with me."

Liam clapped him on the back. "That's tough. Pray about it and ask the Lord to guide you."

He opened the heavy door and stepped out into the night air, leaving Asher alone in his mental prison. He glanced at himself in the mirror, disgusted at the man staring back at him.

Pray about it.

Right.

Like God wanted anything to do with someone like him.

But Liam was throwing him a lifeline. The offer of a friend, a confidant. Someone who knew his secret and still wanted to hang out with him.

Was he brave enough to grab on to it?

Sitting on the bench at the park with her face lifted to the morning sunshine did little to warm the chill wrapped around Sadie's heart.

Two days and still no word from Asher, despite her attempts to contact him. She tossed her phone back and forth in her hands and resisted the urge to check to see if he'd responded yet. The unsettled feeling coiled in the pit of her stomach.

"Hey. Sorry I'm late." Dani dropped on the bench next to her and handed her a steaming to-go cup from Good Day Coffee. "Jill has a new blend in honor of the festival—summer sunset. Tell me what you think."

Wrapping her chilled hands around the warm to-go cup, Sadie inhaled the steam and raised an eyebrow. "Do I smell coconut?"

Dani lifted her cup. "Yep, coconut caramel. Coconut to bid adieu to summer and the caramel to welcome autumn."

"Hmm. Interesting." Sadie took a sip and nodded. "Pretty good. I like it. I'll see if Jill can label it during the festival as a limited flavor. Scarcity marketing will up her sales, especially if people like it and realize they won't be able to get it after the weekend. Maybe she can sell bags of ground coffee, too, for even more sales."

"See, I knew you were the right person to help us with the festival. Martha mentioned the copy you helped her write about the restaurant for the festival advertising. She was pleased, and if you remember Martha well, you know that's not easy to do. You're an asset to this island, Sadie. I hope you can see that . . . and grow your business from here."

"Thanks, friend. So kind of you to say. I've always loved it here. And staying does seem like a possibility." Sadie pushed to her feet and buried her left hand in the front pocket of her hoodie. "Ready to paint?"

Dani patted the bag on her shoulder. "Yep, got my paint clothes right here."

As they headed toward Main Street, Sadie bumped her friend's shoulder. "I appreciate it. And you. Lily's going to join us if she and Declan get back from Port Joseph in time. They're checking out some equipment for sale for the fudge shop."

Dani rested her head on Sadie's shoulder. "Back atcha. I certainly don't mind, but I thought Asher was helping you."

"Me too, but he hasn't responded to my texts or calls since the night on the beach." Sadie stopped and waved her arms, sloshing hot coffee over her hand. She winced and brought the side of her thumb to her mouth. "I've played that night over in my head, trying to figure out what I did to run him off."

"What makes you think you did anything?" Dani looked at her coffee cup, suddenly interested in the pattern of splashed coffee on the plastic lid.

Sadie shoved her sunglasses to the top of her head. "Because things got a little weird after he complimented my singing and I brushed him off."

"Asher's not that sensitive. Talk to him. Ask him. I'm sure he has a good reason. Maybe he isn't even on island right now."

"I've tried, but I can't have a conversation if he's ghosting me." She pulled Gran's keys out of her pocket, unlocked the door and pushed it open.

A wave of lemon cleaner washed over her. She'd spent all day yesterday scrubbing the walls until her arms ached.

Dani lifted her nose as she stepped inside. "Smells good in here. You've been busy."

"Scrubbing's a good way to work out my frustrations." Though the activity had done little to erase the events at the beach playing on a continuous loop in her head.

Dani dropped her backpack onto the front counter, dug out a change of clothes. She returned a couple of minutes later dressed in jeans with frayed holes on the thigh and a gray T-shirt with a white colosseum and *Roma* in script across the top. She twisted her hair and clamped it away from her face with a clip.

Sadie nodded to her friend's T-shirt. "You and Liam should plan a European honeymoon, so you can see those places in person instead of watching them on the Travel Channel."

Dani sighed. "I wish. But that takes time and money. Two things that are in short supply right now. With the festivals I have planned for next year, the hotel renovations, and Liam's business, I don't see that happening."

Rubbing her hands together, Dani glanced at the walls, still a dingy white despite Sadie's hours of scrubbing. "Okay, where do you want me to start?"

Kneeling on the drop cloth on the floor in front of the display window, Sadie pulled a lid opener out of a Smith's Hardware paper bag and pried open a can of bright white paint. She grabbed a stir stick and mixed the separated color. She pointed to the wall next to her. "Let's begin here."

Rocking back on her heels, Sadie placed her hands on her thighs and looked at her friend. "I need to ask you a question."

Dani dug through the paper bag next to Sadie and pulled out a paint roller and tray. "Sure, anything."

"Is there anything going on between you and Asher?"

Dani's head jerked up as an incredulous look crossed her face. She blinked as her mouth dropped open, and a flash of hurt clouded her eyes. "What? Are you crazy? No way. I'm engaged to Liam, remember? Why would you even think that?"

Closing her eyes, Sadie bit her lip. Then she looked at her friend and shook her head. "I'm sorry. It sounded stupid the minute I said it. It's clear you have eyes only for Liam."

"Of course—I love him. Why would you ask me something like that?"

"You and Asher are different together. He talks to you."

"He treats me like a kid sister. We're friends. Nothing more."

Heat warmed Sadie's cheeks, making her wish she

hadn't opened her mouth and voiced the stupid thoughts. "I thought we were too, but every time I try to get him to open up, he shuts down. Is he keeping something from me?"

Something flickered in Dani's eyes, but then it was gone as quickly as it came, so maybe Sadie had imagined it. Dani ran her hand over the roller. "Talk to him."

"I've tried. He won't respond. That's the problem." Sadie pushed to her feet and wrapped her arms around her waist. "I don't want to end up humiliated again."

"Well, I can promise you this—Asher's not married. He's not Garrett, Sade."

"I think you know more about Asher than you're saying. I have to confess, that makes me a little uneasy. Maybe a little jealous."

Dani looked at her, then shifted her attention to the wall. She dipped the roller into the paint and swathed it onto the wall. "It's complicated."

Those two words rocked Sadie back. Her chest squeezed as she struggled to pull in a breath. "So, you do know something."

Dani's face softened, and she put down the roller. "It's not that simple, Sade."

"Secrets never are. They come with a price, Dani. And at what cost?"

"Asher's a good man. Sure, he's a bit standoffish, but he's also kind and generous. His story isn't mine to tell. Please don't be mad."

While her opinion of Asher had changed since that first day she'd met him, and she knew he was a good man, his behavior from the night at the beach had her struggling with her own emotions.

Turning away from Dani, Sadie eyed the walls still needing a coat or two of paint.

A fresh layer would cover the marks and scuffs, but they'd still be there.

Just covered up.

Hidden like the secrets Asher . . . and Dani were keeping.

Sadie crossed her arms. She needed to make a choice—get Asher to talk, since Dani wasn't sharing, or do some digging on her own.

Either decision took courage she didn't have at the moment, but she refused to let her fears or pain from the past keep her in the dark any longer.

The truth of her last mysterious man cost her a lot, and she didn't want to pay that price again.

Twelve

IF ONLY FIXING HIS LIFE COULD BE AS straightforward as replacing a window.

Sadie had texted that morning and let him know she'd returned to the bakery to finish painting—a job he'd promised to help her do—and found a broken window.

After two days of shameful silence, he couldn't ignore her any longer. He'd let her know he'd fix it right away.

Early afternoon rays warmed Asher's back as he stood on the ladder and pried broken glass from the worn frame with a pair of pliers. He dropped the shards in the utility bucket at his feet.

The scent of grilled burgers filtering through the air from Kelley's Bar & Grill made his stomach growl. Once he paused for lunch, he'd grab a bite. First time he'd had an appetite since the night on the beach.

For now, though, he needed to replace the window. He'd given Sadie his word, and he'd follow through.

Once the glass was gone, he pulled the utility knife out of his back pocket and cut away the old caulk, nearly black with age and mildew. Then he inspected the frame to see if it needed to be repaired or replaced.

He ran a finger along the edge. A sharp pain lanced his finger. He pulled it back and found a small cut.

He must've missed a piece of glass.

Asher climbed off the ladder and rounded the front of the building, sidestepping a group of teenagers with their phones above their heads as they took selfies on the sidewalk. Bicyclers pedaled down Main Street toward Blueberry Hill Park. A couple of young kids raced down the cobblestone street as Jack, the island dog, ran alongside them.

Dani's dream of revitalizing the island was coming true. The summer had been more crowded this year. Even though the season was winding down, businesses were booming.

Maybe there was hope for the island after all.

Asher headed inside the empty bakery Sadie had left unlocked for him. His footsteps echoed, bouncing off the freshly painted walls, as he moved into the kitchen. He washed his hands in the deep sink, then grabbed a handful of paper towels.

Leaning against the sink, he pressed one against his finger until it stopped bleeding. He wrapped a clean paper towel around his finger, then secured it with a piece of paper tape from the dust-covered dispenser on the counter. It would work for now.

His phone vibrated in his front pocket. He dug it out and found his mom's picture lighting up his screen.

"Hey, Mom. What's going on?"

"Hi, honey. I sent you a text, but I didn't get a response, so I decided to call."

"Sorry, I was fixing a window and missed the alert."

"No worries. I know you're busy. I wanted to see if you've given any more thought about coming to your dad's party. Abi will be there. She misses you."

Mom's unspoken "too" hung in the air between them.

Asher swallowed a groan as he cupped his palm over his forehead, dislodging his hat. "I don't know, Mom . . ."

"Honey, please. It would mean so much to him. And to me." The way her voice lowered made him suspect his presence would be more uplifting for her.

Asher wanted to argue, but he didn't want to upset his mom. His dad wouldn't care less if Asher showed up or stayed on the ranch where peace reigned.

He filled his lungs with air and released it slowly. "Okay, I'll be there, but one word from Dad about how I'm living my life, and I'm gone."

"I wish you two could put your stubbornness aside and be friends again."

Asher laughed, a strangled sound that caught in his throat. "Dad and I were never friends. I was the son who was a constant disappointment, remember?"

Mom sniffed, and Asher's fingers curled into a fist. He'd upset her and that wasn't right. She had been his champion for as long as he could remember.

"Asher Noble Quinn, you have never been, and you

never will be, a disappointment. You are the son we prayed for. Our miracle baby. We love you."

"Thanks, Mom." He softened his tone. "I'll be there. I promise."

"Thanks, honey. You have no idea what this means to me. I love you."

"I love you too. I'll see you soon." Asher ended the call and gripped his phone.

"Are you involved with someone?"

At the sound of the feminine voice, Asher jumped, then whirled around.

Sadie stood in the doorway, her hands clenched in front of her. Her eyes blazed as her lips thinned into a tight line.

"What'd you say?"

She took a step into the room. "I asked if you were involved with someone. Are you?"

He frowned. "No. Whatever gave you that idea?"

She nodded toward his hand. "I heard you say I love you."

He laughed and shook his head. "I do love someone. My mom." He lifted the phone in his hand. "She called to see if I was going to my dad's birthday party."

"Oh." Sadie's shoulders sagged as she leaned against one of the long stainless-steel counters. Her face softened immediately. "That's great."

Asher closed the gap between them and touched her chin. "You don't trust easily, do you?"

Wrapping her arms around her waist, Sadie shook her head. "Not really."

He didn't want to pry, but if he knew more about her,

then maybe he'd have a better understanding of how to gain her trust.

Sadie pressed her back against the counter. "I worked for a marketing firm in Florida, just outside of Orlando. My boss hired a new guy who had a sharp mind. He could write copy in fifteen minutes—the same assignment that would take me most of the day to complete. He was funny and quick on his feet. Always knew the right thing to say. I won't bore you with the details, but suffice it to say, I fell hard and fast for him. We dated for nearly a year. I really thought he was the one. Took him to meet my family. One night, he called and asked if he could come to my apartment before work. Said he had something he wanted to ask me."

"I can only imagine what you must've been thinking."

Sadie nodded, then gnawed on the edge of her lip. "Like a lovesick fool, I got up extra early and took time with my appearance. I gave myself a fresh manicure. But then he didn't show."

"He ghosted you?"

She nodded. "I was a few minutes late for work because I waited around so long for him. When I got there, I was called into my boss's office. A woman I didn't recognize was there, and if her eyes could beam lasers, I would've been dead on the spot."

"Who was she?"

"My boyfriend's wife."

Asher reached for Sadie, but she took a step back. "Apparently, she found out about us. She confronted me in front of my boss. She screamed at me so loudly that everyone in the office heard. I have never been so humiliated in my entire life."

"And you had no idea?"

Her head jerked up and she glared at him. "Of course I had no idea. If I had, I would've ended things immediately. I don't date married men. I'm not the home-wrecker she claimed I was. I won't be the 'other woman' for anyone."

Asher had up his hands. "Sorry—that's not what I meant."

Sadie raked a hand through her hair. "Don't worry about it. Doesn't matter anyway. To make a long story short, I lost my job that day. With my dignity and reputation in shreds, I packed up my desk and left. Since then, I've been working remotely to cover the rent and basic living expenses. I would never wish anything happening to my parents, but Mom coming down with the flu turned out to be a blessing."

"How so?"

"Gran needed someone to care for her after surgery, and I needed a change of scenery. Lily and Dani had been after me to visit the island, so the timing worked well."

He wrapped his arms around her and pressed a kiss to the top of her head. "This is not your fault."

"I was too naive. Should've seen the signs. Social media is full of memes and reels that talk about cheating red flags. I scrolled past them because I didn't think they pertained to me. What a fool." She lifted her face and looked at him. Her beautiful eyes filled with tears. One slipped down the curve of her cheek.

"I'm sorry, Sadie. I really am." He brushed the wetness

away with the pad of his thumb, relishing the softness of her skin. "You are not a fool."

She gave him a shaky smile as she covered his hand with her own. "Thank you. I appreciate it. It's just that—" Her eyes shimmered as she swallowed.

"What?"

"Sometimes it feels like no matter how hard I try, I keep ending up in the same place." She shook her head. "I know that sounds like self-pity."

"Not at all. Sounds more like you're a little more aware about where you are in your life and where you want to go. But what do you mean by same place?"

She lifted a shoulder, then moved out of his embrace. She turned her back to him and pocketed her hands. Then her shoulders lifted and dropped. "Alone."

The single word, spoken so softly he almost missed it, scored a direct hit to his chest.

He knew that feeling all too well.

Asher moved behind her and placed his hands on her shoulders. "You're not alone. You have your parents, Gran, Dani, Lily. And me."

She turned slowly and looked up at him. "You?"

He nodded but remained quiet.

She lowered her head once again and shook it. "No, I don't. Not really."

"Why do you say that?"

"Asher, I know very little about you. Every time I ask questions, you deflect. You ghosted me for the past two days. To be honest, it makes me wonder what you're hiding."

He lifted his hands and dropped them at his sides. "I promise you, I'm not hiding a wife."

She twisted her face, giving him a look.

"Too soon?"

She held up her thumb and index finger about an inch apart. "Little bit. Besides, Dani said the same thing already."

His eyes widened, and he swallowed. Hard. "You talked with Dani? About me?"

Sadie nodded. "But it didn't do much good. She said your story wasn't hers to tell. And reminded me again that I needed to talk to you. But I couldn't do that since . . ."

"Since I ghosted you."

"Yeah, something like that."

"I'm sorry for not responding the past couple of days. Unfortunately, I ended up getting sick the night we were on the beach, and I wasn't good company."

"I'm sorry. Something you ate?"

He lifted a shoulder, trying to remain non-committal. "It was no excuse—I should've at least responded to your texts. I'm sorry."

She shook her head. "It's okay. I'm sorry you weren't feeling well. I could've left some chicken soup for you or something."

He shook his head. "You are truly remarkable, Sadie. You always think of others. On the way over here, I saw something in the window of Maritime Dreams and bought it for you. I planned to drop it off at the cottage after I was done replacing the window. But since you're here . . ."

Asher headed to the front of the shop and reached

for the small paper bag he'd set next to his toolbox. He hooked the twisted paper handle over the crook of his index finger and turned.

Sadie had followed him out of the kitchen.

He thrust it at her. "Here, I hope you like it."

She frowned and took the bag. "Why'd you buy me something?"

He shrugged. "I don't know. Felt like it, I guess."

She reached into the bag and pulled out an aqua-colored journal with words from Isaiah 43:2 embossed on the cover. She traced the letters as she read, "When you pass through the waters, I'll be with you." She looked at Asher, her eyes bright and expression soft. "Thank you, Asher. I love it. You remembered my love of journals."

Heat warmed his neck. "I don't forget things that matter. And you matter." He took a step closer but didn't reach for her. "You've got a gift, Sadie."

She looked at him with an unreadable expression, a little mix of wonder and . . . fear? "You think so?"

"I've heard you sing." He tapped his chest. "Your singing is real and powerful. Write your songs and sing without fear."

Her fingers tightened around the gilded edges of the journal as she pressed it to her chest. "Easier said than done."

"Open it."

Doing as directed, Sadie opened the cover. Her fingers flew to her lips as she read the words he'd scrawled. "Courage means doing something even though you're afraid. Be brave and write songs from your heart. The world needs to hear what you have to say."

She looked at him with such gentleness in her eyes that his gut turned to mush. Then she pressed a hand to his cheek. "You have no idea what this gift means to me."

"You've got this, Sadie. And you're not alone. I'm here. I'm not going anywhere."

She blinked several times and nodded. "After losing my sister, my desire to write songs died with her. I felt incomplete, you know. It was always our dream—I'd write, and she'd sing."

"Don't allow what happened in the past to keep you from moving forward. Honor your sister's memory by continuing what you both desired."

Asher longed to take her in his arms again, but the mention of her sister created an invisible boundary between them. Until he could follow through with his own words about being brave and confess who he was and his role in changing her family's future, then he needed to put some distance between them.

Problem was, the more he was around Sadie, the less he wanted to retreat.

"I need to finish the window." He glanced across the room to the hole in the wall that gave a perfect view of the island haven.

"Thank you, by the way." Sadie waved a hand toward the window. "I appreciate you fixing it." She tapped the book. "And for this."

"Thank me by following your dream. That's what your

sister would've wanted." He reached for the replacement glass he'd picked up from Smith's Hardware.

Their eyes tangled as Sadie moved toward him. Standing on her tiptoes, she rested a hand on his shoulder, then brushed the lightest of kisses against his lips.

Asher tightened his grip on the glass so he didn't drop it on her foot. He leaned in and kissed her with more depth, more promise, more hope for their future.

He wanted to assure her she'd never be alone if he was a part of her life, but he couldn't promise that.

Not yet.

But soon.

His heart picked up pace as her hand slid behind his neck and pulled him to her. He savored the taste of hope on her lips.

Then she pulled away and pressed her forehead against his. "Thank you."

Her breathy voice curled through him. She had a way of getting under his skin. He swallowed a groan and took a step back as he forced his blood pressure to normalize.

He nodded, not trusting his voice.

Still holding on to the glass, he watched her head out the front door. Then he leaned a shoulder against the wall and sighed.

He needed to come clean and pray she could forgive him. Maybe, just maybe, there was hope for healing and a future together.

Inspired by Asher's faith in her, Sadie felt something she hadn't experienced in years—hope.

Hope in renewed dreams. Hope in new beginnings. Maybe even hope in love.

Was it possible to risk her heart again?

The lines she wrote last night spoke of embracing life, embracing love, and healing the scars from her past.

What would it be like to embrace a future with Asher?

Only time would tell.

She slid the journal Asher had given her into the side pocket of her tote and slung it over her shoulder. Then she reached for the large box containing their costumes that she'd picked up from the post office yesterday after leaving Asher at the bakery. She wanted to pull them out and look at them, but she resisted.

She and Asher could discover them together.

Shifting the box, which was heavier than expected, she headed down Gran's front porch and made her way across the backyard to the ranch.

A light shone in the barn, so Asher was up.

Seemed like the man slept very little.

Even late at night, a light was on either in the house or in the barn.

Morning sunshine hovered over the horizon, cast in a haze with a mix of clouds. While the air was a little cool, the forecast predicted a warm day. As she drew closer to the barn, the scent of hay floated through the air.

She stood in the doorway and searched for Asher.

Gus stood in the aisle, tethered by leads on either side

of him, while a man with salt and pepper hair bent over the huge animal's hoof.

The man looked up, revealing bright blue eyes, deep lines that suggested he smiled a lot, and a graying beard that hung to his chest. Wearing a T-shirt with Foster Farriers written on the back, he nodded, then jerked a gloved thumb over his shoulder. "Mornin'. Asher's in the back."

"Good morning. And thank you." Sadie made her way through the barn, taking a wide berth around Gus, and headed to the back where Asher stored the carriages.

His back to her, Asher rubbed a rag over the glossy black paint of the carriage, filling the room with the scent of some citrusy oil.

"That looks great. Your aunt and uncle will be so impressed."

Asher's head jerked up. A smile crept across his face. He straightened, flung the rag over the carriage body, then moved toward her. Slow and steady, his eyes not leaving hers.

She swallowed and forced the thrum in her veins to calm.

His faded jeans hung low on his narrow hips as his black T-shirt stretched across his broad chest with every movement. He wore a backward baseball hat that had seen better days.

He reached for the box and set it on an old wooden barrel, then he turned back to her. "Good morning."

His voice, low and throaty, sent a shiver skittering down her spine.

She swallowed again and smiled. Oh, she could get used to seeing him every morning.

"Good morning to you too."

Asher rested a hand on the box. "What's in here?"

"Our costumes. I picked them up yesterday afternoon."

"And you brought them by this early?"

She lifted a shoulder. "I was excited to see them. I wanted to wait and look at them together. If this is a bad time . . ." She turned toward the door.

Asher's hand shot out and grabbed her wrist. Gently, he pulled her toward him until they were only inches apart. "No, it's not a bad time. Never a bad time."

He smelled of hay, warm animals, and something a little spicy. His soap, maybe? Whatever it was, it was quickly becoming one of her favorite scents.

She really needed to get a grip.

Sadie opened the box and folded back the white tissue paper, revealing an early 1900s lightweight ivory cotton gown with a high neck, pleated billowy bodice, and lace trim. She let out a little gasp as she drew the dress out of the box and held the flowy fabric against her. She ran a finger down one of the long, fitted sleeves and turned to Asher. "What do you think?"

His eyes searched her face. "Absolutely beautiful." Then he winked. "The dress looks great too."

Her face warmed under his gaze and his words. She draped the dress over her arm, then returned to the box. She pulled out a matching hat with a wide brim, ribbons, and fabric flowers. "Lovely."

Sadie returned the hat and gown to the box, then broke

the tape on the other one. She folded back the paper and found a dove gray tailcoat with striped trousers, a lighter gray waistcoat, white shirt, and black tie. "This will do quite nicely. We'll need to try them on. The practice run is tomorrow, so I hope they fit."

"I'm sure they will be just fine." Hands on his hips, Asher eyed the box, then looked at her. "You sure you want to do this?"

At the questioning in his voice, Sadie cocked her head. "Are you having second thoughts?"

Asher moved away from the box and returned to the carriage. "More like third and fourth thoughts. I want the tour to be a success. I want my aunt and uncle to be proud of what I've accomplished and to be excited about getting the touring company going again."

"I sense a 'but' in there."

"But what if I'm not the one able to pull it off?"

Usually, Sadie was the one who needed to be talked off the ledge, so hearing Asher's doubts made her realize he wasn't as calm and collected as he wanted people to think.

Huh.

Maybe the guy had flaws after all.

She touched his arm. "You are the right person." She waved a hand at the carriage. "Look what you've done. You've taken something that was crumbling and falling apart, and you restored it to its former glory. More than that, you breathed new life into an opportunity to give tourists something fun to do while they explore the island. You put your heart in this, Asher, so that does not make you a failure."

He leaned on the carriage a minute, then turned and slid a hand over her cheek. "Thanks, Sadie. You always know the right thing to say. You're as gifted with words as I said yesterday."

Sadie resisted the urge to cover his hand with her own. She needed to focus. "I talked to Dani yesterday before picking up the costumes. Between her advertising and the posters Lily and I hung up, we have at least forty people signed up."

"Forty?" His eyes widened. "I'd hoped for a handful or so. I can't fit that many people in the carriage."

"We'll do thirty-minute tours throughout the day, then we'll ask for feedback to see what can be improved. How's that sound?"

"Sounds like it's going to be a busy day."

"Do you want to run through the route for tomorrow? I can share my script, and you can let me know of any changes I should make."

For the next ten minutes, they stood side by side as they pored over one of the island maps given to tourists and determined their stops. Sadie recited the script she'd memorized over the past few days, giving highlights to what they wanted to share. She shared information about the hotel, the shops, the park, the fort, and fun legends from the island.

Asher listened, his eyes never wavering from hers.

Sadie gained confidence as she continued to gesture with her hands. Then, she realized what she was doing and shoved them in the front pockets of her blue shorts. "Sorry. I guess I got carried away."

Asher shook his head. "No need to apologize. You are animated and passionate about what you're sharing. The guests are going to love it."

"The island has a lot of fascinating things to share. It's tough to pare it down to thirty minutes."

"See, this is why you're the right person to lead the tour. I'll keep Gus and Ginger on task and allow you to wow the tourists with your words."

"Speaking of words, I did something wildly crazy, and I'll probably end up looking like a complete idiot." Sadie dropped her gaze to her flip-flops as her heartbeat thundered in her ears.

"No, you won't. I believe in you."

Sadie wet her lips and allowed her eyes to connect with his. "Well, um, it's *that* belief that made me think I could actually do it."

He lifted an eyebrow. "Now I'm intrigued."

"I signed up for the talent show." The words came out in a rush, as though if she didn't say them now, then she wouldn't be able to get them out. "If—and that's a big if—if I win, I want to use the proceeds to help with the bakery remodel."

Asher grinned, then let out a whoop. He picked her up and swung her around. "Way to go! I'll be in the front row cheering you on."

Sadie clutched his muscled arms and laughed. "Oh, great. As if I wasn't freaked out enough already."

"It's my privilege to be there. I wouldn't miss it for anything." Asher set her back on her feet, which was a little disappointing. Then his eyes softened as he brushed his knuckles over her cheek. "I'll always cheer you on, Sadie. No matter what. That's a promise."

Her heart slammed against her ribs as her stomach turned to pulp. She slid her arms from his biceps and put them around his neck. "I've never had anyone like you in my corner. The thought of participating in the talent show, though, makes me want to hop on the next ferry off island, but your reassurance keeps me going. Thank you for nudging me to step out of my comfort zone. Because of you, I started writing a new song."

"I can't wait to hear it."

The sincerity in his voice and the warmth in his eyes filled her with such a sense of confidence she hadn't felt until this moment.

As her eyes roamed over the angles of his face, she realized something. And if she wasn't holding on to Asher, her knees probably would've buckled like a heroine in a dramatic soap opera.

She was falling in love with Asher Quinn.

The idea of staying on island after the festival took shape. Maybe she could do more remote work or even partner with island businesses to up their marketing campaigns while writing songs.

Maybe Jonathon Island could become her new home. Gran had said she could stay as long as she wanted. And Sadie would be there to keep an eye on her. Not that Gran needed it . . . if anyone asked. But Sadie loved the time with her. And Gran appreciated the company.

And just maybe Sadie could begin dreaming about a future again.

This time with Asher.

Thirteen

ASHER DIDN'T TRUST EASILY, BUT more than anything, he wanted to trust the weather forecaster's prediction that the storm would hold off until their first tour was completed.

He eyed the dense, steely-gray clouds that lumbered across the sky. The morning air felt heavy and somewhat suffocating. Or maybe that was the bow tie cinched around his neck.

Sweat beaded on his forehead as he fingered the buttons on his waistcoat, or tailcoat, whatever kind of coat Sadie had called it. He just had to remember he was playing a part.

He tried to shake off the apprehension swirling in his gut. Nerves. A lot was riding on this tour.

Eliza had texted to say her parents would be back on island in a couple of days, so everything needed to run smoothly. That way he could share the success with them when they returned home.

The wind stirred the upturned leaves, sending a shower of green over him. He eyed the sky once more and ran a finger between his throat and his collar.

Sadie rested a hand on his arm. "It's just a breeze. Let's keep an eye on the weather and stay with our schedule." She lifted a fabric tote bag. "I bought some emergency ponchos at Smith's Hardware in case we need them."

"Ever the optimist, aren't you? Always prepared." He meant his words to be teasing, but with the tightness in his throat, they came out more as a growl.

The light in Sadie's eyes dimmed as her fingers tightened on the strap of the bag.

Way to go, jerk.

He faced Sadie. "That's not what I meant. Besides, have I told you how beautiful you look today?"

With her dark hair pinned up under her fancy hat and the way her dress highlighted her tiny waist, it would be a wonder if he was able to concentrate on driving the carriage. At least Ginger and Gus didn't need much guidance from him. They could lead a carriage in their sleep.

Her eyes lifted and brightened. "Only about four times already, but I'll take it. Thank you." She ran a hand over the front of his coat. "You look pretty sharp yourself. The hat's going to be a hit with the ladies."

He situated the bowler hat on his head in a jaunty fashion, then raised an eyebrow. "Well, in that case . . ."

She swatted him playfully on the chest. "Your humility is overwhelming."

Asher pulled his phone out of the front pocket of his trousers, the device a complete contradiction to his clothing. He checked the time, then glanced at the crowd forming in front of the livery. Looked like he'd be driving the carriage all day.

Wiping his damp palm on his thigh, he turned to Sadie. "Should we load up?"

Nodding, she smiled. "You've got this."

He appreciated her confidence in him, especially knowing what was at stake for him . . . Or at least all that he'd been willing to tell her.

As he climbed onto the coachman's box and picked up the reins, guilt gnawed at him.

He still needed to come clean.

After his aunt and uncle arrived.

Then he'd be able to pass the carriages over to them and take a step back. He'd confess everything to Sadie and let the chips fall where they may . . . or whatever that cliché was.

Truth was, keeping secrets was a burden he was ready to release.

Behind him, the carriage squeaked and swayed as the passengers boarded under Sadie's calm instructions. As they settled in their seats, she offered coffee and hot chocolate from Good Day Coffee, passed out lightweight blankets to stave off the chill in the air, and gave an overview of what to expect.

She was definitely the right person to partner with for these tours. Maybe she'd consider staying once Hetty was moving on her own.

The wind picked up, causing the tree limbs to bow. A strong gust flicked his hat off his head and sent it rolling down the cobblestone street.

He hopped down and glanced at Sadie. "I'll be right back."

Laughter from the passengers followed him as he chased the hat down the street like something from a cartoon. He finally caught it, perched it on his fist, and used the sleeve of his coat to brush off the leaves and dirt.

As he approached the carriage, he raked his hair off his forehead and placed the hat more firmly on his head.

One of the female teenagers sitting in the front row looked at him. Then her eyes widened, and she let out a squeal. "Oh my gosh, I don't believe it! You look just like Eli Noble. I mean, like, you could be his twin and everything. Except he had longer, blond hair."

An older man with a balding head and a paunch sitting next to her, maybe her dad, scowled. "Who?"

"Eli Noble. You know, that lead singer in the band I love. Phoenix." While flapping one hand, her thumb moved across the screen on her phone. Then she held it up to the man. "See?"

The man took the phone, then lifted the glasses hooked on to the collar of his shirt and placed them on his nose. He peered at the phone, then over the top of the glasses at Asher. Then he nodded and handed the phone back to the giggling, red-faced teenager. "Sure. Sure. I see it."

Asher silently begged for a sinkhole to appear in the street. He pulled himself up onto the bench and reached for the reins. "Let's take a tour of the island. Who wants to see the fort?"

The girl placed her hand on the back of Asher's seat, leaned forward until her head was near his, then shoved her phone in front of him. Her thumb pressed the button before he had time to react. The girl sat back in her seat. "I'm sending this to my friend who has all things Phoenix in her room."

Asher whirled around, an arm pressed on top of the seat. "I didn't give you permission to take my picture. Please delete it."

"No way."

Asher's jaw tightened as his eyes clashed with the guy sitting next to her. Asher could certainly take the overweight, middle-aged man, but that would only tank any online reviews he'd hoped the tour would generate.

An older woman leaned forward and looked at the teenager's phone. She looked at him. "Same nose, dark eyes. You *could* be twins. But you have scars, and this person doesn't."

The teenager sucked in a breath. "Scars. That's right. Oh, man. Those must be from the fire."

"Fire?" Sadie reached over and took the girl's phone out of her hand.

"Hey, give that back to me."

Ignoring her, Sadie stared at the phone, then lifted her face and locked eyes with Asher, the horror of what she'd just learned so very evident as the color drained from her face. The optimism she'd shared at the onset of the tour vanished. Instead, she stared at him with a mix of shock, disbelief, and maybe something else . . . fear?

Raindrops fell gently from the bloated clouds, drumming steadily against the carriage roof.

"Sadie." He reached for her, but she leaned away from his touch.

He wanted to reassure her that he wasn't the same guy as the photo, but what could he say? Really?

Her eyes shuttered as she thrust the phone at the girl. Without a word, she turned her back to him and welcomed their guests. As she began her rehearsed script, he took that as a cue to drive the team.

For the next thirty minutes, Asher guided them past the highlighted areas of the island and listened as Sadie shared fun facts about the founding of the island and unique highlights about the different quirks, like the fudge wars that Lily and Declan longed to forget.

And not once did she include him in her conversations with their guests.

Probably a good thing. The less they focused on him, the better.

Asher brought Gus and Ginger to a stop in front of the livery where more people waited to board for their scheduled ride. He climbed out of his seat and helped the passengers disembark. The redheaded teenager who started the whole Eli Noble nonsense shot him a wide grin, then squealed as she followed her father down the sidewalk.

As soon as the final passenger disembarked, Sadie looked at him for the first time. Fire blazed in her eyes.

"You lied to me. I thought you were different, but I was wrong. You're no different from Garrett." Then she lifted her skirts and hurried down Blueberry Boulevard toward Main Street.

"Sadie, wait!" Asher started after her, but then one of the guests caught his arm. Sadie turned the corner and disappeared. He stopped and looked back at the guests, still waiting for their discounted tour.

They could wait another minute.

More than anything, he wanted to chase after her and let her know the man in those pictures wasn't the same man she'd gotten to know on the island.

But it wouldn't matter.

The damage was done.

Thunder rippled across the island as jagged streaks of lightning lit up the sky. Heavier winds blew pelting rain through the open carriage, soaking the seats.

Asher remained rooted on the street as the storm raged over him, soaking his hair, his clothes, and his hopes for the future.

He'd failed.

His family.

The island.

But most of all, Sadie.

With the festival only days away and tourists beginning to converge on the island, he had nothing of value to offer anyone.

Today's tour was a catastrophe. Once the girl's pictures swarmed social media, his privacy that he'd worked so hard to protect would be jeopardized.

The paparazzi would hover like vultures, waiting to pick at the bones for a good story.

He had only one option of salvaging the touring company and protecting his family.

It was time to leave.

Sadie was a fool. How could she have been so blind?

With her soaking wet hair falling in her face and clothes dripping, she struggled to unlock the bakery door. At least she'd had the common sense to carry her phone and keys in the matching mint reticule that hung from her wrist. Otherwise, she would've had to run all the way back to the cottage in the rain.

She'd go anywhere to escape Asher and his deception.

Rain pounded against the glass as she hurried inside the room that smelled of fresh paint and . . . she lifted her nose. What was that weird, dank smell?

She couldn't worry about that. She needed to get out of her wet clothes and hide out until the storm passed. At least she had decided to change at the bakery instead of walking through town dressed as someone ready for some sort of reenactment.

She hurried through the store to the back storage room that she'd turned into a makeshift dressing room and reached for her hat only to find it wasn't there. It must have flown off during her escape.

Releasing the hairpins, her hair tangled around her face. She brushed it aside and tried to unbutton her blouse, but she couldn't quite reach the buttons in the back. Dani and Lily had helped her into the gown.

She wanted nothing more than to rip off the buttons, shed herself of the dress like a snakeskin, and pitch it in the trash along with her memories of her most recent time on island.

Dropping on a box full of baking pans, she buried her face in her cold hands. A chill slithered through her as a wave of anger and betrayal washed over her, humiliating her in the worst possible way.

She shivered and her teeth chattered as she pulled out her phone. She stabbed Dani's number and put their call on speaker.

"Hello?" Dani's voice sounded thick with unshed tears.

"I need you. Can you come to the bakery?"

"Yes, I need to talk to you anyway. I'll be there in a minute."

Sadie stood and pulled herself together the best she could. She hurried to the front of the shop and unlocked the door just as Dani appeared, enveloped by a light-blue rain jacket and matching umbrella.

Wind howled and blew rain inside as Dani pushed through the open door. Sadie closed it and pressed her back to the glass. Then she turned the deadbolt. Lights flickered a moment but remained lit.

Sadie grabbed Dani's hand and pulled her toward the storeroom. "I need your help in getting me out of this thing."

Dani grabbed Sadie's wrist. "Wait. I have to tell you something."

Sadie turned and found Dani looking at her with wide eyes as tears drifted down her cheeks. Sadie frowned. "What's wrong?"

Shaking her head, Dani rubbed her fingers over her eyes. "Everything's ruined."

That was an understatement.

"Ariel had to back out of the music festival."

"What? Why?"

Dani lifted a shoulder. "I don't know. She didn't go into details. Something about having an unexpected medical procedure done. Now we don't have a headliner. Even though Caleb Kennedy was able to talk Drake Hamilton into showing up, he'll be here for one set, and that's it. The concert's going to be a bust. After I refund all of the tickets, we're going to be so broke. Not to mention our—make that *my*—reputation will be ruined. No one will want to return next year, and I'll be another Sullivan destroying the island with my crazy schemes."

Any other time, Sadie would've been quick to encourage her friend, but Dani's news simply poured gasoline on the fire that Sadie had no way to put out.

"You could always ask Eli Noble to fill in." The words dripped off her lips like poison.

Dani's head shot up, her eyes wide. "Eli No—Asher told you?"

A sickening feeling churned Sadie's stomach as she opened her mouth to speak, but the words wouldn't come. She could only stare at the person she'd considered one of her few friends on the island. A vise gripped her chest, making it difficult to breathe.

"You . . . you knew." The statement came out as a gasp. "That's what you meant before when you said it wasn't your story to tell."

The shock of the double betrayal within minutes sent ice coursing through her veins.

Dani's face paled as she took a step toward her. She stretched out a hand. "Sadie . . ."

Sadie stepped back and wrapped her arms around her waist. "I don't know what's worse. Asher keeping his identity from me, or the fact that you, one of my best friends on the island—and probably off, for that matter—knew and didn't tell me. How could you?"

Dani dropped her hand and lowered her chin to her chest. She shook her head. "I promised him I wouldn't say anything, and I had to keep my word. You value integrity, so surely you can understand that."

"What I understand is you knew I was falling for him . . . Stupid me. And you stayed quiet. You knew what he'd done to our family. I thought you were my friend." Sadie's voice rose as burning tears clouded her vision.

Fresh tears flowed down Dani's face as she grabbed Sadie's arm. "I *am* your friend. And I'm Asher's friend. I wanted to tell you. So many times. Especially when I realized you had feelings for each other."

Sadie shook her head so hard her wet hair slapped her in the cheek. "No worries about that now. I want nothing to do with the lying jerk. He's responsible for my sister's death."

"No, he's not. He took the blame, but he wasn't responsible. I know you're hurt and angry, but I do hope you can see the truth."

Pounding on the front door echoed through the shop. Sadie whirled around and found a hulking shadow looming behind the glass.

Asher's hair was plastered to his head. He pressed a fist against the doorframe. "Sadie, let me in. We need to talk."

Wrapping her arms around her waist once again, she shook her head. "There's nothing to say. You lied to me."

"Please let me explain."

"What could it hurt to hear him out?" Dani's voice was nearly a whisper behind her.

Sadie spun and faced her so-called friend. "Hurt? What could it hurt? I can't believe you just said that." She jerked a thumb over her shoulder. "My sister is dead because of him."

Thunder shook the building as lightning lit up the sky in an eerie grayish-green cast. Somewhere in the building, the pipes rumbled back a response.

Dani pushed past Sadie and hurried to the door.

"Dani, if you unlock that door, I swear I will never speak to you again."

Dani looked at her with sadness in her eyes. "That's a risk I'm willing to take for you to learn the truth." She flicked the lock and pulled open the door.

Asher slid inside and closed the door. He held her muddy, sopping hat. Chest heaving, he swiped a hand over his dripping face and raked his wet hair off his forehead. Then he took a step toward Sadie.

She flung both hands up. "Don't come any closer."

Asher stopped and dropped his shoulders.

"Did you know who my sister was when you met me?"

He gave her a long look, then shook his head. "Not at first."

"Then when."

"The night in the barn when we—" He paused and glanced at Dani.

"You knew after you kissed me? After I bared my soul to you?" Her voice trembled as the hurt and anger twisted around her windpipe.

"I didn't know until you told me about how Lauren died. Then, I wanted to come clean. So many times."

"Why didn't you?" The weight of his betrayal compressed her chest, leaving her gasping for air.

"I didn't know how, because I knew the moment I did I would lose you." His last couple of words had been spoken so low she'd barely heard him.

"Lose me? Didn't you think I'd learn the truth eventually?"

"The truth isn't what you think it is, Sadie." Dani moved between them.

Sadie glared at Dani. "You stay out of this. You're nearly as guilty as he is."

A drop of water hit Sadie on the nose. She wiped it away and ran a hand over her destroyed Gibson Girl-style updo.

Asher took a step toward her. "Dani had nothing to do with this except in keeping her word to me. I planned to tell you right after my aunt and uncle returned to the island. I wanted them to see what I'd achieved with the tour." He glanced out the large storefront window. "Looks like that's pretty much destroyed too." He turned back to her. "You were so vocal in how much you hated the band and me that I wanted to prove I could be trusted. And maybe you'd be able to see who I am today, not who I used to be."

Sadie's eyes widened. "So, your lies are my fault?"

Asher's face twisted. "That's not what I said. You claim to want a real relationship, but you don't trust well."

"With good reason. People can't be trusted. You and Dani proved that." She pulled the keys out of her pocket and slapped them on the counter. "I'm done with the festival," she said quietly, her voice barely audible over the patter of rain. "And I'm done with the both of you."

Dani shot Sadie one last sorrowful look and ducked under Asher's arm. Wrenching the door open, she grasped the brim of her hood and hurried down the sidewalk into the storm.

"Be mad at me as much as you want, but Dani doesn't deserve that." With that, Asher walked out the door.

Somewhere in the building, the pipes groaned and rattled, nearly shaking the walls. A loud pop exploded in the kitchen.

Sadie hurried to the swinging kitchen door and pushed it open as a burst of water showered over her from the ceiling. Water quickly pooled at her feet and formed streams coursing out into the dining area.

She looked for the water main but couldn't see where to turn anything off. Picking up her skirts, she raced for the door, trying not to skate in the river of water streaming through the shop.

Defeat chased her out into the storm as she headed for Martha's to get some help.

With her trust shredded and the bakery ruined, what hope remained for her to stay on island?

And Gran wouldn't be able to stay in her cottage now.

Fourteen

WHY DID SHE ALWAYS FALL FOR THE liars?

All cried out, Sadie was left with nothing but a raging headache and a broken heart scattered across the island.

Late afternoon shadows cloaked Gran's guest room as Sadie sat on the bed with her back pressed against the headboard. With her computer on her lap, she scrolled through the numerous websites that showed images of a burned bus and told the story of the tragic accident. Then she slipped down the rabbit hole of forums that thrived on conspiracy theories and speculation. So many people questioned the rumors of drugs and alcohol and wondered where Eli Noble had been hiding for the past five years.

His most recent exposure had been plastered on social

media, showing him sitting on the carriage with headlines screaming, "From Rock Star to Carriage Driver."

Lily and Mia had stopped by earlier and mentioned people were coming to the island in droves, hoping to catch a glimpse of him, but she didn't want to hear it.

She was done with Eli Noble. And Asher Quinn.

He was no better than Garrett. Maybe even worse.

But she had no one to blame for the deception but herself. She should've learned her lesson with Garrett and followed her instincts by keeping Asher at arm's length.

But no . . . Like a lovesick teenager, she succumbed to his charms.

Her phone vibrated again.

She lifted it off the bed and glanced at the screen. Another message from Dani, wanting to talk.

Forget that.

She shut off her phone, opened the nightstand drawer, and dropped it inside. She slammed it shut and returned to her computer where words like reckless, blame, and irresponsible jumped out at her. She moved her finger over the keypad and closed the browser.

Setting the laptop aside, she rested her head against her pillow and longed to dive deeper under the covers. After yesterday's rain, she didn't think she'd get warm again. But she couldn't stay holed up in her room. Gran needed her attention. After all, that was supposed to be Sadie's main purpose for being on island.

She started down the hall, then froze when someone laid on the doorbell. Georgie barked, and Gran opened the front door. Then Sadie heard a familiar deep voice.

Goosebumps prickled her skin as she slunk deeper into the shadows.

"Give her the envelope and ask her to call me please."

"I will, Asher. You take care of yourself now, you hear?"

Their voices faded as Sadie retreated and dove back onto her bed.

A moment later, a light knock sounded on the door. It opened, and Gran stood in the doorway, leaning on her four-footed cane. She held an envelope in her other hand. "Asher stopped by. Again. How long are you going to hide from him?"

"I'm not hiding."

"You've barely left this room since yesterday."

"I've had a migraine."

"Mm-hmm." Gran's eyebrow raise showed she didn't believe Sadie. "Doris and I are heading into town to meet with the insurance adjuster at the bakery. Wanna come?"

And witness her pinnacle failure? No, thank you.

But she should. Even if only to learn what could be done to save the flooded store. But Sadie shook her head.

Being in town meant running into Dani.

She pointed to her computer. "I'm going to catch up on some work, then take a shower."

"Sounds like a good plan." Gran smiled and set the envelope on the end of the dresser. "I'm going to leave this right here."

Sadie watched her retreat. She wanted to call out and ask how Gran could stand the sight of Asher after he lied to her all this time. But truth was, she didn't really want to hear what Gran would say . . . which would be that Sadie needed to forgive him.

After Gran hobbled back down the hall, Sadie swung her legs off the bed and grabbed the envelope. She stood in the open doorway and made sure Gran made it safely back to the living room.

Now that Gran was able to manage more on her own and even take short trips into town, maybe it was time for Sadie to consider what was next. After all, if the insurance would cover the damage at the bakery, then Gran could find someone to fix it properly and sell it for a higher amount.

She opened the nightstand drawer, pulled out her phone, and tapped on Lily's number.

"Sadie! It's about time. Why have you been ignoring my calls and texts? I stopped by the cottage, but Gran said you were sleeping."

"You talk to Dani?"

"Yes." The single word, spoken quietly and without judgment sent another surge of tears pressing against the backs of Sadie's eyes.

"So you know what's going on."

"I'm so sorry. Declan and I headed to Port Joseph, and we're on the ferry now to return to the island. I'll be over as soon as we dock."

"I need a change of scenery." Sadie pressed a hand against her pounding forehead. "Maybe spend some time with my parents."

"You want to exchange one island for another."

"Staying on island's out of the question." Sadie reached

for her AirPods and inserted one in her ear. Then she dropped her phone on the bed and tapped the envelope against her palm as she paced the room. "Dad has two more months on his enlistment, then they'll be leaving Oahu. If I want to visit, now's the time. Want to go with me?"

"Sadie, sweetie. You know I'd do anything for you, but you're running away. And that's not going to solve anything. Plus, I don't want you to go. I'm sure your grandma would say the same thing. Have you talked to Asher yet?"

"No, and I'm not going to." Opening the nightstand drawer once more, she dropped the letter inside. Then she picked her phone up off the bed and opened her bank app. The shrinking numbers did little to settle the anxiety building behind her rib cage. "You know, I paid for the touring costumes, thinking Asher had only a couple of pennies to rub together." She scoffed, tears burning her eyes once more. "Eli Noble, on the other hand, could afford a warehouse full of costumes—and even the manufacturing company that produced them. I'm such an idiot."

"No, you're not. You're hurt and angry."

"How could I be so clueless? You know, there was something that bugged me about him from the very beginning. After seeing the pictures that girl on the tour flashed, now I can't believe I'd been so blind." That same sickening feeling she'd experienced yesterday curdled her stomach.

"Well, for one thing, no one expected Eli Noble to be hiding out on island."

"Dani knew." The two words reinforced the betrayal

she'd felt from the moment she realized her friend was aware of Asher's alter ego.

"From what Dani said, she'd given her word to Asher. And you know Dani won't go back on that."

Sighing, Sadie dropped on the edge of her bed. "I know . . ."

A horn blasted, and Sadie's shoulders bunched around her ears.

"Hey, we're about to dock. I'll head to the cottage shortly." With that, Lily ended their call.

Sadie put her AirPod back in its case, then did a quick search on her favorite travel app for flights. She had just enough in her bank account for a one-way flight to Oahu, but then what?

Mooch off her parents? That felt more like a concession to defeat.

She needed to find a job.

Exchanging her phone for her laptop, Sadie skimmed listings for copywriting jobs that would take her far away from Michigan. Maybe back to Florida. She could stand a healthy dose of sunshine and sand right about now.

She dreaded walking back into that world, but a girl's gotta eat and make her own way. She couldn't rely on others. Other than Gran, her parents, and Lily, there wasn't anyone else she trusted anyway.

The desire to write songs had been snuffed out. Before, they reminded her of Lauren. Now they were a reminder of Asher's lies and betrayal.

Getting off island and returning to a nondescript cubicle would help her leave behind the complications of falling in love and getting her heart broken a second time.

If only it were that easy.

The vultures were descending, and Asher had to figure out where to go before they desecrated him even more.

Remembering Liam's lifeline, he reached out and asked for help.

For a moment, it felt good not having to work everything out for himself. But then the reason he needed to leave crashed over him, reminding him what a terrific failure he truly was.

With a baseball hat pulled low over his forehead and dark sunglasses on his face, Asher sat at the back of Cody Hart's boat and scanned the horizon as Port Joseph came into view.

The scent of fish and sunshine wafted over him.

Maybe he needed to get a boat.

Then he could keep it in the marina and escape into the deep whenever he liked.

Problem was, he wouldn't be returning to the island.

After trying for days to talk to Sadie, he realized there was no reason to stay. Time to cut his losses and find another spot of solitude.

Wearing a backward baseball hat over his dark-blond hair, Cody tied up the boat in the marina, and Asher tossed his duffel on the dock next to Cody's slip.

His stomach nothing but a ball of knots, he held out a hand to Cody. "Thanks, man. I appreciate it."

"Sure thing, brother. Take care. And don't be a stranger."

Asher smiled but refused to commit. Returning would simply remind him of what he'd lost.

Several hours later, he pulled his rental into his parents' driveway.

He hadn't driven in over a year, having remained holed up on his uncle's ranch.

Part of him wanted to accelerate and keep driving, but no matter how far he went, he wouldn't escape the disaster of his choices.

Somehow, though, he had to put Jonathon Island and Sadie out of his mind for now.

He climbed out of the black SUV and approached the front door of the brick ranch that had been his home for the first eighteen years of his life. Multicolored flowers grew in decorative pots on the front steps. His mom's favorite rocker still sat in the corner of the covered porch next to a small table that usually held her cup of tea or novel she was reading. An autumn wreath in reds and golds hung on the front door with *Welcome to the Quinns* centered in the middle.

His parents, Noble and Pamela Quinn, welcomed people through the years into their home. Him, not so much. At least, not anymore.

Music and laughter sounded from the backyard. He rounded the house and found his parents' back deck lit up with strands of lights and candles on small round tables. At least twenty people milled around, drinks in hand, talking and laughing with one another.

The party.

Oh man. With everything that happened with Sadie, he'd forgotten today was his father's birthday party.

And he wasn't exactly dressed for a celebration.

He glanced down at faded jeans, beat-up loafers, and wrinkled button-down shirt open over a gray T-shirt.

It would have to do.

Scents of seared steak spiraled toward him, scoring a direct hit with his taste buds.

The party for his dad was in full swing.

Maybe he could stay for a bit.

He removed his sunglasses, hooked them on the collar of his shirt, then crossed the yard to the slim, dark-haired woman wearing a blue floral dress. He tapped her on the shoulder. "Hey, Mom."

She whirled around. Her blue eyes lit up as she flung her arms around his neck. "Asher, you came!"

Her expensive floral perfume tickled his nose as he buried his face in her neck, careful not to dislodge the clip holding back her hair. "It's great to see you."

And he meant it.

His dad, on the other hand, eyed him from his position at the grill but didn't approach them. He lifted his chin in greeting.

Asher nodded in reply.

Dressed in khakis and a light-blue short-sleeved button-down, his short dark hair combed back, Dad manned the grill at his own party. Was it an excuse not to mingle, which Asher knew his dad hated? Or did he need to control everything?

Including trying to direct Asher's life. Which was why

their conversations had been limited to a few words each year. Usually at Christmas. Although he did send the perfunctory birthday text and received "Thanks" as a reply.

Asher scanned the guests and frowned. "Where's Abi?"

"She and Blake are running late."

"That guy put an engagement ring on her finger yet?"

Mom shook her head, then turned toward someone calling her name.

"Asher!"

With an arm around his mom's shoulders, Asher turned and found Uncle Terry moving toward him, his beefy arms outstretched. Asher walked into his uncle's bear hug.

The older man with thinning hair that held more gray than when Asher had seen him ten months ago clapped him on the back. "So good to see you. Glad you made it."

"Thanks, man. It's good to see you." He took in his uncle's tanned face, lined blue eyes radiating peace, and the grin that wouldn't disappear anytime soon.

Uncle Terry shifted his hand off Asher's shoulder to the back of his neck, giving him a light squeeze. "I have a bone to pick with you."

"Take a number." Asher longed to disappear into the woods rimming his parents' backyard. "What did I do now?"

"I was under the impression we'd discuss the *idea* of reviving the tour company. Then I got a call from Sawyer Hastings, wanting my permission to release some horses to Eliza. I called my daughter, and she told me everything."

Asher raked a hand over his face. "I wanted to prove I

could do it—generate an income for the ranch so you'd want to stay on island."

Terry dropped his hand and slid it into his pocket. "Why do you care so much?"

"It's your home. Why would you want to leave it?" Gone less than a few hours and Asher missed it already.

His uncle chuckled. "This coming from a guy who traveled the world."

"Right. Which is why I see the value in putting down roots."

"I've had roots most of my life. Now it's time to see what's out there. Angela and I had a blast touring the country in our RV until recently." Some of the enthusiasm left Terry's voice as his face took on a subdued expression.

"What's going on?"

Terry breathed out a sigh. "Looks like she's having some problem with her thyroid. May need surgery. She wants the comfort of the ranch and being a ferry ride away from her doctor in Port Joseph until things get figured out."

"I'm sorry." Asher stuffed his hands in his pockets. "That's tough."

"So is she." Uncle Terry scratched the back of his head. "So, this tour business . . . I'd be open to reviving it, if you'd be willing to stay on and lend a hand. Maybe we can expand down the road and bring on more drivers."

Asher kicked at the grass with the toe of his leather flip-flop. "Listen, Unc, I want to help. I do. And I'll do whatever I can from the mainland, but I won't be returning to the island."

"Not returning? Why not?" Terry shot him a puzzled look.

Asher glanced over his uncle's shoulder at his mom and aunt in conversation with another woman. "The trial tour didn't go as planned." He explained what happened, the humiliation rubbing him raw. "I'm better off staying away."

"Because of one tour?"

"People know who I am now. Reporters are already swarming the island. There won't be any privacy for you and Aunt Angela."

"Come on, kid. Whose privacy are you really trying to protect? No one's going to bother us."

"They will if I'm there. People will hound you to get the dirt on me. They'll be relentless, doing anything for a story. Just like they did after . . ." Asher ran a hand over his face. "Just like they did after the accident. Remember that? You don't need them stirring up the past."

"Is there more that you're not telling me?"

Sadie's devastated look swam into focus. Asher shook his head. "My time on island is over."

"Well, then. If you're done hiding out on Jonathon Island, then maybe it's time you joined the family business." Dad joined them, hands in his pockets, as he shot Asher a calm but cool look.

Perfect.

He had to choose that moment to pull himself away from the grill.

"You can put your construction skills to good use. Find some purpose in your life."

Asher ground his jaw and considered his words. He

looked at the man who did little to try and understand him. "Thanks for the offer, but I'm not joining your construction business, Dad."

Dad's smile faltered. "What's the matter? Getting your hands dirty too good for you? You have something against hard work?"

"I've been working hard all my life." Asher's voice rose as his fingers curled into fists. "Just because you don't approve doesn't mean my life doesn't have purpose."

Conversations quieted around them as the party guests pretended they weren't staring and listening to the same old father-son argument.

Mom left her group of women and hurried over to them, her mouth tight. "That's enough. Both of you. This is not the time or the place for this discussion."

Dad strode back to the grill without another word.

Asher hugged his mother. "Sorry, Mom. I gotta jet."

She held him at arm's length, the disappointment on her face adding to his feelings of failure. "But you just got here. And your sister's on her way."

He kissed her cheek. "I'll call you."

With a nod to his uncle, he headed to his rental and slid behind the wheel. As he headed back in the direction he'd come, Asher sagged against the seat.

Home for less than fifteen minutes, and he and his dad couldn't manage a five-minute conversation without jumping at each other's throats.

He shouldn't have even bothered to show up. He had

no idea where he was going from there, but he knew one thing. He had no real place to call home.

Not anymore.

Fifteen

SADIE HAD TRADED ONE DISASTER FOR another.

Pools of stagnant water puddled on the worn tile floor in the bakery. No matter how much she mopped up, the water still seemed to settle in the cracks and crevices.

Her freshly painted walls had been splattered with grimy water from the pipe that burst in the kitchen and poured gallons of water through the store.

Hunter Barrett came out of the kitchen, his face grim.

She tightened her grip on the mop. "How bad is it?"

Rubbing a hand over his forehead and dislodging his Barrett Construction hat, he shook his head. "It's not good, Sadie."

Her shoulders slumped as she lifted the industrial mop into the metal bucket on wheels and pushed it to the corner. She lifted her hands and dropped them to her sides. "Might as well let me have it."

Hunter proceeded to lay out the cost for all new plumbing, not to mention the cost of replacing some of the equipment that had gotten fried as the bursting pipe created minor flooding in the store, leaving several inches of water in its wake.

Maybe new owners wouldn't want the equipment anyway. Maybe that didn't matter as much as replacing walls and flooring. Maybe she was kidding herself into not panicking.

His estimate was a crushing blow, each number chipping away more and more at her goal to keep Gran on island.

Tears filled her eyes as she wrapped her arms around her waist.

Her phone chimed from the front counter. She picked it up and found Mia's number on her screen. "Hello?"

"Hey, Sadie. Just passed the bakery on my way to Martha's and saw your lights on. How bad is it?"

"Well, Hunter gave me an estimate with way more zeros than I cared to hear."

"Henrietta's business insurance should cover most of the damage, if not all. I'm sure they'll send out an assessor and work up a claim."

Sadie ran a hand down her thigh, not wanting to share Gran's previous issue with her insurance. "Yeah, the thing is, the insurance adjuster met with Gran yesterday. I don't know how much they're willing to pay out, but it's safe to say the building can't be sold right now. It's such a mess with puddles of water everywhere. Even with windows open, the place reeks. We have no choice but to take it off the market since there's no one available to do the work right now."

"I'm sorry. Let me grab a few people and we'll come over and help with the cleanup."

Sadie shook her head. "No, not until we know it's safe. I can't risk anyone getting sick or hurt."

Besides, Sadie had no doubt that Dani would be one of the first people to show up. Because that's what Dani did—she showed up to help, no matter how full her own plate was. And Sadie wasn't ready to talk to her yet.

They ended their call, and Sadie returned her attention to Hunter. "Sorry about that. What would you recommend?"

"Talk to Henrietta's insurance agent and see what they're willing to do. I know the figures I gave seemed a little high, but they were a rough estimate. The insurance company may want to use one of their own contractors, and you can go from there." He pointed to the top of the sheet. "My contact info's right there if they want to get in touch with me."

Go from there . . .

Tired, so very tired of water, Sadie needed a break. After Hunter disappeared out the back door and up the stairs to his apartment over the bakery, which now lacked water, she grabbed her phone and headed back to the cottage.

With each step down the sidewalk, questions swirled around in her head as she tried to come up with different scenarios for everything to work out. By the time she reached Gran's front porch, she had more questions than answers, and her nerves were frayed.

She stepped inside Gran's living room and breathed in the familiar fragrance of vanilla and sugar wafting through the air.

Sadie kicked off her shoes by the front door and started for her room and the bliss of a hot shower, but the sound of metal sliding into the oven redirected her to the kitchen.

She found Gran plopping balls of dough onto a baking sheet with smooth, practiced adeptness. Behind her, a light breeze cascaded through the open window and ruffled the leaves of Gran's African violet sunning itself on the sill.

Gran looked up and smiled, her blue eyes full of peace and vibrancy. "Sadie, good morning. I thought you were still sleeping."

Shaking her head, Sadie pulled out a chair and sat. She stared at the woman who was one of the most important people in her life, and the stress of the events from the past couple of days crashed over her.

The ache of Asher's betrayal, the damage at the bakery, and the fear of the unknown bore a hole so deeply in her chest that she pressed a hand over her rib cage to hold in the pain.

Her eyes burned with tears that fought to be released. She swallowed several times, but it wasn't enough to prevent the dam from breaking.

One by one, tears slipped over her lids and slid down her cheeks. She buried her face in her hands as a sob broke from her chest.

"Love, what's going on?" Gran moved in front of her and pressed a hand against the back of Sadie's head and drew her against her waist. Her fingers moved through Sadie's hair in the same comforting gesture she'd known as a child.

Sadie shook her head. "I failed, Gran."

Wood scraped against wood as Gran pulled out a chair and sat in front of her. "What do you mean, failed? Failed at what?"

Dragging the back of her hand across her face, Sadie sniffed and looked at the woman who'd always been there for her. "I failed you. The bakery. My life."

Gran reached for a napkin off the holder on the table and pressed it into Sadie's hands. "I'm sorry you feel that way. Tell me what's going on."

Sadie wiped her face and proceeded to tell her about her plan to get the bakery fixed up so it would bring in a higher price. "With the way Asher and Dani betrayed me, I want nothing more than to leave the island, but I barely have enough money for a ticket to Hawaii. Everything's falling apart, and I don't know how to fix it."

Another sob rose in her chest as she mopped her eyes, but it wasn't enough to stop the steady stream exposing her broken heart.

Gran scooted closer and drew Sadie into her arms. "Oh, love, you're carrying many burdens that don't belong to you. It's not your job to fix any of it. I never should have saddled you with my financial woes. I blame it on those pesky painkillers that lowered my defenses. You are not responsible for the consequences of my actions—mine and Grandpa Hank's. He was a brilliant baker but a frustrating businessman. And I'm sorry for asking you to keep things from your parents."

"They'd want to help you."

"Yes, I know. When I broke my hip, I listened to a couple of friends who vented about their kids wanting to shuttle them off to the old folks' home." Gran waved a hand around her kitchen. "I'm not ready to leave this house or the island. I like my freedom. I do need to make some changes so I can stay. I've already called your dad and told him we need to make some decisions as a family, but I made it clear no one is booting me off my island."

Sadie smiled through her tears at the conviction and spunk in Gran's words. "I don't think anyone wants to see you leave either."

Gran cupped Sadie's face in her soft hands. "I appreciate that more than you will ever know. The Quinns' insurance covered the tree damage, and my insurance company will cover the other storm damages to the cottage."

"But I thought you lost your insurance."

Gran frowned. "Why would you think that?"

Sadie jerked her head toward the front porch. "When the tree fell, you learned your policy had lapsed."

Gran scanned her face, then her eyes lit up. "Oh! Goodness me! I didn't tell you. I called the company and explained about my fall and subsequent surgery. I reminded them I had been a customer for over fifty years. I caught up my payment, and things are as right as rain."

Sadie stared at Gran as she tried to process the news.

She sighed and lowered her eyes to the shredded napkin torn to bits in her lap. "Well, that's a relief."

Gran lifted Sadie's chin and caught her gaze. "You are not a failure. You are sweet and kind and brilliant."

Sadie shook her head. "I put my trust in the wrong person. Again. When will I learn that men are nothing but liars?"

"Sadie girl, that's not true. And it's not fair to sweep all men together because of the actions of one man."

"Two men. Garrett and Asher."

"Well, truth be told, I never cared for Garrett. He was too slick. But Asher, on the other hand, he's a good man."

Sadie jumped to her feet and paced the kitchen, arms wrapped around her waist. "No, Gran, he isn't. You wouldn't say that if you knew what I know."

"I know what I need to know."

Biting her lip, Sadie shook her head. She pressed her back against the kitchen sink and closed her eyes as images from her web search about the bus crash flickered through her head. "He's the reason Lauren's dead."

The words sent a spike through her chest, flaying it open for all of her pain to be exposed once again.

Gran moved in front of her and took Sadie's hands. "He's not, Sadie. Lauren died in a tragic accident. It wasn't Asher's fault. You need to talk to him and forgive him so you can find your own healing."

"Forgive him?" Sadie's words came out in a gasp as her eyes widened. "Are you crazy? He destroyed our family."

Gran looked at her with patient eyes, but the light had dimmed. She shook her head. "No, he didn't. Our family is still intact. We still love and support one another, even across the miles. There's no distance that love can't bridge."

Sadie pushed away from the sink and paced between the table and the stove. "I read the articles. I saw the pictures."

"Speculations. Not facts. Talk to Asher and learn the truth. Forgive him so that bitterness doesn't consume you."

"Dani knew and didn't say anything either."

"Forgive her too." Gran released a sigh and reached for her hand. "And you'll need to forgive me while you're at it."

Sadie's eyes jerked back to Gran. "Forgive you? For what?"

The timer dinged, and Gran slid her hand into an oven mitt. She pulled a pan of oatmeal chocolate chip cookies from the oven and set them on the cooling rack, then faced Sadie, a hand on her hip. "Because I've known who he was from the moment he stepped foot on island."

Sadie's eyes widened, and all the words on her tongue disappeared as her jaw unhinged.

Gran lifted the baking sheet off the cooling rack and started removing cookies. Her face didn't bear any malice as she mentioned Asher. How could that be?

"How did you know?"

Gran removed the last cookie and set the sheet on the stove. Then she returned to her chair and rubbed her left hip. She pointed to Sadie's empty spot. "Sit, and I'll tell you."

Sadie did as directed and waited.

Gran's eyes locked with hers. "Angela Quinn has been my prayer partner since she and Terry bought the ranch.

She was a young mom who felt in over her head. Jared's death was hard on them, but they leaned into their faith. When they considered asking Asher to join them on the ranch, Angela came to me and we talked. I had to pray and ask the Lord to uproot any seeds of bitterness and to show nothing but His love and grace to this tortured young man."

"I can't imagine it was easy."

"I didn't think it would be either, but God is good. Always. I've come to see Asher as a remarkable young man. Caring and generous with his time. He's being chased by his own demons and doesn't need anyone else adding to that race. Forgive him, Sadie. For your sake and for his. Forgiveness doesn't happen overnight. It can be a process, but once you start, then the healing can begin."

Sadie nodded as she digested her grandma's wise words. "His betrayal hurt, especially after what Garrett had done."

"I know, love. I'm sorry for the pain you're feeling. Just know, God will never betray you. Or humiliate you. His love will sustain you and give you the strength to move forward. You can always go to Him for wisdom and guidance. He will never leave you nor forsake you."

"Thanks, Gran." Sadie stood and leaned over her, wrapping her arms around Gran's small frame. "I love you so much."

"I love you too, and that's why I want to see you face your fears so you can have the life that God longs for you to have. Did you ever read that letter that Asher dropped off the other day?"

Remembering the envelope she shoved into the night-stand, she shook her head. "I'll do that now."

In her room, Sadie opened the drawer slowly and stared at the envelope with her name written in Asher's handwriting. She removed it and slid her finger under the flap. She pulled out the papers, unfolded them, and started reading.

Sadie,

There aren't enough words to express how sorry I am. You don't have to believe me, but I didn't set out to deceive you. The more I got to know you, the harder it was to tell you the truth because I knew how you felt about Eli Noble and Phoenix. I tried showing I wasn't that guy anymore. But it wasn't enough. I get that. I hope you can forgive me someday. I found this poem in my cousin's guitar case. After reading it, I realized it belonged to you. Not sure how it ended up there, but I thought you'd like to have it back.

All the best,

Asher

She slid his letter aside and found a worn piece of paper with very familiar words.

Her eyes scanned the words she'd penned so long ago as a memory of Lauren surfaced. Her sister had come into her room as she was writing and jumped on her bed. She'd snatched the paper out of her hands and danced around as she put Sadie's rough words to music.

Sadie had forgotten about them, but Lauren must've kept the paper with the lyrics. But why?

How did they end up in Asher's cousin's guitar case? Had her sister hoped to get Phoenix to sing one of *her* songs? Is that why Lauren was on that bus in the first place?

A chill snaked through Sadie.

If she continued to blame Asher, then she'd have to blame herself too. But it was no more his fault than it was hers. A tragic accident, like Gran had said.

The irony sent a sharp pang through her chest.

Burying her face in her hands, she drew in a lungful of air and released it along with a prayer. "Help me, Lord. I don't even know where to begin."

As she sat in the quiet of her room, a peace she hadn't felt in quite a while wrapped around her.

Gran's words tiptoed through her thoughts, poking at the questions that lingered. As Sadie untangled her knotted emotions, she realized she had two options. She could make a choice to forgive Asher and Dani and choose love and friendship, or continue to allow those seeds of bitterness to take root, destroying what could be.

Each choice came with a cost, and she had to decide which one she wanted to pay.

She picked up the papers again and reread Asher's words. Then she reached for the poem written during a time when her worries seemed frivolous compared to the burdens she carried today.

She opened the nightstand again, removed the journal Asher had given her, and turned to the page where she'd started writing.

Slowly, letters came together in her head and formed

words. Those words stood together and completed some of the lines she'd been missing from the lyrics she'd started a few days ago.

She grabbed a pen and wrote, allowing the words from her heart to flow through her fingers and make their way onto the page.

With her pulse racing and fresh tears blurring the words on the page, she realized she'd written a song for Asher.

And he had to be the one to sing it.

Now it was time to face the music and make a choice . . . for both of their futures.

Asher had no place to go but no desire to stay where he was.

He'd figure it out. Find some place to hole up where nobody knew or cared who he was.

He jammed the last of his clothes in his duffel, zipped it closed, then glanced around the hotel room to make sure he'd gotten everything.

The unmade bed with blankets twisted spoke of his night of very little sleep. At least nightmares hadn't unleashed their wrath.

His dad did that on his own.

He tossed a few dollar bills on the dented pillow for housekeeping and spied a stray sock on the neutral carpet that blended with the beige-lined wallpaper. Nothing in the room stood out. It was as if the room itself was trying to be as unobtrusive as possible.

Asher got it. He wanted nothing more than to blend in.

Swiping his phone off the dresser, he slung his duffel over his shoulder and headed for the door. Ensuring he had his key card, he turned the knob.

And found his uncle Terry standing in the doorway, his fist poised to knock.

Asher took a step back. "What are you doing here?"

"Checking on you. Mind if I come in?"

"Mom told you where I was." Once he'd settled in his room, he texted his mom, told her where he was staying, and promised to meet her for coffee before he headed out of town.

"I was about to check out, but I have a few minutes." Asher stepped aside and let his uncle pass. "I wasn't expecting you."

Uncle Terry glanced around the room, rested a shoulder against the wall next to the bathroom and shoved a hand in his front pocket. "You should've stayed at the party. We missed you."

"Define 'we.'"

"Your mom tried to put on a happy face for everyone else, but she was hurting. And your sister was upset you left before she got there." Terry leveled him with a direct look. "How long are you going to let this feud between you and your old man continue?"

Asher tossed his bag on the bed and sank onto the mattress next to it. "When we're together, it's always the same thing. He only respects me if I do what he wants, not what I want."

Terry pushed away from the wall and pulled out the office chair at the small desk next to the dresser. He sat and leaned forward, resting his forearms on his knees. "What do you want, Ash?"

Man, that was a loaded question.

So many things . . .

Asher rubbed his forehead, then looked at his uncle, who acted more like a dad than his own father. Grief and years of being outside had etched deep lines in the man's face. His dark hair, streaked with silver, had been combed off his forehead. His blue eyes radiated something Asher longed for.

Peace.

Asher stared at his own hands, nicked and calloused from months spent working with the horses. Months of trying to escape his past mistakes. His throat thickened as his vision blurred. He ran a hand under his nose.

"I want to be enough." The whispered words tore at the wound festering deep inside him. "I want to be redeemed from past mistakes. To make up for everything I've messed up. I keep feeling like I'm just . . . failing . . . and falling into this pit with no way of climbing out."

"Wasn't your fault, Ash."

Asher shook his head against the same song and dance. He looked at his uncle. "My bus. My fault."

Terry stood and moved to the window, his back to Asher. "I wanted it to be. I wanted to lash out and blame someone for my boy's death. Maybe then it would keep the pain in my chest from crippling me, from destroying my wife, from crushing my daughter. I wanted someone to take the blame so I could feel better."

"Then blame me." Asher jumped to his feet and

pounded a fist against his chest. "I'm the reason Jared is gone."

Terry looked at him, his eyes glittering and a tortured expression on his face. Then he reached out and placed a meaty hand on Asher's shoulder and shook his head. "No, son, you're not."

Son.

He didn't deserve to be anyone's son. Especially his uncle's, who lost his own flesh and blood.

Terry squeezed gently as his jaw clenched. "I read the police report. Studied the accident investigation notes. The accident happened because of the storm. Lightning struck a tree and fell on the road ahead of the bus. Because of the darkness and rain, your driver couldn't see it until it was too late. He tried to overcorrect and ended up sliding on the slick surface. The back end came around, hit the tree, then the bus rolled. Leaking gas ignited with sparks and started the fire."

Asher slammed a clenched fist against his chest, his breathing constricted. "But I was the one who agreed to let them drive so we could make the next venue. Me. I made the decision to keep going. We had to make time on the road. The guys were over their hours, but I allowed them to keep driving. They were tired. Their reflexes were slower. If I'd said no, then we would've hung out at the hotel and woken up safely the next morning. I'm the selfish one who needed the roar of the crowds like an addict needs a hit. I got so lost in my own self-importance that I endangered everyone. Got so caught up in the lifestyle that I lost sight of what mattered most."

The memory of that night ravaged Asher's brain as the squealing metal, screams, and roar of the fire echoed in his ears. His own screams as flames seared his skin. The anguish of recovery. Because of his pride and selfishness, he lost some of the best people in his life.

"You don't know that. You may think that, but who knows what could've happened had you spent the night? You're not God, Ash. You need to let go of something that wasn't your fault. The accident was a tragedy. No one's denying that. But no one blames you but you. Let it go."

Let it go.

Three words that were easy to say but so hard to do.

Asher lifted his eyes and searched his uncle's face for condemnation, but all he found was compassion. He swallowed, the boulder in his throat growing. The anguish in his chest twisted his heart so tightly that Asher winced at the pain. "You lost your son. How can you stand to look at me?"

A lone tear trailed down Terry's cheek as he nodded slowly. "I did. And I miss him every single day. But that doesn't dilute the love I feel for you, Asher. You've locked yourself in this emotional prison for the past five years and refused visitors."

"I couldn't stand to see anyone's judgment, so it was better to be alone where I couldn't cause any more pain. Even you and Aunt Angela split soon after I showed up at the ranch. I figured you couldn't stand the sight of me. Of what I cost you."

"Oh, man." Terry sighed and lifted his hand off Asher's shoulder. He dragged it over his face, wiping another tear off his cheek. "We didn't leave because of you—at least, not for the reasons you're thinking. We left because we trusted you to take such good care of the place. I told you that."

Asher nodded, then shook his head. "I didn't believe you. Figured you were just being nice."

"I'm sorry our trip left you with those feelings. You weren't meant to live out your days being a recluse burdened by the past. God created us for relationships, first with Him, then with others. Your family loves you. Not for what you've done or didn't do. But for who you are." Terry strode across the room and opened the door. He stepped outside, then returned carrying two guitar cases and set them on the bed next to Asher's duffel.

Asher's heart dropped to his feet as he caught sight of the black cases laying side by side. The same cases he'd opened a few days ago for the first time in five years. He looked at his uncle. "You've gone back to the ranch?"

"We made a short trip back before showing up to your dad's party. Found this open on the couch in the living room. Gotta admit—felt like a sucker punch to the gut. Too many times, Jared sat in that same spot, ankle on his knee as he strummed chords and worked out lyrics. I grabbed his case, then headed to your room and found yours." Terry shoved a hand in his front pocket. "You weren't meant to be a solo act either. Not in life or in your career. You were meant to play with other people. You thrived on that stage with others playing around you. That's just how God created you. Jared's gone, but you're still here. It's time to embrace that again and stop going through life as a one-man band."

One-man band.

He didn't want that either. He longed for relationships again.

"I don't know what to do. Where to go from here." Asher flipped the latch open on his guitar case and ran a finger around the curves of the body and across the soundboard. "I feel like I have to constantly prove myself, to measure up, to be enough. I keep thinking if I do more, then maybe that will be enough to earn my dad's respect."

"You're a young dude with plenty of options. Take some time and explore what's out there." Terry clapped a hand on his upper back. "Your dad is proud and stubborn, but I have no doubt about his love for you. You don't need to perform to be loved and valued. God gave you a gift—a talent for music. You can use it to honor Him and bring light to others. But do it for the joy and not for trying to earn your place anywhere . . . or with anyone. Decide where you want to go but leave the baggage of the past behind."

Asher's eyes shifted to the packed duffel sitting on the bed. He pulled in a deep breath and released it slowly, feeling lighter than he had in a very long time. He turned back to his uncle and threw his arms around him. "Thanks, Uncle T."

"Anytime, man. You're a great kid, Ash. A fine man. Now you need to embrace that and move forward."

Move forward.

He wasn't quite sure how to do that. How to release

the past and people's perceptions of him. But more than anything, he wanted to shake off the shackles of his own grief and start fresh.

But not by himself.

He lifted the guitar from the case and closed his fingers over the neck. The weight felt right as his fingers touched the strings.

The itch to play came back with a vengeance, something he hadn't felt in a very long time. "Mind if I crash at the ranch for a little while longer?"

"You're always welcome at the ranch." Terry raised an eyebrow and shot him a pointed look. "But you need to straighten things out with your dad first."

Asher nodded. "I will. I promise. But first, I need to finish what I started on the island, then I'll clear the air with Dad."

Terry smiled at him. If Asher were a hopeful man, he'd hope it was pride beaming from the older man's eyes. "As long as you're not running anymore. Face your future with faith and courage. I'm proud of you, man."

Hope exploded in Asher's chest. He returned the guitar to the case and snapped it shut.

For now.

Then he slung his duffel over his shoulder. This time, though, he wasn't heading for a place to escape, to get lost in the crowd, to blend in.

He was going home.

Sixteen

S ADIE HOPED CHAI LATTES AND A thousand apologies were enough to mend her friendship with Dani.

If not, then she got what she deserved.

For someone who valued integrity like Sadie did, she should've listened instead of placing blame.

Dani was being a true friend. In hindsight, Sadie admired that.

Juggling the cardboard holder with two iced chais, Sadie tapped on Dani's open office door at the Tourism Bureau.

The vintage anchor print that papered the walls went well with the worn secretary desk and the scent of old books. Dani had added personal touches with a framed photo of her and Liam and a potted plant with bright green leaves that hung down the side of a wooden file cabinet.

With her phone to her ear, Dani spun in her chair and faced the door. The moment she saw Sadie, though, her animated expression shut down. She murmured something into her phone and ended the call. Then she stood, straightened her royal blue polo shirt with the Jonathon Island logo over her light-gray shorts, and flipped her long braid over her shoulder.

Sadie took a tentative step into the room. "Hey."

Dani smiled but remained quiet, her eyes wary.

"I brought you a latte from Good Day. Figured you could use a break." Sadie removed one of the dripping cups and held it out to her.

Dani stepped forward and took it. "Thanks."

"I know you'd never betray me, and I'm sorry for the awful things I said." The words came out in a rush.

Dani used the straw and scooped up a dollop of whipped cream and put it in her mouth, then she looked at Sadie over the edge of her cup, her eyes tinged with pain. "You really hurt me."

Sadie's shoulders sagged. "I was shocked to learn about Asher's connection to my sister, and when I learned you knew, I just lost it. I'm sorry for the way I reacted. You were only trying to protect Asher and me."

Dani's shoulders relaxed as she set her drink on her desk. "I wanted to tell you so many times, but it wasn't my place. I made a promise to Asher. I'm sorry too. I never wanted to hurt you."

"Never apologize for your integrity. I can only imagine how hard it was to stay quiet."

"It was the worst, especially when I saw the way you looked at him." Dani opened her arms. "Forgive me?"

Sadie shook her head as she walked into her friend's embrace. "No need. You did nothing wrong."

They broke apart and reached for their drinks. Sadie took a sip of the icy sweetness. "How's everything else going?"

Dani waved a hand over her messy but organized desk. "About the equivalent of a dumpster fire. You know, just another day at the office."

"The concert?"

Dani nodded and glanced at the clock above her desk. "Still waiting to hear if Dahlia Denton will sing without Ariel. She's supposed to return my call within the hour. If she says no, then the concert is off, and I have to refund our sold-out tickets, which will wipe us out and ruin my rep with the community."

"What if I can help you get someone else, just in case. Or even in addition to?"

Dani furrowed her brows. "Who? Especially at the last minute? The concert's in two days."

Sadie pulled her journal out of her tote bag, opened to the page she'd completed that morning, and handed it to her friend.

Dani took it. "What is it?"

"Read it."

Dani read the words, then looked at Sadie with wide eyes. "You did it. You wrote a song. Not just any song either. A great song. I mean it, those lyrics are amazing."

"I don't know about amazing, but thank you." Sadie

took her journal and ran her finger over the embossed words on the cover. "I'm going to ask Asher to sing it at the concert."

Dani's face fell as her enthusiasm from seconds ago disappeared. "Have you talked to him?"

She shook her head. "Not yet. Going there now."

"I'd really hate to see you get your hopes up. Besides, Mia mentioned Cody snuck him off island in his boat the other night, and that he had no plans to return."

Sadie lifted her hands, then dropped them again. "Well, I'll go to the ranch and talk to his aunt and uncle. Maybe they'll let me know how I can contact him. I know they're back, because Angela stopped by to see Gran."

Dani reached for Sadie's hand and gave it a gentle squeeze. "Good. I hope you're able to talk to him. Promise to keep me updated."

"Absolutely. It's time for both of us to come out of hiding, to embrace the life God has called us to live."

Dani nodded, her smile bright. "I'll help you however I can."

Sadie's phone rang. She pulled it out of the pocket of her sundress and found Gran's number on the screen. "Hey, Gran."

"Sadie . . ." Gran's voice fractured.

Sadie tightened her grip on the phone. "Gran, are you okay?"

"Yes." The word came out in a sob.

"You don't sound okay. I'm with Dani. I'll be there in about ten minutes. Do you need me to call an ambulance?" Her heartbeat thundered in her ears as she headed for the door.

"No, no. I'm fine. Just a little overwhelmed." Gran cleared her throat. "I just got off the phone with Mia."

Sadie slumped against the wall. "Well, that's a relief. What did Mia have to say?"

"Someone made an anonymous offer to buy the bakery for twice the appraisal amount."

"What?" Sadie nearly dropped the phone as her pulse spiked. She straightened and glanced at Dani, who watched her with a frown. "Who?"

"I don't know. The condition of the sale is the buyer remains anonymous until I accept the offer and sign the papers."

"Is that legal?"

"I'll have my lawyer look everything over to be sure."

Sadie couldn't stop the excitement that crowded her voice as she did a little dance in the middle of the doorway. "That's so great, Gran. I can't even tell you how excited I am that you get to remain in your house."

Hearing Sadie's reply, Dani let out a whoop and did her own dance.

"Who was that?"

"Dani. I'm at the Tourism Bureau."

"So, everything's fine between you two?"

"More than fine."

"What about Asher?"

Sadie's excitement dimmed. "Dani heard he left the island."

"He did. But he's back. Angela said so herself. Talk to him, love."

"I will. I promise." She ended the call and released a squeal as she raced across the room and hugged her friend. Tears warmed Sadie's eyes as she relayed the conversation.

"So your grandma doesn't know who?"

Sadie shook her head.

Dani scrunched up her face, then smiled. "Mia wouldn't be involved with anything shady, so we need to trust her to have Henrietta's best interests in mind."

"Exactly." Then Sadie remembered Gran's other revelation. "Oh! Asher's here. On island. Angela said so."

Dani waved her toward the door. "Then get out of here and fix things with him. We have a show to put on, and I'm not willing to let anyone down if I can help it."

Raising her latte in a salute, Sadie left the hundred-year-old building with more excitement and energy than when she had entered.

For the first time in a while, things were really coming together.

Now if only she could convince Asher to say yes . . .

It was time for a new beginning, but that couldn't happen until Asher worked up the nerve to talk to Sadie.

He snuck back on island last night the same way he'd left—by Cody's boat. As he expected, reporters camped out in front of the ranch, so Cody snuck him up through the state park and the quiet beach where his life imploded only a few days prior.

Once he finished feeding Gus and Ginger, he'd head across the fence and see if Sadie was still at the cottage . . . and willing to hear him out.

He scooped grain into buckets, then poured it into the horses' feeders. After filling the troughs with fresh water, he broke apart a bale and dropped biscuits of hay in their stalls. While they ate, he reached for a broom and started sweeping hay out of the aisle.

He caught a movement in his peripheral vision and turned. He sucked in a breath. "Sadie."

Standing in the open doorway, she lifted a hand. "Hey."

Everything in him wanted to sprint down the aisle, crush her against his chest, and beg her to forgive him.

She smoothed down the front of the pink and yellow flowered sundress she wore with a short jean jacket, looking even more beautiful than ever. Her long hair had been gathered in a messy knot on her head with a few loose strands framing her face.

She clasped her hands in front of her. "Can we talk?"

"Sure." He returned the broom to the tack room, then headed over to her. "Want to take a walk? We'll have to stay in the pasture. Too many people camped out by the gate."

"I saw that. I'm sorry. I'm sure that's tough." The look of compassion on her face had him wanting to sweep her into his arms all over again.

Instead, he pocketed his hands. "There's a reason I try to protect my privacy. Who wants every moment of their lives splashed across the media for criticism or speculation?"

Sadie shook her head. "It would be a terrible way to live."

"I used to crave it, you know. From the moment I stepped into the spotlight, cupped my hand around the mic, and belted out that first note . . . well, I came alive. Almost like some sort of monster fueled by the screams of adoring fans. I wanted—almost needed—it more and more. Then when I lost everything, I craved the bottle to drown out the haunting screams. I've learned that's not the kind of person I want to be or the life I want to live. Being on island taught me what's important—real, lasting relationships, helping people, giving back to my family and community."

Asher placed a hand at the small of Sadie's back and guided her around the barn and to the pasture where Gus and Ginger enjoyed their free time. Noticing Sadie's flip-flops, he decided to walk along the fence line, where the grass was shorter.

She stopped and adjusted her bag on her shoulder. Crossing her arms over her chest, she glanced at him, then looked away, shaking her head. "I'm sorry—I can't do this."

"Do what? Take a walk?"

Still shaking her head, she made a circular motion around them with her hand. "This. You. Me. Us. The polite talk." She shoved her sunglasses on top of her head. "May I ask you something?"

The moment he'd been waiting for—to come clean, bare his soul, seek her forgiveness, and find the redemption his heart had been craving since the accident. He planted his feet shoulder-width apart, then stretched his arms out at his sides. "Yes, you can ask me anything, and I promise to answer. No deflection. No evasion. I'm an open book."

Her eyes searched his, then a slow smile spread across her face. "Good, then I guess I'd better make it count. Will you sing for me?"

The words, spoken almost in a whisper as if she were afraid to voice them out loud, nearly stopped his heart. His eyes widened as his brain comprehended what she was asking.

"Sing for you? Like right here? Right now?"

Reaching into the navy tote bag slung over her shoulder, she withdrew a book.

But it wasn't just any book—it was the journal he'd given her.

She opened it and turned it to face him. Then she looked at him with eyes full of nervousness and maybe a little wonder. "I wrote a song. For you. For us. I'd like you to sing it at the concert. Maybe the talent show? Not as Eli Noble but as Asher Quinn. Will you do that?"

"Why me?" A chill washed over him despite the warm sunshine streaming over them. Did she realize what she was asking?

She pressed the journal into his hands. "It's time for both of us to come out of hiding, to reveal our scars, and embrace the life God has called us to live."

With his limbs quaking, he took it. As he read the words, the uneasiness loosened in his chest.

As if his hand had a mind of its own, his fingers tapped

a beat against the back cover of the journal as the rhythm of the lyrics came alive inside his head.

He imagined reaching for his guitar, wrapping his left hand around the neck, and caressing the frets and strings. Closing his eyes a moment, he visualized his fingers reaching for his pick and strumming the chords to create a melody worthy of the beautiful words Sadie captured on the page.

Humming, mostly to himself, Asher tapped his foot in time to the music playing in his head. Opening his eyes, he pulled in a breath and softly sang the first verse. "Share the scars, share the fears. Bring them all, bring them near. You are healed, you are Mine. In My love, you will find."

His throat thickened as tears burned the backs of his eyes. He looked at Sadie standing in front of him, arms around her waist and biting on the corner of her lip.

"Sadie, this is beautiful. Truly remarkable."

Her shoulders sagged as a hand flew to her mouth. "You mean it?"

He nodded and closed the distance between them. He ran the backs of his fingers over her petal-soft cheek. "Yes, I do. I wouldn't lie to you. Not about this. Or anything for that matter. I'm so sorry for hurting you. Please forgive me for deceiving you."

With her eyes closed, she covered his fingers with her hand and nodded. Then she opened her eyes and looked at him. "I forgive you."

The three words spoken softly but with conviction were like a sharp knife slicing through the invisible cords that had cinched his chest for nearly five years.

He gathered her in his arms and crushed her to his chest. With as much strength as he could manage, he did his best to hold it together. To his horror, a tear rolled down his cheek and disappeared into his beard.

"You need to forgive me too. For leaving. For not hearing you out. For blaming you. I'm sorry, Asher. So sorry." Sadie placed her hands on his chest and looked up at him. She touched his face, her fingers trailing down the puckered skin along the side of his neck from his ear to his collarbone. "Tell me what happened."

For years, he'd tried to stuff the memories away, to keep from reliving the horror that changed his life and created so much unnecessary grief. And now he wanted to talk about it, to share with her so she'd understand. But it needed to wait.

Asher took her hands in his and gave them a gentle squeeze. "I will. I promise. But I realized I didn't answer your question."

She frowned. "My question."

"You asked if I'd sing at the concert."

"Oh, right. Will you?"

"On one condition."

"What's that?" She raised her eyebrows.

He pulled her toward him. "You sing with me."

Sadie's hopeful expression fell as she turned away, pulling her hands from his grasp. "Asher, I don't have talent close to matching yours. If I mess up, then people will laugh. I'll be humiliated, and I'll let you down."

"You will never let me down, Sadie." He stepped closer, his voice steady and encouraging as he lifted a hand and ran a thumb over her cheek. "You can do this. I will be at your side the entire time. As your grandma likes to remind me, God will never leave you nor forsake you. And I won't either. That's a promise. It's time I stop being a one-man band, and I can't imagine anyone else I'd rather sing *our* song with than you."

"You really think I can do it?" Her large, blue eyes full of uncertainty searched his face, looking for what? Courage, maybe?

"I don't think—I know." His hand cupped the back of her head. "You have a gift, and it's time to share it with others. No matter what happens, we'll do it together."

"Together. There's no harmony without other people."

"Exactly."

"Okay, I'll sing with you. I'm scared, but you give me courage. You help me to feel brave. It's time to put our pasts to rest and find healing together."

Asher drew her closer and lowered his mouth to hers. He captured her soft lips as her arms slid round his neck.

He hadn't performed on stage in years, but something told him this concert would be different. It wasn't about him needing to see his name in lights, to hear the applause, to feel the rush of adrenaline.

This time, singing with Sadie would be a celebration of overcoming what they'd lost and the new beginning for their future.

Together.

Seventeen

FOCUS ON ME."

The three words Asher whispered in her ear before running onto the wooden stage set against the backdrop of the lake gave Sadie the courage to put one trembling foot in front of the other and take her place next to him.

A canopy of stars and the glow of the full moon cast subtle light over the park on Blueberry Hill where tourists, islanders, family, and friends sat on blankets and chairs scattered on the grass.

Twinkling lights had been strung through the trees and around the park to create a radiance that was almost ethereal.

Water lapped the shore, adding to the rhythm of excitement pulsing through the park.

Asher handed her a mic, then reached for her hand and gave it a gentle squeeze. "Ready?"

Sadie pressed a hand to her quaking stomach. Feeling like the ten-year-old playing a tree in her school play, she couldn't stop shaking. "Not really. Sure you need me?"

His eyes darkened as he lowered his head to her ear. "I'll always need you. You can do this. Sing from your heart. That's what matters."

Asher slung his guitar over his neck, then lifted up both arms as he stepped closer to the microphone. "Hellllooooo, Jonathon Islannnndddddd!"

Cheers exploded from the grass as people jumped to their feet.

"I'm Asher Quinn, and this lovely lady next to me is the ridiculously talented Sadie Hudson. Tonight, we're singing a song called "Share Your Scars," written by Sadie, and it's dedicated to Jared Quinn, Lauren Hudson, and the rest of the Phoenix crew."

Asher took a step back as the crowd quieted and the two of them stood in the spotlight, darkening the world around them.

He fitted his long fingers over the fretboard, then began strumming the first notes. His rich, melodic voice nearly whispered the first few lines of lyrics that she knew by heart.

Sadie closed her eyes, took a deep breath, and released it slowly.

Sing from your heart.

Focus on Me.

Even though Asher had spoken the words just moments before, this time, she didn't hear his voice. Instead, she felt the presence of the Lord, and His confidence gave Sadie the courage she needed to open her eyes and hold the mic close to her mouth.

As she opened her heart, the words written for the one she loved flowed from her mouth. Their voices harmonized at the chorus, the lyrics washing over her and healing the pieces of her wounded heart, note by note.

The others drifted away as her eyes tangled with Asher's and they were the only two in the park. As he sang, every note spoke of hope and love and touched her soul.

They sang the final chorus and brought the last note to a hushed finish. The crowd roared. Jumping to their feet, exclamations muffled by clapping exploded throughout the park.

Asher swung his guitar around to his back and closed the distance between them. He wrapped her in his arms and swung her around. He set her back on her feet, slid a hand behind her neck, and claimed her lips for his own. Then he pressed his forehead to hers. "You were brilliant."

Tears flooded her eyes and coursed down her cheeks. Not caring who witnessed this emotional moment, she didn't bother wiping them away. Slightly breathless and a little overwhelmed, Sadie wrapped her arms around Asher's waist and pressed her cheek to his chest. "I don't believe it. I sang in front of a crowd. And it wasn't horrible. All because of you."

Asher tipped up her chin. "No, because of you. You are strong and brave, and I love you."

The sounds of the crowd melted away as she closed her eyes and absorbed his words.

"I know we haven't known each other that long, but I can't change how I feel."

Sadie nodded. "I get it. I love you too."

Someone cleared their throat, and Sadie and Asher jumped apart. She turned and found her parents holding hands and standing in front of the stage with Gran.

Sadie practically flew off the platform and into their arms. "You're here! You came! Why didn't you say anything?"

They glanced at one another and smiled. "We wanted to surprise you."

Mom gave Sadie another hug, her eyes sparkling with unshed tears. "That was beautiful, sweetheart. Absolutely beautiful. Lauren would be so proud."

Fresh tears warmed Sadie's eyes. "Thanks, Mom."

Dad dropped a kiss on her cheek. "Looks like those porch concerts finally paid off, eh?"

Sadie laughed, tears blurring her vision, and wrapped her arms around their necks. "So how long are you staying?"

"How about permanently?"

Sadie jerked back, her eyes wide. "What? Are you serious?"

Dad, standing tall with the same military bearing as he'd had for as long as she'd been alive, ran a hand over his short, dark hair threaded with silver. "Your mom and I talked and chose not to say anything until closer to the date, but I've decided to retire. Thirty years is plenty of time to serve my country. Now it's time to serve my community."

"Community? What do you mean?"

Gran reached for Sadie's hand. "Remember my anonymous buyer for the bakery? Imagine my shock when I went to Mia's office today and found my son and daughter-in-law sitting there, ready to take ownership." She scowled at her son. "I would've given it to you, you know."

Dad pressed his cheek on the top of Gran's head and wrapped an arm around her shoulders. "Of course, Mom, but this way, you get to stay in your home."

Sadie held up her hands. "Wait a minute—you bought the bakery?"

Dad thrust his hands in his pockets and rocked back on his heels. "Sure did. Your mom and I sold the house in Hawaii, and we wanted to invest in something meaningful. Seemed like a great retirement project."

Sadie glanced at her mom. "And you're okay with this?"

She smiled, tiny lines deepening her blue eyes very similar to Sadie's. Mom's dark hair, cut in a chin-length bob, brushed across her cheek as she nodded. "Absolutely. We spent many years being away from family. It's time to come home."

Home.

Sadie scanned the park that had always been one of her favorite places when visiting the island. She could certainly settle here, especially if Asher decided to stay.

"You know, when we open the bakery, we're going to need help with marketing to grow the business again. Interested in a job?"

"Absolutely. Just as long as I have time to write songs on the side."

"Yes, of course." Dad wrapped an arm around Sadie and drew her to his side. "I'm proud of you."

Sadie wrapped her arms around his waist and leaned her cheek against his chest. "Thanks for believing in me, Dad."

"Always."

As her parents wrapped her in their embrace once again, Sadie reached for Gran's hand. Over her shoulder, her eyes connected with Asher's, and he winked as he disengaged himself from signing autographs and started toward her. Dani stepped in his path, caught him in a hug, then talked to him for a couple of minutes, her back to Sadie. Asher's eyes widened, then he nodded as he grinned. He gave Dani another hug, then pointed at Sadie.

Dani waved to her, and Sadie gestured for her to join them. Dani shook her head and pointed at Liam.

Asher appeared at her side and reached for her. "Dani just asked us to sing the closing set with Dahlia Denton."

Sadie gripped Asher's arms as her heart thundered in her ears. "Are you serious?"

His grin widened even more. "Yes, Miss Dahlia watched the talent show and loved our song."

Sadie pressed a hand to her chest. "I can't believe it. You should do it."

Asher's grin faltered. "Not without you. We are a team, remember?"

"But—"

Asher pressed a finger to her lips. "No buts. You can do this, Sadie. Sing from your heart."

For the second time in the last hour, his words permeated her soul. An almost supernatural burst of courage surged through her, and she nodded. Then she curled her fingers through Asher's. "Come and meet my parents."

"Mom, Dad, this is Asher Quinn." Then she glanced at Asher. "These are my parents, Colonel Greg and Joanne Hudson."

He extended a hand to both. "Pleasure to meet you both. And thank you for your service, sir."

As Asher talked with her parents and accepted a hug from Gran, Sadie's heart swelled with pride.

Scars would always be a part of their story. They nearly destroyed what could have been. But healing brought them together and offered a new beginning.

Asher had performed around the world, but nothing gave him greater joy than singing with Sadie.

Still buzzing from adrenaline and the applause still echoing in his ears and the gushing from a few fans, Asher tightened his arm around Sadie's waist as they talked with her family. Thankfully, other concert attendees had given them privacy.

"Asher!"

He turned at the sound of his name, and his heart slammed against his ribs.

Bending his head, he whispered in Sadie's ear. "Excuse me a moment. I'll be right back."

She nodded and returned to talking to her parents.

Asher strode across the grass. His sister and his mom hurried over to him. Mom's dark hair pulled back in her favored ponytail that emphasized her high cheekbones and was strung through a white hat she usually reserved for playing golf with Asher's dad. She wore a pink Summer Sunset MusicFest T-shirt purchased from one of the vendors on the lawn and a pair of white, cropped jeans. Abi wore a matching shirt in light blue and a pair of jeans with frayed slices through the thigh. Her hair, the same color as their mother's, had been pulled back and fastened with a decorative clip.

"Ash, you were really great." Abi hugged him, then she smacked his chest. "I'm mad at you for ditching Dad's party before I arrived."

"Sorry, sis. I had to get out of there." Not wanting to let his still-fresh argument with his dad dampen what he was feeling after singing with Sadie, he slung an arm around his sister's neck and faced his parents.

Pulling Dad along with her, Mom dropped his hand, then flung her arms around Asher's neck as she had done at his father's birthday party.

"Sweetheart, you were wonderful. I'm so proud of you."

Dad remained a few steps behind her.

Par for the course.

But then to Asher's surprise, Dad moved next to Mom, slid an arm around her waist, and thrust out his right hand. "Great job, Ash. Really great job."

Asher glanced at his mom and then back at his dad. A beat passed, then he took his father's hand. "Thanks, Dad."

Instead of shaking his hand then dropping it, Dad jerked Asher closer into a one-armed man hug and thumped him on the back. "So proud of you."

When was the last time his father had hugged him? Or told him he was proud of him?

The compliments swirled around in Asher's brain. The warmth of his father's praise washed over him, then his eyes narrowed as he cracked a smile. "Are you dying?"

Dad's head jerked up, then he scowled. "Dying?"

Then his eyes lit up, and the crinkles at the corners deepened as his tanned face split with a grin and laughter rolled out of his barrel chest.

Shaking his head, he rested a hand on Asher's shoulder. "No, definitely not dying, but I certainly haven't been living either. I owe you an apology. Your mother gave me an earful about what happened at my party . . . and the past fifteen years. I'm sorry for not being the kind of father you deserve. If you'll let me, I'd like to make up for that."

The glistening in his father's eyes rattled Asher. In all his thirty-three years, he'd never heard such a humble apology. His uncle's words from the other day about reconciliation sifted through Asher's head.

He wrapped both arms around his dad and hugged him. "No apologies needed, Dad. I'm the one who's sorry. I disrespected you by leaving your party instead of talking it out like a man. You're a great dad and a hard worker who always provided for his family. I didn't always appreciate that. Even though I still don't want to work construction every day, you've taught me plenty through the years, and I've been able to help others. Thank you for everything. I'm honored to be your son."

Dad dragged a hand over his face. "So, uh, I guess now's

a good time to let you know I have every album you've put out."

"Yeah, I know. Mom displays them in the living room." Much to Asher's embarrassment. Her own private Hall of Fame, she called it.

Dad nodded, then shook his head. "Right, she does. But I bought my own—the covers line the walls of the trailer I haul to construction sites for every job."

Asher opened his mouth, but the words died in his throat at his father's admission. He looked at his dad, who had his hands in his pockets, studying the tips of his worn leather deck shoes, then Asher glanced at his mom, who brushed a tear off her cheek and nodded at him.

Wow.

The admission rocked Asher to the core, and he didn't quite know how to respond.

"Thanks, Dad. I appreciate it." The words sounded so hollow, but he didn't know what else to say.

Dad lifted his shoulder and chuckled. "Wasn't like you needed the money or anything, but I could brag on my kid at work."

His dad bragged about him?

The weight of his father's words hit him in the chest.

Maybe he'd been underestimating him all these years.

"Listen, Ash, I know I've been hard on you. I'm not against your career. In fact, I'm proud of what you've accomplished. I think I was a little jealous."

"Jealous? Why?"

"You stood up to your old man and followed your dreams. When I was in high school, I didn't want to follow in my dad's footsteps either. I didn't want to drive the carriage or give tours and couldn't wait to escape the island. I played guitar and wanted to strike out on my own, but my dad said a man needed to earn a living and take care of his family. So, I traded my guitar for my hammer. More so out of spite, but I love the company I've built." Though his voice remained steady, Dad's eyes softened. "I was too harsh on you about your dreams. I let my own fears cloud my judgment. I'm proud of you, son. I really am."

"Thanks. That means a lot." Asher took a deep breath. "I just wanted to play and pushed you away because I didn't think you believed in me. All these years, and I never knew you played."

"It was in the past so no need to bring it up."

Asher caught the wistfulness in his father's voice. "Doesn't have to be." He glanced at his parents. "Listen, Dad. A few minutes ago, Dani Sullivan asked Sadie and me to sing the final song with Miss Dahlia. After the rest of the acts play, she'll close with her traditional 'Amazing Grace.'" Asher jerked his thumb toward the stage where local boy and lead guitarist Caleb Kennedy played with his band. "Join us on stage and play with me."

Dad's eyes widened as he scanned the crowd dancing and singing along with Drake Hamilton, then he shook his head. "I can't—I haven't played in years."

"So, you're a bit rusty." Asher lifted a shoulder. "Once you pick up that guitar and put your fingers on the frets, I bet those chords will come back to you. What do you say? Father and son playing together for the first time. And with Dahlia Denton, Dad." He glanced at the platinum-haired woman with her tiny waist, huge personality, and wearing her signature sequins talking with Dani, Liam, and Seb Jonathon.

A genuine smile spread across Dad's face as he followed the direction of Asher's eyes. "Okay, yeah. Let's do it."

Sadie and her parents approached. While her parents caught up with his—apparently they knew each other years ago from the island—Asher draped an arm over her shoulder and drew her into his embrace. He dropped a kiss on the top of her head. "You okay?"

"More than okay." She shook her head and laughed. "To be honest, words escape me. Tonight was even better than I could've imagined, thanks to you and your belief in me."

"We believe in each other. A storm brought us together, but I'm so thankful the last one didn't tear us apart. I love you, Sadie."

"I love you too, Asher." She looked at him with a wicked glint in her eyes. "Or should I start calling you Eli."

He shook his head. "Eli's in the past. While a phoenix may rise out of the ashes, it's time for me to be the man God called me to be—Asher Quinn, the real man behind the mask. No more secrets."

Sadie pressed a hand to his cheek. "I didn't know Eli Noble, but I'm looking forward to getting to know Asher Quinn even more, who is the same fine young man that Gran claimed from the moment I met him."

Asher didn't deserve her, but he would be forever thankful she didn't walk away from him for good.

He dipped his head and brushed his lips over hers, sealing the promise of their love.

They'd weather whatever storm came their way. Together.

Eighteen

SADIE HAD NO IDEA WHY ASHER wanted her to meet him at three o'clock in the morning at the park. And on this particular day, no less. But when he asked her to simply trust him, she did. No matter how crazy she felt his request was.

Despite her desire to be tucked safely in her warm bed at Gran's cottage, Sadie rode her bike—a gift from Asher since she'd decided to remain on island and needed wheels to get around—down Sugar Maple Lane and cut to Blueberry Boulevard. With the stars shining her path, she passed the livery and stables, the Island House Inn, the Little Stone Bible Church, and headed to the park on Blueberry Hill.

Downtown was silent except for the sounds from the marina—the water lapping at the shore and against the boat hulls, the gentle breeze smacking lines against the masts of the sailboats, and a few stray seagulls dipping and soaring for an early breakfast.

A light beckoned closer to the water.

Sadie parked her bike in the rack at the entrance to the park, then followed the sidewalk past the volleyball nets, clusters of white Adirondack chairs, and the playground to a canopy of lights strung through the limbs of the majestic pine where Asher had kissed her after their concert.

Even though it had been nearly a month, the memories of the concert remained fresh in her mind—one of the most pivotal and exciting days of her life.

With Asher by her side, she confronted her fear of singing in public, then soared on those feelings of exhilaration as she walked across the stage and received the grand prize check for winning the talent show.

The weeks following had been a whirlwind as she helped her parents find a place so they could move in once Dad's retirement was official at the end of the year. Plus, Miss Dahlia, *the Dahlia Denton*, had approached her and Asher after the festival about co-writing songs with her and singing on her new album with Dani's cousin Ariel.

And none of it would've been possible without the man standing under the radiance of lights, hands holding on to a large manilla envelope and waiting for her to come to him.

Even though she and Asher had spent nearly every waking minute together since the night of the concert, her legs turned to jelly as she covered the distance between them.

Caught in the shadow of the tree, the lights created a halo over his dark hair, turning the top of his head nearly blond. He tucked the envelope under his arm, then reached for her and brushed a kiss over her lips. "Good morning."

His smooth, rich voice flowed over her like the warm glaze on a conveyor of freshly baked doughnuts.

"Good morning to you, you crazy man." She gripped his muscled upper arms and stood on her tiptoes to brush another kiss across his lips that tasted faintly of mint. "Why did you drag me out of bed and ask me to meet you on Blueberry Hill at three o'clock in the morning?"

He looked at her, his eyes dark and questioning. "Do you trust me?"

"Absolutely." No hesitation in her voice, because he'd proven himself over and over to be the kind of person she could rely on with her life . . . and her heart.

Asher ran his fingers over her cheek and brushed a wisp of hair off her face. "Do you remember the night of the storm, when we first met?"

She nodded, captured in the spell of the whisper of his voice.

"Do you remember what time I pounded on the door?"

Sadie looked over his shoulder and drew her brows together as she thought back to the night he'd entered her life. Then she jerked her gaze back to him and gasped. "Three a.m."

He nodded, then his mouth tightened. "What I never told you—or anyone else, for that matter—was five years ago today at three a.m., I was thrown out of my bed when the Phoenix tour bus rolled, crashed, and caught on fire."

Sadie's hand flew to her mouth as a rush of tears blurred

her vision. "Oh, Asher. I've been dreading today all week, but I didn't realize the significance of the time."

He brushed a thumb over her cheek, removing a tear that escaped. "I hated this date and time on the calendar so much. The nightmares. The guilt. The shame. I wanted to run from it. But I've learned that hiding and cutting myself off from the world to punish myself doesn't change what happened."

She grabbed his hand. "But it wasn't your fault, Ash."

He reached for the envelope and tapped it against his palm. "This is the police report of the bus crash. My uncle gave it to me when I first came to the island about a year and a half ago, but I was too chicken to read. Last night, I finally summoned the courage to read it for myself." He held it out to her. "I want you to read it so there are no doubts in your mind about me . . . If you're interested, that is."

Sadie took the envelope, the few pages suddenly feeling like an anvil in her hand. Then she looked at the man with anguish in his eyes. She brushed her fingers across his jaw. "That's not necessary, Asher."

He caught her fingers in his hand. "I'm so very sorry for your sister's death. If I could bring her back, I would. But I'm not God. I don't know why He chose to spare me when Lauren, Jared, and the rest of my band and crew weren't. I'm sorry for the heartache that your family endured." Asher's voice caught on the last words, and he coughed.

Now it was Sadie's turn to dry the wetness on Asher's face. She pressed the envelope into his hands. "I don't need to read this. In fact, I don't want to. I trust you with my whole heart. You've walked through your own grief, and I'm sorry for what your family has gone through. The accident wasn't your fault. I know that now. And I believe it. I'm sorry I ever blamed you."

Asher crushed her to his chest and tightened his hold around her. "I don't know whatever I did to deserve you, but I'm so thankful for you, Sadie."

Taking a step back, he reached into his pocket and pulled out a small black box. Getting down on one knee, he looked up at her, his face framed in the glimmer of the lights, his eyes full of love. "I know we haven't known each other very long, and I'm okay with waiting—as long as it's not too long—so we can get to know one another even better, but I love you, Sadie Mae Hudson, and I want you to be my wife." He cleared his throat. "Dead in flames, given new life. Trust the One who sacrificed. In His grace, we find our way. From the dark to the light of day."

Hearing Asher sing the second verse to the song she'd written for them sent the rest of her tears cascading down her face. She engaged her diaphragm and sang the chorus with him. "Embrace love, embrace life. Up from the ashes we rise. Together, we will find a new life. We are reborn. We are reborn."

As they brought the final note to an end, Sadie lowered herself to the ground and reached for the man who had proposed to her in the most unexpected, yet most romantic way, and nodded. With tears in her eyes and an outpouring of love in her heart, she nodded again. "I want to be your wife more than anything, Asher Noble Quinn."

As he opened the small box in his hand and pulled

out the ring, her breath caught in her chest as he slid the sparkling diamond on her finger. "It's beautiful."

"It belonged to my grandmother. I always loved her ring, and when my grandparents passed away, my dad, uncle, and Aunt Sally asked if there was anything Jared, Eliza, Abi, or I wanted from their estate. I asked for Grandma's ring to give to my future wife someday."

Sadie's chest shuddered as she blinked back a fresh wash of wetness. She laid a hand against her fiancé's cheek. "You're such a romantic."

Instead of responding, he brushed his lips across hers, then pressed his forehead to hers. "I know we haven't known each other very long, and I meant what I said about waiting until you're ready, but I'm old enough to know what I want, and I want you. As my wife. As my friend. As the future mother of our children."

The thought of being the mother to his children sent her heart stumbling against her ribs. She rested her cheek against his chest, listening to the steady beating of his heart. "I want all of those things too." Then she lifted her head and looked at him. "I don't need to wait to get to know you better—we have a lifetime for that. But I want my parents to be here, and they won't be on island until after Thanksgiving. What do you say to getting married on New Year's Eve so we can begin the New Year as a married couple?"

Asher intertwined his fingers through hers and gave them a gentle squeeze. "I say that's a most excellent idea. I can wait three more months to claim you as my wife."

Asher stood, then pulled Sadie to her feet. He shook

out a blanket and draped it around her, then he drew her against his chest and rested his chin on the top of her head. His arms wrapped around her, cradling her in the warmth of his embrace.

Sadie sighed, her heart full. Memories of the concert washed over her again as she looked at the space where the wooden stage had sat with the lake as a backdrop. "This is where it all changed, isn't it?"

"Maybe for you. For me, it was when you opened the door and nearly growled at me for waking you up."

She twisted and looked at him. "I didn't growl. Looking back on that night though, I appreciate how you braved the storm just to check on Gran."

"I love her as if she were my own."

"She feels the same about you. I know my parents will too."

Sadie wrapped her arms around his waist, taking the blanket with her. "We've encountered several storms this summer, haven't we?"

"Yeah, we have. But we made it through each one." He stepped closer, his gaze locked on hers. "And I'll always be by your side, no matter what. Singing those first notes with you freed me from a prison of my own making. After the concert, my uncle told me Isaiah 43:2 was my cousin's favorite Scripture—'When you pass through the waters, I will be with you: and when you pass through the rivers, they will not sweep over you. When you walk through the fire, you will not be burned; the flames will not set you ablaze.' I can't think of a more fitting verse for our lives.

The Lord met me in a storm of my own making, took my hand, and brought me to you."

The conviction in his voice deepened the trust in her heart. "Your cousin would be so proud of who you are today, Ash. You've been my anchor this past month. You've taught me that love is stronger than fear, that it can guide us through the darkest days. I can't imagine my life without you. I don't want to imagine it. I know we'll face many more storms in our lives, but we need to keep trusting the Lord for His protection and His provision and not allow them to sweep over us."

"I never thought I could be this happy again." The warmth of his breath caressed her skin as he kissed the curve of her neck. Then he guided them deeper into the burrow of the trees where he'd spread out blankets and small pillows. He sat and then pulled her down to him where she fit so perfectly into the curve of his arms.

For the next few hours, they talked and planned for the future as the moon bid goodnight and drifted into the light cascading across the water.

The morning dawned, marking five years since both of their lives had been turned upside down. Dreams crushed, hearts fragmented, family dynamics altered.

But today was about fresh starts and new beginnings.

About healing and hope.

Sadie held out her hand and admired the delicate ring in the dawn of the new day.

The promise of a future with Asher filled with love, making music together, and raising a family happened because she released her fears with courage. Now they would embrace whatever came next. Together.

293

Bonus Epilogue

Thank you for reading *Meet Me on Blueberry Hill*. We hope you loved this story. Find out what happens next for Asher and Sadie with a Bonus Epilogue, a special gift, available only to our newsletter subscribers.

This Bonus Epilogue will not be released on any retailer platform, so scan the QR code to get your free gift. You acknowledge you are becoming a Sunrise Publishing, Lisa Jordan subscriber. Unsubscribe from any newsletter at any time.

Thank You

Thank you so much for reading *Meet Me on Blueberry Hill*. We hope you enjoyed the story. If you did, would you be willing to do us a favor and leave a review? It doesn't have to be long—just a few words to help other readers know what they're getting. (But no spoilers! We don't want to wreck the fun!) Thank you again for reading!

We'd love to hear from you- not only about this story, but about any characters or stories you'd like to read in the future.

Contact us at www.sunrisepublishing.com/contact.

Jonathon Island

Return to Jonathon Island in book 5
Meet Me at Sunset Cove
by Sarah May Warren.

She needs a house to rebuild her career. He needs a fiancée to keep his home. Neither planned on rebuilding their hearts in the process.

Daisy Decker didn't plan to ruin her career by making the network execs of her hit home renovation show choose between her and her cheating co-host, but she's got a plan to fix it. Step one, find herself a cute little house on the world's most adorable island. Step two, film herself giving the house a total "Decker" remodel and use it to restart her YouTube channel. Step three, absolutely annihilate her ex in ratings and followers until the network execs realize they made the wrong choice and come crawling back.

The problem with this plan? The only house she could possibly afford belongs to the guy who got away.

Local contractor Hunter Barret is not letting his family's legacy go without a fight, and he's especially not going to sell it to Daisy Decker, the woman who ruined his future and broke his heart. But the family trust states that the house will hit the market the moment he turns 31, and there's nothing he can do to stop it. That is, unless he can miraculously find a fiancée overnight. He's out of options and out of time...but maybe there's a way Hunter and Daisy can both get what they want.

With power tools in hand and walls coming down, Daisy and Hunter discover that sometimes the strongest foundations are built on second chances.

One

DAISY DECKER HAD ALWAYS BEEN A girl with a plan.

So why did she feel like she was drifting aimlessly in the middle of nowhere?

Outside the window, gusts of wind sprayed icy water against the side of the vessel, carrying the scent of pine and autumn leaves through the nearly empty ferry. Daisy let out a shiver and wrapped her sweater closer to her body, wishing she'd taken more than five minutes to research her destination before tossing a few "cute fall girlie" outfits into her suitcase and fleeing the city. Apparently, Michigan had a very different definition of fall than California.

A vibration from her smartwatch tugged her attention away from the mesmerizing swells of Lake Huron, and she glanced down to see the preview of a text.

Robin ♥

Stop hiding from me. Answer your phone.

Daisy rolled her eyes, cracking a smile for the first time in what felt like days at her friend-slash-agent's dramatics. She was not hiding. She was just taking a strategic retreat while she tried to formulate a plan to salvage the wreckage of her career.

That's what she was good at. It was sort of her "thing": Daisy Decker—the girl with all the plans. She cringed at the memory of that slogan being slapped across half the HGTV billboards in the Midwest a few years back.

Her watch buzzed again, flashing the name Robin ♥ across the screen.

Taking a breath, Daisy fished out her phone and winced as she answered it. "Hi . . ."

"Hi?" Robin asked from the other end. "You dump your boyfriend, quit your job, and then vanish into thin air for forty-eight hours, and all you have to say is 'hi'?"

"Hi . . . How are you?"

Her friend let out a groan. "You infuriate me."

Daisy grinned, relaxing for the first time in twenty-four hours at the sound of a friendly voice. Well . . . friendly-ish. "I'm sorry, Robin. I should have talked to you before bolting." A swell of water splashed against the glass as the ferry passed beside an enormous bridge. In the distance, the outline of an island was just starting to come into view. "I just . . . I had to get out of there." Like, immediately. Because the moment she'd stood up in that conference room and laid down that ultimatum, making them choose between her and her hunky costar-slash-very-fresh-ex-boyfriend Logan, she'd known it had been a mistake.

"I know," Robin said softly, followed by a heavy pause. "He's a jerk. And they're idiots for picking him over you."

Daisy sucked in a breath, trying her best to smother the sudden ache in her chest. "Thanks, babe . . . but honestly, I think I'm over him."

"Sure. Because it's just that easy to get over someone you dated for over two years."

Daisy stared out across the choppy water, searching for the right way to explain it. "Really. I think we've been over for a while now . . . I just didn't want to admit it, you know? It felt like we were this package deal—Double and Decker—but something was never quite right. And I kept waiting for things to click, but they just . . . never did."

The truth was, it wasn't seeing Logan with his arms around another woman that had made her run. It was her pride. It was standing in that boardroom, Jerry McGuire–style, with the heavy silence of rejection pressing in on every side, that kept her awake at night. She couldn't let that be the end of her career.

She heard her friend take in a breath of her own and then, "Okay, so what's next? I can start making calls . . ." Her tone turned suddenly optimistic.

"I'm glad you asked," Daisy said as the docks came into view. "Priority number one is damage control. I'm sure social media is already spinning out stories about the way I stormed out. The longer I avoid the public, the more power Logan has. That brings me to priority number two. If I'm going to get back on the radar without the network's help, I need content. And I need it ASAP. So, the plan is as follows:

"Step one, find myself an adorable little house on an adorable little island. Step two, film myself giving the house a total 'Decker' remodel and slap it up on YouTube. Step three—"

"Absolutely annihilate Logan and *Double Decker* in ratings until the network realizes they made the wrong choice and comes crawling back?" Robin suggested.

Daisy grinned. "Bingo."

"I guess it's a start," Robin said. "So where are you going to find this adorable little house?"

Before Daisy could answer, an automated voice echoed through the ferry speakers. "On behalf of everyone at Jonathon Island, we'd like to welcome you to the island. We'll be docking in just a few minutes, so please remain seated until the vessel has been secured to the dock and luggage carts have been unloaded. Please take this opportunity to collect your things. And lastly, please be courteous to your fellow passengers as you exit the ferry. Thank you, and have a nice visit."

"What was that?" Robin asked, her frown sounding through the receiver. "Daisy, where are you?"

Daisy shifted in her seat, trying to get a glimpse of her destination. "Jonathon Island, Michigan."

The ferry slowed as they passed a pair of buoys bobbing in the water. Daisy's eyes trailed up to the shore, where the water faded from blue to teal, lapping against a white pebbly beach. Above that, a wall of pine trees hugged the shoreline with pops of orange and red.

"The place Eli Noble was spotted a few weeks back?"

"That's the one!"

"It's a little off the beaten path, isn't it?" Daisy's eyes trailed the shore, catching on a Victorian-style turret poking through the trees as the ferry rounded the edge of the island. "It is. But I've got a good feeling about it. Who knows, maybe this place has exactly what I need to make a comeback."

The boat passed the breakwater as their destination came into view, and Daisy's breath caught in her chest.

Tucked in the crook of the bay, Jonathon Island sprawled out along a picturesque boardwalk. Blue and yellow storefronts lined Main Street, while sailboats bobbed along the marina. Victorian-style homes climbed the hill that rose up behind the town, and at the end of Main Street stood a massive historic-looking hotel. Although the structure was obviously still under construction, it didn't take much for Daisy to imagine the completed estate.

It was breathtaking.

It was no wonder the townsfolk had been working so hard to rebuild. It was a place worth fighting for. And from what Daisy had learned from the news article covering Eli Noble's recent reappearance here, the townsfolk were doing everything they could to do just that. Including selling houses for a dollar.

What better way for her to make her HGTV comeback?

"I gotta go," Daisy said, slinging her backpack over her shoulder.

"Call me when you're ready to put this plan of yours into action," Robin said, her voice touched with worry.

"You know that I'm still your best friend first. Agent second. I just want you to succeed."

There was that word. *Succeed.*

Daisy smiled. "I know. I'll call you." She ended the call, watching through the window as a rough-looking man pulled her lone piece of luggage out from the cargo space and set it on the dock for her, and she felt a flurry of excitement as she made her way to the door.

Please, God, don't let this be a dead end.

She sucked in a hopeful breath.

The ferry worker stood at the gap, his calloused hand extended to help her down the ramp.

Here went nothing.

That hopeful feeling followed her as she stepped out of the Island House Inn onto its charming wraparound porch the following morning. From the front steps of this historic building, Daisy could see the entire harbor laid out ahead of her, the late sunrise spread across the water in hues of blue and purple. A light fog crept across the pebbly beach, dissipating at the cobblestone street and the docks where the ferry, with its faded blue stripes, sat waiting for the commuters making their way down the boardwalk, chatting each other up with neighborly smiles and rosy cheeks.

This place really was a dream.

Daisy slipped her phone from her pocket, turned so the water lay behind her, and posed for a picture. The morning light touched her cheeks, giving her practiced smile a hopeful glow.

This was going to work out. It had to.

She opened up her socials and posted with a caption that read:

Big things coming, friends! Stay tuned for more from the girl with a plan!

And it was time for the first step of that plan.

Daisy dialed the number she'd looked up after settling into her hotel room the night before.

A woman's voice answered the call. "Hello?"

"Hi, this is Daisy Decker. I left a voicemail last night, but—"

"Oh, hi! Of course," Mia said warmly from the other end of the phone. "I—" She broke away, her voice suddenly distant. "Maggie, sweetie, let's keep our food on the table"—and then back to Daisy—"Sorry about that. Yes, I was just about to call you back. I hear you're interested in moving to Jonathon Island?"

Moving to Jonathon Island? Daisy bit her lip. "I'm definitely interested in buying a house…" Moving to an island a thousand miles from her home and her career, not as much.

"Great! I've got a couple hours—Finn, off the chair. Feet on the floor, bud—free next week. When can you get out to the island?"

Daisy felt a little of her excitement deflate. "Actually, I'm on the island right now. Any chance you might be available today?"

"Today?" Daisy heard a rustling of papers and then, "I've got a couple of minutes open this morning. But I've got to catch the ferry at ten-fifteen. I can give you a quick show of the houses available so you can get a look before we take the next steps. How does that sound?"

A grin split Daisy's face as she pushed away from the railing. "That sounds perfect! Thank you so much!"

"No problem. I'll drop the kids with a friend for a while and meet you at the corner of Jonathon Boulevard and Main in twenty."

"See you then!" Daisy agreed and ended the call, slipped her phone back into her pocket, and practically skipped down the remaining steps.

"Morning," a gruff voice called from the cobblestone walkway leading from the street. Augo, the man who'd been working the front desk the evening before, stood outside the white picket fence, a bundle of flowers in one arm and a paper sack in the other. The man looked to be in his eighties, with a flat cap, thick white mustache, and flannel. A small red-haired Dachshund padded along at his heels, her tongue contentedly lolling from the side of her mouth. If Daisy remembered from the night before, the dog's name was Lucy.

"Working again this morning?" Daisy asked, hurrying down the path toward the gate, swinging it open for him. Lucy ran through first, her little tail wagging as she looked up at Daisy, expecting pets. Daisy happily obliged, giving the dog a scratch behind the ears.

"Thank you, Miss . . ." The man paused, shifting the paper bag in his arm. "Remind me?"

"It's Daisy." She smiled.

He returned the smile, his own buried under his bushy mustache. "Thank you, Daisy." He turned back toward the inn. "And to answer your question—Sarah's our regular day shift. But Caleb said she's not feeling too great, so it looks like you're stuck with me again." He grinned, pausing at the first step of the landing. "You up for some breakfast? I just stopped at Doug's Market on my way in, got some eggs, some smoked salmon. You like salmon?"

Daisy cracked a genuine smile at the man's candid invitation. "Sounds amazing, but I've got somewhere I need to be—Actually, you wouldn't mind telling me how to get to Jonathon Boulevard, would you?"

"Big plans, eh?" Augo raised an eyebrow, grinning mischievously.

Daisy shrugged. "Something like that." Everything like that, actually.

He tilted his head. "You know what they say about plans."

"No, what?"

"If you want to make God laugh, just tell Him your plans." The old man let out a hearty hoot, giving her a warm wink before finishing his ascent up the stairs, Lucy once again at his heels. "Head down Blueberry Boulevard, when you find a turn, take it and keep walking. You can't miss it!" he called back over his shoulder as the front door shut behind him.

"Can't miss it, indeed," Daisy grumbled as she spun on

the heel of her Dr. Martens once again. The wind swept her ponytail across her shoulders, and Daisy adjusted the neckline of her turtleneck sweater, wishing once again that she'd brought something a little warmer than a cardigan and high-rise, ripped jeans. If this thing panned out, she'd have to stock up on a few choice clothing items, starting with a warm jacket.

Admittedly, Daisy had never been great at directions, but she shouldn't have needed a GPS to take a single-turn walk through a zero-stoplight town. She huffed again, tucking her chin into her collar.

Per Augo's directions, she'd gone "up" Blueberry (whatever that meant) and taken the first turn she could find, which had brought her down to the marina and right up to the water until she couldn't "keep walking," so she'd hopped onto the boardwalk and followed it toward town.

On her first pass up the boardwalk, Daisy had stopped to admire the stunning views. The golds and reds of the trees poking around the Victorian houses up the hill. The picturesque sight of wooden boats bobbing in the bay. The pops of blue and yellow winking from the main stretch of buildings in town.

It was all much less charming on her third pass through.

Finally, after popping into a cute little coffee shop and being given three simultaneous sets of directions by three different well-meaning townsfolk, none of which were the same, proceeded by a handful of probing—also well-meaning—questions about who she was and what she was doing, she arrived on the corner of Jonathon and Main.

A woman rose from a bench under a nearby awning, her warm plaid jacket of gold and blues complementing the fall decor peppered throughout Main Street. Daisy stepped toward her, assuming she must be the realtor.

"I was starting to wonder if you'd changed your mind," the woman said with a smile. She held two coffees, one extended toward Daisy as she stopped at the curb. "Got you some coffee. It's a chilly day, and we'll have some walking to do, so I thought you might need something warm." This with a glance at Daisy's ripped jeans, the skin beneath already turning a rosy pink.

"Thank you," Daisy said, taking the cup in her chilled hands. "I'll admit, I did get lost. But it's not my fault—I think the front desk guy gave me bad directions."

The woman frowned. "Caleb?"

Daisy winced as she took a sip of her coffee. "Augo."

"Ah, well, that explains it," she chuckled. "Augo can't be trusted with directions."

Daisy raised her brows.

"He likes to make them intentionally vague. Says it helps people 'find the town.'"

Oh, Daisy had found it all right.

"We should get going," the woman said, nodding toward the street hidden between two false-front buildings. "I'm Mia, by the way."

"Daisy." She held out a hand and Mia shook it.

"I'm excited to show you around, Daisy," Mia said, leading the way up the cobblestone street. Daisy took a hesitant sip of the still-scalding coffee as the fall breeze nipped at her neck. "What brings you to Jonathon Island? Other than your house search, of course."

Daisy's coffee caught in her throat.

That was a big question.

She went with the simple answer. "I'm a designer. I'm on the hunt for a renovation project."

The cobblestone street soon gave way to a residential neighborhood. A row of cozy houses sat nestled between a mixture of maple and pine trees. Many of the yards here were overgrown, the picket fences wrapped with invasive vines, boxwoods stretching toward the sky in front of empty bay windows. But Daisy could see it. The potential was there in every property they passed. The potential for these houses to become homes again, with the right kind of love and care they'd obviously once had.

"That sounds like a really fun job," Mia said, stopping in front of a faded-blue craftsman-style house, the covered porch overtaken by foliage that climbed toward the second story.

It looked the way a perfectly rainy day felt.

It reminded Daisy of the first house she had ever remodeled. Warmth grew in her chest at the memory.

"Well, we have a few cute little options to take a look at. Do you have a budget in mind?" Mia asked.

Daisy shot her a tentative look. "Um . . . well, I heard about the dollar house program . . ."

"Oh." Mia blinked, her eyes widening. "I'm so sorry for the confusion. The dollar house program is over. There aren't any more storefronts left."

Daisy tilted her head, her brows drawing together. "Storefronts?"

Mia matched her confused expression. "Yeah, you know. To open your business . . . That's the dollar house program. It was for business owners who wanted to open shops on the island. They all had to apply and get approval from the town council. But all the spots have been filled. I'm so sorry. We do still have houses for sale though." She gestured toward the craftsman hopefully.

Daisy's heart sank, the plan slipping. "I don't have a very big budget . . ."

The wind picked up, shaking the trees. Through a gap in the tree line, Daisy spotted the same Victorian-style turret she'd seen from the ferry the day before.

Mia followed her gaze. "Let me make a call. I might just have something."

The fifteenth time's the charm—or so Hunter Barrett kept telling himself as he stared at his father's red ink massacre of yet another perfectly good blueprint. The red marks on his latest blueprint were becoming almost comical at this point. Three weeks, fifteen revisions, and his father had rejected each one for increasingly microscopic issues—a quarter-inch variation in the support beam placement, a slightly too-wide window trim, and yesterday's complaint about the "aesthetically concerning" spacing between floor joists that literally no one would ever see. But version fifteen? Hunter had spent half the night adjusting measurements that were already well within code, knowing his father would scrutinize every detail like he was renovating the White House instead of a midwestern-suburb, ranch-style house.

He carefully rolled up the document and slid it into his backpack. The old man couldn't possibly reject this one.

Hunter groaned as he stepped over his brother's gym bag in the hallway of their small two-bedroom apartment. "Come on, Waylen," he grumbled as he slid the bag out of the traffic zone.

"Talking to yourself again?" Waylen asked from the kitchen table, where he sat with his dirty-socked feet kicked up on the handcrafted oak, one arm slung over the back of his chair, eating an Eggo waffle with his bare hands.

Hunter slapped his brother's feet to the floor as he crossed to the fridge. "I'd talk to *you* if I thought you'd listen," he grumbled into the dark refrigerator. "And I thought you were going to fix the light in here?"

Waylen balked. "Why me?"

Over his shoulder, Hunter cast him a look of disbelief. "How about because *you're* the one with time on your hands?"

Waylen scoffed. "What's that supposed to mean?"

"It means you could afford to take a minute to fix a lightbulb between shifts of donut eating down at the police station. Or is there a recent crime streak I haven't heard about?"

"You know, the whole cops and donuts thing is a common misconception," Waylen said, threading his hands behind his head as he leaned back again. "I'm more of a Danish guy myself."

Hunter shot him a teasing glare over his shoulder. "How about you become an electrician guy, or I'm gonna start charging you your full half of the rent."

"Yeah, yeah . . ."

Hunter cracked a smile, rolling his eyes.

Giving up on a nutritious breakfast, he snatched a bagel from the top of the fridge and popped it in the toaster.

"Speaking of appointments," Hunter said, leaning back against the counter. "You said you'd help out at the Riverfront project tomorrow. Dad really can't afford any delays, so don't forget."

Waylen appeared completely taken aback by the reminder. "What makes you think I'd forgotten?"

The bagels popped out of the toaster, and Hunter spun to retrieve them, butter knife in hand. "Because one of the sticky notes you use to keep appointments ended up on the bottom of my shoe last night."

Waylen shrugged. "So?"

"That, and you forgot to show up to the last two projects you agreed to help out with." He finished slathering the bagel with butter, wrapped it in a napkin, and stuffed it into the pocket of his jacket. "I mean it, I don't want the demo team giving me any dirty looks by association when you forget again."

Waylen waved him off with a sheepish grin. "Thanks, *Mom*."

"You joke, but maybe if you had a mom around, you'd know better than to put your feet up on my handcrafted hardwood table." He pushed Waylen's feet aside again and picked up a stack of papers from the table, sliding them into his backpack. "You need anything from the mainland today?"

"I'll survive," Waylen replied, finishing his last bite of waffle.

Hunter gave a nod and checked his watch. Right on time. He'd have exactly forty minutes to catch the 10:15 ferry.

Hunter soaked in the morning light as he stepped out of Good Day Coffee with a warm cup of joe steaming into the air. Overhead, the sound of seagulls mixed with the lapping of water on the shore, and across the street, Jack, the town dog, was getting some morning affection from Dani Sullivan. She rose, giving him a wave as she stepped into the Tourism Bureau.

It was another beautiful day on the island.

Hunter made his way down Main Street, his eyes gazing over the wild blue of the water. The wind flicked at his hair as he rounded the corner at the end of the street and hurried up the hill. His boots creaked over the wooden ramp, leading up to the old post office building. The small, cream-colored house sat nestled on the corner with lilac trees, now past bloom, framing the walkway. A bell rang out as Hunter stepped inside.

"Morning, Hunter!"

"Morning, Roger," Hunter replied, waving at the white-haired man behind the counter.

"Some exciting mail today!" the older man said, leaning over the desk to watch as Hunter opened his PO box.

"I keep trying to tell you, Rog." Hunter slid the contents out of the small metal box and closed it back up. "You're not supposed to look at people's mail while you're sorting it."

Roger scoffed. "First of all, I'm too old to waste away of boredom. Second, it just jumped out at me."

Hunter frowned. "What did?"

"See for yourself." He rapped a knuckle against the counter and wandered back into the office.

Hunter sorted through the pile, not sure what he was looking for.

And then he did.

His address was written in gold cursive, with a floral stamp in the corner. A wax seal weighed it down, but that was nothing compared to the weight of the sender's address.

Hunter's heart jumped into his throat as he opened the envelope and pulled out the thick cardstock.

Lisa Sherman
And
Carlisle Hansen
Joyfully Invite You
To Celebrate Their Wedding
Saturday, December 7th,
Twenty Twenty-Four
Four o'clock in the Afternoon
The Teachout Building
Chicago, Illinois

Hunter dragged a hand through his hair and flipped the card over, half expecting some sort of handwritten note with something like *I know I abandoned you and your brothers, but I'm sooooo much happier. Please bring gifts.*

He was going to throw up.

His phone rang, pulling his attention away from the invitation long enough to catch his oldest brother's name flashing across the screen.

"She's out of her mind if she thinks I'm going to her wedding," Hunter growled into the phone.

"Wow, and good morning to you too," Miles said on the other end.

"It was." Hunter stuffed the mail into his backpack, unable to summon the energy to look at the rest. With his luck, the rest were probably all consecutive jury summonses or IRS audit notices. "Until I checked the mail."

Hunter pushed back through the door, sucking in a breath of cold air as he started back down the hill.

Miles paused. "I think you're being a little hard on her, Hunt. She's still our mom."

Hunter couldn't help the eye roll. Miles had always been too forgiving for his own good. Together, his brothers could cause a real mess. Evan and Jude found the strays. Miles and Waylen kept them. And Hunter cleaned up the pieces when it was all said and done. Mom was no exception.

He rounded the corner, the docks coming into view. Across the boardwalk, commuters and a nearly non-existent handful of tourists were gathering for the 10:15 ferry. He crossed the street to join them.

Hunter stopped at the docks, out of earshot of the crowd gathering below. "Listen, Miles, you can go if you want, but you can count me out."

His brother's silence spoke volumes. "Okay."

Hunter pushed out a breath, trying to force the tension out of the conversation. "How are things out there? Gone on any fancy hippie retreats lately?"

"Oh, ha ha. I go on one nature retreat and suddenly I'm a hippie."

"Your words, not mine!" Hunter chuckled, relaxing just slightly.

"For your information, the adventure tours are going well. I led a kayak group out this morning for the sunrise."

"Brave kayakers. It's freezing on Lake Michigan."

Miles barked a laugh of agreement. "You should come out here sometime."

Hunter made a face despite knowing his brother couldn't see it. "Eh, I think I'm still a little jaded toward the Windy City."

"Still hung up on that stupid contest?" his brother teased. "You know, it's not the city's fault."

"Even so, I'd prefer not to relive my greatest embarrassment every time I come to visit you. You'll have to come to us. Dad's been perfecting his smoked ribs for just such an occasion."

"How is Dad?"

Hunter turned, leaning his elbows on the edge of the boardwalk railing, switching the coffee to the hand that had grown cold. "You know Dad. He works too hard. I wish he'd take a break."

"Sounds like someone else I know," Miles poked.

Below, Mia Franklin caught his eye from the dock and gave him a wave, gesturing for him to come down and talk to her. "Hey, Miles, I wish I could catch up more, but it looks like Mia needs to talk to me."

"No problem, let's talk later."

"Sure thing." He hung up and strode down the dock as Mia made her way to meet him, two kids in tow. It was still hard to see an old friend, now a widow, managing on her own. Then again, she wasn't on her own anymore. She and Cody Hart were getting pretty serious, from the sound of it.

"Hey, Mia, what's up?"

"Sorry to cut your call short. Was it important?"

"Nothing to worry about." Hunter shrugged. "What's going on?"

She released her son's hand to brush a strand of dark hair behind her ear, and he dropped into a crouch, stalking the seagull a few feet behind them. "I was hoping you might ask your dad to give me a call. I couldn't get through to him just now, but I have someone who's interested in the house."

Hunter frowned. "Interested?"

"Finn, honey, leave the bird alone." Mia waved her son closer and turned her gaze back to Hunter. "Yeah, some designer. I told her where to find the house so she could take a look. But I think she's looking to buy immediately, so I really need Joe to call me back."

The prerecorded announcement interrupted over the

speakers. "On behalf of everyone at Jonathon Island, we'd like to thank you for coming to the island . . ."

Mia began ushering the children onto the ferry. "Come on, kids, time to go." When Hunter made no move to follow, she paused, turning back toward him. "You're not coming?"

"My first meeting's not until two o'clock. I'll catch the next one."

The ferry pulled away, and Hunter turned toward home.

No way he was letting someone take his house.

Acknowledgments

Lord, may my words glorify you.

Patrick, Scott, and Mitchell—I love you forever.

Special thanks to Tari Faris for sharing some of her family's history. Without your idea, this story would've fallen apart. Thanks to Wendy Galinetti for sharing Old Dominion's "One Man Band" that cemented Asher's spiritual journey. Thanks to Lindsay Harrel, Rachel D. Russell, and Dalyn Weller for brainstorming and research help—any mistakes are mine.

Heart, home, and faith have always been important to **Lisa Jordan**, so writing stories with those elements comes naturally. Represented by Cynthia Ruchti of Books & Such Literary Management, Lisa Jordan is an award-winning, PW-bestselling author for Love Inspired and an author and line director for Sunrise Publishing's contemporary romance line, Hometown Hearts. She is also the operations manager for Novel Academy, an online writing academy powered by My Book Therapy. Happily married to her real-life hero for over thirty-five years, Lisa and her husband have two sons. When she isn't writing, Lisa enjoys quality family time, being creative with friends, or getting lost in a good book.

Learn more about her at lisajordanbooks.com.

Jonathon Island

Where faith, family, and romance meet small-town, beachside charm. Whether you spend a weekend at The Grand, take a stroll down Lilac Lane, or cozy up in the Christmas Cottage, you'll fall in love with this heartwarming contemporary romance series, full of second chances and unforgettable love stories!

Check out the full series at sunrisepublishing.com.

We solve the problem of what we read next.   Available on Amazon

MAGNOLIA BAY

Where southern charm and romance intertwine...

"Heartwarming, genuine, and utterly captivating."

–SUSAN MAY WARREN
USA Today bestselling author

We solve the problem of what we read next.   Available on Amazon

Home to Heritage

SUSAN MAY WARREN and **TARI FARIS**

with **Mandy Boerma** and **Andrea Michelle Wood**

**WHERE EVERY STORY IS A FRIEND,
AND EVERY CHAPTER IS A NEW JOURNEY...**

Subscribe to our newsletter for the latest news, weekly giveaways, exclusive author interviews, and more!

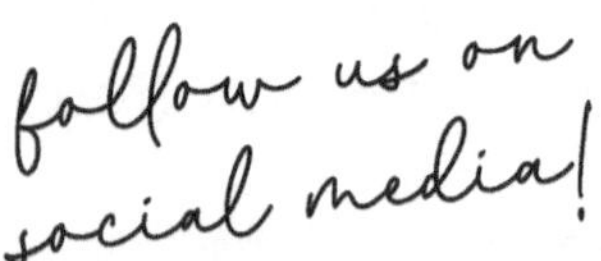

Shop paperbacks, ebooks, audiobooks, and more at
SUNRISEPUBLISHING.MYSHOPIFY.COM